A GENTLEMAN IN HELL

Elena Sandidge

This is a work of fiction. All the characters and events depicted in this book are either products of the author's imagination or are used fictitiously.

A Gentleman in Hell

ISBN: 0992807034

ISBN-13: 978-0992807030

First Edition: March 2016

Printed in the United States of America

For Brad and Kit

A Gentleman in Hell

CHAPTER ONE

Doc Holliday's eyes were the most memorable trait that he possessed. In bright sunshine they were light blue but when angry, his eyes seemed black. His body was skeletal, wasted by tuberculosis and alcohol. The only depth to his chest was the derringer that he hid in the top pocket of his silk vest. He sat at the poker table dressed in gray. His back was straight and his long fingers rested against the table. The silver ring on his right hand reflected the light from the gas lamp and the cards of a player on the other side of the table. Doc's index finger flicked through the stack of cards, feeling the edges for recent cuts, folds and tears. He played with the corners. He threw gold dollars into the center of the table and waited.

He peered over the top of his brown tinted spectacles. Everything red in the lower half of the room was magnified. The colors of the queen on the card beside him jumped up to kiss his cheek. The red mark, indistinguishable to the naked eye, shone in the top corner of the card. The top half of the room was tinged in yellow warmth from the gas lamp and was filled with the faces of strangers who wanted his money. His right hand moved over to the glass of whiskey and lifted it. It appeared golden from a distance, blood red near his face when he drank. He returned the glass to the table, and coughed. He wheezed and pressed his back against the chair to support his lungs. It stopped the pain. He brought his right hand to his chest and clutched his side, until the fit passed and his straining chest muscles relaxed.

The young cowboy watched Doc with scared brown eyes. "Don't go for no guns. I know you got a derringer in that pocket of yours."

Doc rolled his eyes and watched his opponent. The cowboy was typical of the type that drove cattle through Wichita day in and out. He was young for twenty, brave on cheap whiskey and full of talk. He was a Texan, maybe from Dallas or some where close to the Louisiana border. The boy's eyes were restless and rolled backwards and forwards looking from gambler to gambler. When a card fell on the felt, the boy would twitch and goggle at the card as if he could see through its back to the picture on the other side. Doc felt pity for the boy, cowboys made a dollar a day he doubted the boy had seen so much money before in his life.

Doc leaned forward and peered over his dark glasses. His eyes focused on the boy's head, as if just by looking at the he could cause his head to catch on fire. "You miss your Mother?" Doc said grinning.

"What in hell do you mean by that?"

Doc's kept his eyes on the boy but poured his glass full of whiskey and placed the bottle down by his side. "I mean," he continued. "You're kind of young to be playing these stakes without parental supervision. I understand that the gun l that I'm carrying in my top pocket concerns you. I'd like to inform you son that I am the dealer at this table and any derringers I carry are my business and mine only. I have no need for shooting little crawdads. So long as you're a clean player, you have no occasion to worry at tasting any of the lead that I carry."

The boy's nose twitched. "I don't want trouble. I just want to win this here stake."

"Well, quit bellyaching and play the game."

The other men kept quiet. The cards whispered as they hit the felt and floated on their sides. The gold coins chinked together and joined the glowing pile in the center of the table. Despite blank expressions, you could tell who wanted the money. Everyone eyed the gleaming pile of coins with a nervous twitch, all except for Doc. Doc's hands worked without visual aid, shuffling, dealing, skimming and dividing the cards.

A door in the saloon slammed closed. The players took their attention off their cards and listened. A man was searching for someone. The door to the poker room rattled, opened and hit the wall with a bang. A drunken cavalryman entered. He pointed a finger at Doc.

"You Southern dick. I didn't ask a drunk to pull my teeth, I want a refund."

Doc peered over his glasses but didn't respond.

"What? You mute or something?"

Doc heard something click. Under the table his fingers brushed the leather holster and wrapped around the cold metal army revolver. He drew the gun and fired it. The bullet left the gun's chamber and spliced the soldier's leg. He fell backwards, his face contorted in pain and collapsed on the ground.

The players pulled back from Doc and the table, running from the room. Only the trooper remained on the ground. He reached with some difficulty for his pistol and aimed his tired arm up at Doc.

Doc's fingers moved along the gun. His long, thin arm reached out and flicked the pistol down. The gun engaged and fired. The bullet flew through the air. A cloud of dust surrounded the burning tip and lodged itself in the trooper's blue coat. Small flames leapt from the soldier's chest. He hit his coat with his gloves and choked as the warm blood flowed to his lips. The gun was still warm in Doc's hand. Blood dripped onto his wrist. He shivered and wiped the substance away. His breathing was rapid and noisy. His face paled as the shock hit him. He placed his gun back into the holster. He covered himself in his long, gray overcoat. 'I'm still alive,' he thought. He shuddered. The hairs on his neck bristled and his skin grew cold. He left the poker room in a daze and drifted out of the saloon and on to the bright street.

A horse roared. Doc ran towards the noise. His knees gave way. He tripped and faltered. He grabbed the horse by the bit shanks. The horse reversed with a snort. It reared up, pinning its ears on its dappled neck. Doc reached for the horn of the saddle and swung his left leg into the stirrup. The horse pivoted around in a tight circle. Doc slid down towards the ground and tried again. He could feel the blood drain from his body. His legs sank.

Men swarmed from the saloons, shops and hotels, led by the town Sheriff. "That's him, we've got him," he said.

Doc crawled into the saddle. There was a loud bang as guns fired behind him. The horse lunged forward with him hanging on. It straightened out and with a final kick, galloped as fast as it could. Doc clung to the horse's neck and beat his spurs against its side. The dust rose in clouds behind them. Down the street they galloped and out onto the prairie. Doc turned back to see if anyone was following but could only see the gray tail of the horse and the thorny scrub. His ears buzzed, his head grew heavy and he dropped his face deep into the dark mane. The horse felt the weight on its neck and galloped faster.

After a couple of miles of hard galloping, Doc's mount grew tired. The horse had run alone out of fear for the first mile and had burnt up any stamina that it had left in his lungs. Doc clung on for most of the ride. He was too tired to fight the horse and was as scared as the horse was. Now exhaustion created a bond between them. Doc slowed the horse to a steadier pace.

The animal heaved and strained, breathing hard. The horse's breath and hoof beats echoed in Doc's head. He heard whistling from the horse's nostrils and the heavy snorts as each hoof hit the ground.

Doc pressed his heels harder against the horse's ribs but there was no more energy to take. They slowed down to a trot. Foamy spit flew backwards from the horse's mouth and hit Doc's overcoat. The horse moved with a slow stumbling gait. It puffed hard, veins raised in its face and its nostrils fluttering with every stride.

The dentist dropped his reins in disgust. He was tired too, the sweat dripped down between his eyebrows, over his nostrils and deep into his chestnut mustache. His heart was still pounding and his chest was tight and heavy from the effort. He wheezed, coughed and spat over the horse's shoulder. He slowed the horse down to a walk. The horse dropped pace with gratitude and pulled its neck to the ground, snorting. Clouds of steam rose from its back. Doc patted the horse's wet shoulders and turned to look back at the trail that he had ridden. He dearly wished he had stolen a faster horse. He had spent long enough as a farm boy to know that his horse was broken-winded. He felt the irony of his situation, fate had teamed him with an equine asthmatic. Were there still people after him? Doc couldn't be sure. Where was he? He didn't know that either. He had been too distracted to follow any particular direction and had no time to plan any route. He rode until the sun retreated from the sky and left the clouds to float in the growing darkness.

Doc pulled the collar of his overcoat high up around his neck. From the far distance the thunder rolled and crept closer to the trail. There was an eerie silence before the first flash of lightning. The horse startled and roared. The second flash was closer still and broke the little horse into a shuffling jog. The rain fell. Icy droplets found a gap in Doc's overcoat and ran down his neck. Doc shivered and tensed his back against the cold. He pushed the horse back to a gallop. It slid down the trail before Doc felt it lose balance in the muddy ground and steadied it back. They were lost. Doc saw a clump of trees at the side of the track and rode towards them.

The ground was soft and dry beneath the trees. Doc was happy to get some shelter and take a break. He kicked his feet free of the stirrups and dismounted. His knees buckled as he landed. He grabbed hold of the horn on the saddle to steady himself. His body buzzed and tingled as he fought pain and exhaustion. He led the horse over to one of the biggest trees and he flopped down in the dirt. He kept his eye on the horse and stared at the rein until the leather slipped from his hand and exhaustion dropped him into a shallow sleep. He woke up cold and hungry. He took a long drink from his flask of whiskey. A warm glow spread through his body and took some of the numbness away. Why had he been so stupid? The whole day had been a disaster. He had woken that afternoon with a warm bed, a hangover and winnings from the poker tables the night before. He had even earned some money from a dental job that had come his way. He had never dreamed that he would ever hit someone in the stomach with his bullet let alone kill anyone out right. Now he sat, cold and wet, miles from the nearest train station, guilty of murder with a stolen, worn out, horse for company. He moved his head to see where the horse had wandered off to but he was still dizzy and unfocused. He had felt lonely and depressed many times before but never had he wanted to die as much as now. He knew that suicide was cowardly but could see no other way out of his dilemma. He pulled his pistol from his coat pocket and placed it to his head. The shiny metal barrel sat heavy in his hand and his wrist wobbled as he fingered the trigger. He choked and felt tears of shame run down his face. His father gave the gun as a graduation present back home in Georgia. He closed his eyes and aimed the gun. The hammer pulled back and clicked against the empty chamber. He tried again with increasing desperation. The gun was empty. He searched in his pockets for ammunition. His pockets were empty. He threw the gun down with disgust, whimpered and clutched his chest, rocking himself, until he cried himself to sleep.

Raindrops dripping on the ground from overhanging branches woke Doc. He moved with a clear head and noticed for the first time that the trooper had shot him in the side. The wound was not deep but painful enough to make any movement slow and awkward. His body would have to wait for attention. He would be able to patch himself up once he reached a town.

He looked around for his horse and saw it grazing on a clump of grass at the side of the trees. He hauled himself painfully off the ground and limped towards it. His leg moved stiffly at first, his clothes were still wet from the night before and his muscles were cold. He moved a couple of strides and winced in pain. He watched the horse and wondered if he could get the animal to come over to him. He pursed his lips and whistled. The horse's ears pricked forward. Doc whistled louder. The horse lifted his head and turned around to look at him.

He whistled again and halted in mid flow to cough. The horse pricked both ears, took a stride forward and stopped.

"C'mon now."

The horse shook its head in disapproval, swatted a fly with its tail and continued grazing with a snort. Doc cursed and sighed.

He reached into his pocket and found a cigarette that he had rolled the night before. He smiled at his luck when he found a match to light it with. He took a suck of the end and blew the smoke out. The nicotine hit his bloodstream. He wheezed and choked between puffs. He had almost reached the drags when he felt a nudge in the shoulders. He looked up at the horse with surprise. The horse nudged him again.

"What is it? You want a cigarette?"

The horse poked its nostrils forward to sniff the smoke and jerked its head back at the sour smell. Doc smiled.

"Oh now honeysuckle you don't want to smoke this, it'll do bad things to your health."

He grinned and placed the butt in the corner of his mouth.

He pulled the reins up and across the horse's neck. He leaned against the saddle, shifting and hopping until he was in a better position to mount. He placed his boot into the stirrup and hauled himself up. He made some progress and then slipped back to the ground. He gritted his teeth and tried again. He grabbed the sides of the saddle for a better grip and used all his strength to pull himself up. The pain oozed from his side. Doc grimaced and held on with determination. His hands shook and his knuckles paled. With his weight leant over the saddle he moved his leg over the horse's side and lowered himself on to the saddle. The horse grew restless and walked away. Doc lost balance and leaned his weight down on the gelding's neck. The pony scared and moved with a shuffle into a trot.

"Wait."

He grabbed the reins and a piece of mane and pulled himself up into a sitting position. The horse trotted with speed through the long grass and hit the mud slick road in a rocking canter. Doc slipped his feet into his stirrups, took a quick puff of his cigarette and then took charge of the business of steering.

The pair of runaways galloped at their leisure along the track. Doc relaxed and enjoyed the ride. The pain in his side finally subsided, least he felt that it had, or perhaps he was numb to the sharp sensation. He felt completely at ease. He wasn't worried about where he was going any more. He really didn't care. He clicked his tongue and urged the cow pony across the open country.

CHAPTER TWO

Doc felt he had been riding for an eternity. How long would it be until he could have a drink of whiskey? His flask had been empty for hours. Surely he must be getting close to a town soon? The noise of the rushing water of the Arkansas River broke the silence. The river bubbled and frothed in a dangerous manner. Ahead lay a massive wooden bridge, big enough to take a line of traffic in both directions. The horse's hooves thudded on the wooden boards, dust rose with every step. Dodge City opened up before Doc, sprawling out on the banks of the river. His horse hopped off the bridge and strode out into Front Street. A huge wooden sign declared that carrying firearms was prohibited and that bitter was selling a couple of cents cheaper than anywhere else in Kansas. Bulls roared and horses snorted as buckboards and buggies trotted past one another in the street. A barbershop door lay open, a businessman leaned back in a chair, chin covered in soapy foam. Doc could hear the trade of the saloon as confidence men won over potential suckers.

Riding across the railway tracks, Doc looked down the line to the train station. He watched a group of Texan cowboys stare at the afternoon train as it chugged into the station, steam and smoke billowed down the line. The cowboys gawked at the strange machine, pointing and dropping jaws. Doc thought back to when he had seen a train for the first time, when he was a child in Georgia. It was difficult to remember how he had felt and although he tried, it was hard to relate to the cowboys' feelings. They were the stupidest looking rabble of individuals that he had laid eyes on in a long time.

Outside the pharmacy, Doc swung his legs stiffly down from the saddle. His right leg buckled as it hit the ground and he stumbled. He limped to the boardwalk, climbed the steps and opened the door.

The shop was dark. On the shelves above were brown jars filled with drugs and remedies each one neatly labeled. A set of measuring scales sat on the wooden counter. The air smelled strange, scented with a musty sweetness from the contents of the jars. The dentist smiled when he spied the jar of candy balls sitting at the back of the counter along with a small arrangement of other confectioneries. Candy balls indicated that the town would be in need of a dentist sooner or later. The store was warm and familiar. It brought back memories of a time when his father had run a similar store in Georgia. A man with a walrus mustache lifted the hinge on the counter and let himself out to be beside the dentist.

"How can I help you Sir?"

"I've been shot. I was hoping you'd be kind enough to suture the wound for me."

"Gun misfired?"

"I'm sure you understand Sir, it was an accident. I'm not the kind to involve myself in bar room brawls of any kind. I merely have been having difficulty with my gun engaging during awkward situations."

"Well, that happens sometimes. Come on through the back and we'll get you cleaned up."

He ushered Doc through to a back room and sat the dentist down in a polished wooden chair. The pharmacist left to get a basin of water and some clean rags. He returned and sat down in front of Doc.

"Take your jacket off and open your shirt."

Doc obeyed and eyed the man as he undid the little mother of pearl buttons on his silk vest. The pharmacist gazed down at the dentist's protruding ribs.

"Consumptive huh?"

"Yes Sir I am," said Doc.

The pharmacist focused his attention on the wound. The blood had clotted around the edges. In the middle there still seeped a trail of blood. Around the mouth of the wound were a few bruises and a yellowing burn mark. The man studied the flaps of torn flesh.

"That'll need a couple of stitches. Don't see any sign of a bullet in there or serious damage."

The man washed the wound over and cleared the sticky puss from deep in the center. Grit fell further into the wound before being washed out and caused the mouth of the wound to sting. The man took a needle and thread and proceeded to sew. Doc gritted his teeth and winced.

"Hold steady now," said the man.

Doc growled as the needle went into his skin and came through the other side. The man seemed hesitant in the way that he sewed. The dentist wished that he could clean himself up. It never seemed to hurt so much when he sewed his own wounds. He sighed, gulped, and then closed his eyes and chewed down against the constant pulsing coming from the wound. He concentrated on blocking out the pain. The man finished sewing and wiped little dots of blood from the edges of the thread. He knotted the end and broke off the excess around his fingers. The stitches pulled tight. Doc flinched with a snort.

"Hurts some don't it?" said the man.

"Yes sir it does."

"Well gettin' shot will do that for a man. This your first time?"

"No, no, I've been shot before."

"Hold on a second. I have somethin' that'll help."

The man went back through to the store and brought back a small brown bottle of laudanum.

"Now, you take six to eight drops of this whenever you get sore and you won't feel a thing soon enough."

Doc reached into his coat pocket and pulled out a large wad of hundred dollar bills. He separated five dollars with some effort and laid them down for the pharmacist. "Will this be enough?"

The man gazed down at the large sum of money that Doc held in his hand. He then turned his attention to the five dollars pushed before him. He swallowed and thought it best not to ask the stranger why he was carrying such a large amount of money.

"That ought to do it," said the pharmacist.

Doc took the bottle of laudanum and wet his lips with the bitter substance. He felt the warmth sink into him and hoped that the pain would ease quickly. The pharmacist fussed over the wound and put a light dressing on in the hope of keeping it clean. The chore finally over, Doc was able to pull his shirt back on in peace.

"Thank you Sir," he said, easing his satin vest over his shirt and fastening the buttons. He moved his gun into his overcoat pocket, away from his wounded side.

"Don't you go doing anything stressful now. You could burst your stitches. Just take it easy."

Doc laughed. "I don't think you have to worry about that. The idea of leaving this chair pains me."

"Well now, you let me know if those stitches get ripped or if you run out of laudanum or anything. The store is open most of the time."

"I'll do so Sir. I believe I have enough here to keep me for a while. I can always suture anything that comes loose."

"You're a doctor?"

"No I'm a dentist."

"You need a supplier?"

"Not at the moment perhaps later."

"I supply opiates and cocaine to the Doctor here and the one in Fort Dodge. Just let me know."

"Thank you. I'll certainly keep you in mind. Your

prices are reasonable."

"You got a place to stay?"

"Nowhere at the moment."

"You may want to try the Dodge House it's the best rooming house in Kansas. They do a fine meal there most days."

"Thank you."

"No thank you. It's been quiet today. I was glad to see you. Hope you get to feeling better."

"So do I."

Doc eased himself from the chair and walked stiffly towards the door. He could feel the stitches pull in his side. It was a strange, painful sensation but his mind rested with the knowledge that the wound was clean and treated. It was one less thing to worry about. He could feel his senses blur as the laudanum numbed the pain.

The sleigh bell hanging from the store door rattled as the door closed. Doc walked out into the early evening with his overcoat slung over his arm. A chill ran through his body, his clothes were dry enough to wear but still retained some dampness from the rains the night before. The temperature outside was dropping. Doc could feel the wind rattling his bones. He walked along the boardwalk and tried to forget the pain that caused him to limp when his right foot hit the ground. He crossed the street to where lines of bars and brothels stood waiting. He had wanted to behave and get a bed for the night, eat supper and retire, but his curiosity was killing him. He had seen some interesting saloons a few hours before on the ride into town. One saloon would not be wrong, he was too tired for poker, he wanted only to buy a couple

of bottles of whiskey and get settled down for the
night.

He stepped through the mud to the far side of
Front Street, trying not to slide through the wetter
areas. The street was more than just puddles. The
rains had mixed sand and water together, forming
a frothy brown slime that would send any sure-
footed individual flying with the shortest of notice.
A horse and cowboy cantered down the street with
splashing strides. Doc moved away from spraying
distance and climbed the steps that led him to the
boardwalk on the other side.

Light oozed out from the Long Branch Saloon,
making the puddles shine. Doc made his way
through the smoky crowds to the bar. He found a
place at the far corner of the bar and waited for
someone to take his order. As he stood waiting he
took a look at his surroundings. The bar was by no
means fancy, but comfortable enough. He looked
down towards the floor. The bar was lined with a
brass surround. Muddy boots sat in a long line.
Spur rowels balanced on the wooden floor-boards,
only spittoons interrupted the line. Paneled wood
and deer skulls of different shapes and sizes
covered the walls. A heavy mirror lined the back of
the bar. Reflected in the mirror were glass shelves
holding hundreds of shot glasses and tumblers.
The gas lamps that hung from the ceiling bounced
light against the mirror and up against the
bartender's bald head. The barman worked
methodically, remembering each customer's order,
refilling glasses and taking money. He stood in a
striped shirt with a long white apron. His
mustache was long and bushy and his eyes were

almost black. He stood with his arms folded
waiting for a sign of a new order. Doc tipped his
hat to get the bartenders attention and ordered two
bottles of bourbon and waited.

A gun hammer pulling back with a click sent a
shiver down Doc's back. He turned and saw a
cowboy raise a gun in the air. The cowboy's
drunken arm wobbled backwards and forwards.
The barrel of the colt was pointed at the back of a
tall, lanky man with dirty blond hair, who was
sitting at the other side of the bar drinking coffee.
The cowboy pulled the trigger was back, grinning
with satisfaction.

Doc reached for a pistol that hung on the side of
the bar, prayed that it had bullets and took his
chances. He pulled back the trigger and took a shot
at the cowboy. Both guns fired at the same time,
the two bullets flew in opposite directions, but Doc
was faster. The cowboy was hit in the shoulder and
dropped his gun as it discharged. The cowboy fell.
The tall man got up and stared down at the
cowboy on the floor who had tried to kill him. Doc
saw the badge on the tall man's chest and
shuddered. He had no need to involve himself
with the law. He hoped that the marshal had no
contacts in Wichita.

The lawman nodded his appreciation, walked
over to Doc and shook his hand vigorously.

"Thank you. I thought I was as good as gone."

"Well you would have been. I couldn't bear to see
a coward shoot a man in the back like that."

"I appreciate it."

"Do you need help disposing of this gentlemen?"

"Are you volunteering? Grab a hold of his arm

for me and we'll drag him over to the jail."

Doc held the cowboy's bleeding shoulders in his arms. The lawman took the man's legs. Doc could feel his stitches stretch as the weight of the cowboy was distributed across his shoulder blades. The weight was painful, but he was too proud to admit it to the lawman. He walked in silence with the man against his chest, out to the open air and back across the muddy street that he had crossed earlier. He knew that the weight of the prisoner in his arms was causing him to drag his feet in the mud but he didn't care. He thanked God for such muddy ground that allowed him to slide across to the jail as if he were on ice. He watched the lawman carry the other end of the prisoner's limp body. He made it look effortless. He even stopped at one point to allow Doc to readjust his grip. The dentist struggled with the weight. He didn't dare show his lack of strength or the pain that grew from his sides as the stitches chaffed and rubbed the bullet wound.

The light from the jail shone out onto the street. It was the first time that Doc had ever been happy to see a jail in his life.

"You can let him down now," said the lawman. Doc was relieved to drop the man to the ground. Beads of sweat dripped over his back and shoulders. He stood wheezing, trying to breath normally. He reached for his handkerchief and dabbed the sweat from his face and wiped his mouth. The lawman grabbed the cowboy by the shoulders and dragged him to a cell. Two other men were waiting, he flopped him down on a grimy bunk and slammed the door shut.

It was easier to see the lawman in the light of the jail without smoke getting in the way. The man was tall and lean but not bony. Every muscle in his body had been earned by labor. His white shirt was collarless and tainted with blood from the prisoner. His hair was long at the back, in need of some attention from a barber. His mustache swept down to his jaw line and his light blue eyes held a perpetual squint that gave him a look that was both inquisitive and perplexed at the same time.

"First time I'd seen you," he said, "What's your name?"

"Doc Holliday, I rode into town today."

"Well, I'm sure glad that you did. I'm truly grateful Doc, you saved my life tonight."

"It was nothing."

"The hell it was. I almost got killed." The lawman offered his hand to shake. "Wyatt Earp call me Wyatt. I'm the Deputy Marshal here in Dodge. If there is anything you need, come over to the office and I'll see what I can do. Nothing is too big a favor after tonight. I'll never forget what you did."

"That's a kind offer Sir. I believe you're a man that keeps his promises."

"You can bet your ass I am. You know, your name sounds familiar. What do you do for a living?"

"I'm a dentist."

"That doesn't answer my curiosity. Are you a saloonkeeper? Do you gamble?"

"I gamble some."

"That may be where I heard of you then. It's a pleasure to meet you Doc."

The men shook hands and eyed one another

strangely. Doc was amused by the incident but thought little of it. He could feel the laudanum drain the remaining energy that he had in his body. In other circumstances he would have been more polite, but the desire to eat, drink and sleep were overwhelming. He nodded to the marshal, said his goodbyes, turned and left the jail.

Doc Holliday checked into room twenty-four at the Dodge House. Despite the laudanum in his body he remained tense and alert. He walked into the dark room with his right hand resting on his gun. He felt stupid doing it. He knew that he had no ammunition and he knew that no one was waiting for him. It was his routine to check every door and every closet. Only after he was sure he was alone could he relax and lock the door.

He removed his shirt and winced as the material got caught on the bullet wound and almost ripped off the dressing. The blood had seeped through the bandage making the surface sticky. He was sure that some of the stitches had burst after his adventure down at the jail. The other stitches had tightened and pinched the skin together. He would have to re-suture the wound again. He was too tired to be bothered. He sat down on the bed and kicked his muddy boots off onto the floorboards.

He lay down and thought about his first evening in Dodge. He regretted helping Wyatt. He knew that the Marshal probably had friends in Wichita that would know about him shooting the soldier. Surely it wouldn't take them long to ride to Dodge. Why had he been so stupid?

CHAPTER THREE

Doc glanced at the Dodge City Times that lay on the bed. He had bought the issue early one morning on the way back from an all night poker game. It lay open at a story about the city police, Jim Masterson and Wyatt Earp, and how a risky arrest had almost ended in tragedy. According to the paper, it had been the second time in so many months that someone had tried to shoot Wyatt. The town hadn't forgotten Deputy Marshal Ed Masterson's death. A cowboy had gunned him down in the middle of Front Street after an ordinary arrest had gone wrong.

Doc admired Wyatt's guts and as a gambler he fully understood risk. There was instant fame for the successful man who tried to kill him. The easiest form of assassination was to shoot someone in the back. Doc wondered if it was the same for Wyatt and smiled. It was comforting to think that Wyatt was as vulnerable as he was. No matter which side of justice a man was on, he would always be a target if he had a reputation to keep.

Doc pushed his thoughts aside and got ready for work. He slipped his gun down into his shoulder holster. He winced as the weight of it rubbed the holster against his recovering bullet wound. The damage to the wound was repairing well, but the area around his ribs was still bruised and swollen and the stitches were itchy. He brushed the dirt off his jacket and pulled it. The butt of the gun rubbed against his side. Without thinking, he caught the gun before it had a chance to catch on his wound. He closed the newspaper and looked at his advert for dental services in amongst the other Dodge classifieds, on the front page. The advert had generated little reaction from anyone. In one week, he had made three hundred and fifty dollars. Five dollars earned pulling teeth, the rest from gambling profits. The money was a fortune to most people but Doc knew that he could lose it gambling as fast as he had made it. He needed a money supply that he could depend on day to day - dentistry was not the source. He questioned the apathy of the people. The good Christian citizens of Dodge considered Doc as a drunkard and devil. Doc thought it strange that they felt that way. When he was a child in Griffin, the minister lectured the same moral lectures, virtues and sins at church every Sunday. The devil had rested on every corner back in Georgia. It was only a matter of time before you'd succumb to his vices. It had been easy for Doc, all he had done was curse one Sunday and the devil guaranteed him his place. It was funny to think that he was now a sinner and was going to burn in hell if the advice the church had preached was any where near the truth. Was it any wonder that the Christians of Dodge would not let their children, mothers or fathers near Doc for dental duties? It was understandable. As for the cowboys, they preferred alcohol as a cure. They had their fair share of knocked out teeth, cavities and tooth-aches, but they had no desire to wear gold fillings. A cook and brander at the chuck wagon could burn and punch out the offending piece of enamel.

Doc gazed down at the pitiful amount of money he had gathered that week working as a dentist. He sighed and reached for his hat. He would need to work hard at the poker tables to pay his way. He smiled and tried to be positive, he was lucky to get any dental work at all. Perhaps he would buy a bottle of Bourbon to celebrate. He closed the door and checked that he'd locked it. The door to the room next to his was wide open and Doc caught a vision of two hunting dogs lying stretched out on the bed. One lifted its head, yawned and howled. It rolled upside down on the bed with its back legs spread open and a length of drool soaking into the bed covers. Doc sighed at the sight, slung his overcoat over his shoulder and went down the stairs to the lobby of the Dodge House.

At the reception desk two men argued with the proprietor over a shortage of beds. They were told that they would have to share. The first man pulled his gun on the other and threatened to shoot him for the bed. The other's hound dog growled and bit the man's ankles. The man aimed his gun but the dog pulled at his ankle and threw him off balance. A shot went through the ceiling, causing a prostitute upstairs to scream. The proprietor and his fat wife laid their hands on the fighting men and pulled them apart, ending the argument. The men were told that they would share the bed or leave. The man admitted that was fine so long as his hunting dogs could sleep with him. The other man frowned and took the key. Doc showed little interest and continued on his way down the stairs and out the front door. He was lucky to have a room to himself. Few people wanted to share a bed with a consumptive, let alone a murdering one.

Doc walked out into the warmth of the summer night. He stood taking in the atmosphere, rolled a cigarette with his bony fingers and set off down the street, lighting a match. The wind blew in a weird concoction of aromas. When the air was dry, there was always a faint smell of sandy soil and horsehair as it lifted in dust devils along the city streets. Other evenings would bring the sweet smell of wild sage. On this night, the scent of steak frying wafted up into Doc's flared nostrils and made the dentist wish that he had time to stop and eat. He walked on and ignored his hunger.

He walked down the street until the misty haze of cigarette smoke beckoned him into the Lady Gay Saloon. He wandered in through the elegantly carved bat-wing doors. The smoke rushed out to great him. He stood for a while, mapping a route through the Faro banks, drinking tables and standing, crowds of cowboys. After some consideration, he proceeded forward and made his way through the crowds. On each side of the saloon, different games progressed.

There must have been at least three Faro banks running that night. In the far corner a roulette game rattled and down beside the bar, a game of 'chuck-a-luck' was in action. Cowboys huddled around the little cage that held three dice. The dealer brought the cage down onto the table with a clunk and everyone scrambled to see the faces of the dice. Two dice showed one dot, the other showed five. Words of 'hard luck' and 'better luck next time' were called and the next cowboy stepped forward, pushing his coins to the dealer. Doc pushed his way through the crowd, to the edge of the long, mahogany bar. He ordered bourbon, took the bottle gladly and handed over his hard-earned money. He gazed around the bar for a table but was out of luck, there wasn't much room to stand. He took a deep breath and headed towards a door at the back of the saloon. Every step was littered with discarded cigarette and cigar butts giving him a spring in his stride. As he moved towards the door, the cigarettes disappeared. He pushed the swing door open and stood on the mud encrusted, red carpet.

The sudden silence after the noise and bustle of the main saloon was shocking. Doc stood in the darkness and took in the scene. The smoke reflected off the lantern light and cast ghostly shadows on the walls. The poker table stood illuminated in the darkness, its green felt shone brightly. Doc walked through the shadows, trying not to disturb the players. He studied the game in progress, a maneuver that only true poker sharks practiced. He examined each interaction, noiseless conversation between players, movement on movement. From high above, a smart player could absorb the styles of his future opponents. He could scan for signs of nervousness and subconscious actions that tell stories of losing hands.

Doc walked out of the darkness, into the light. Three men sat at the table, gold coins littered the center. Laughter broke the silence. A young man of twenty-seven years leaned back in his chair, tears of laughter rolled down his face. The other players studied him in dismay.

"What in hell are you laughing at?" said Jim Masterson.

The young man smiled and laid his cards down, one by one. He had a Royal Flush. "I guess that's about a hundred dollars you owe me."

Jim stretched his arms and shoulders and got up to put on his coat. "I'll owe you later Morg. I've got to get back on duty. Wyatt got touchy last time I was late."

"You're just scared I'll whip you another time."

Jim turned towards the door. For the first time Doc was able to read the deputy badge pinned to the man's shirt. He wondered how many other members of the police force sat around the table. He stepped forward into the light. Jim smiled and tipped his hat on his way out. "Good luck sir. I hope you've you're feeling lucky. You'll need it against that boy."

Doc nodded.

The table took a short break to allow everyone to get up and stretch. Luke Short accepted his financial loss. He removed a lacquered box from under the table and offered cigars to everyone. Doc saw his chance to introduce himself.

"I do believe someone was needing one hundred dollars. I'll lay you down three hundred if you give me a cut of the game."

Morgan waited until he had counted the money before looking up at the dentist. He smiled at Doc. The other men watched Morgan's reaction.

The dentist waited for his offer to be accepted. Deep down he wished he hadn't wagered so much money. He had promised himself that he would be more prudent and had offered to lose all the money he had. He told himself that he had to continue; to lower a bet was against his principles.

Morgan laughed and reached for the pack of cards. "All right then. I guess you've got enough. Lay your money down and take a place."

Doc sat down in the empty chair that Jim had left behind him. Morgan shuffled the cards. Doc watched his new players carefully, if he was going to be a fool with his money, he may as well commit to the game. Morgan was a tidy dealer but not stylish, he was efficient and workmanlike. The cards purred like a cat as he took the split deck and shuffled them back together. The first card slid across the table on its belly. One by one the cards drifted into piles in front of each player. Doc flexed and stretched his hands and wrists until his index finger popped with a crack. He stretched each finger independently and waited. He remembered the bottle of whiskey that he had bought earlier and poured a shot into the scratched glass.

Morgan finished dealing and watched Doc carefully. "Doc isn't it? You're the killer dentist, from the South."

Doc looked at Morgan in disgust. "Is that what they're saying? And you are?"

"My name's Morg. It's a pleasure to beat you.

Let's kick this game into action."

A smile of cunning ran across Doc's face. "Morg, the pleasure's mine."

Poker games have a tendency to be a tad unpredictable, as are the players that partake. Some games take hours and some take days. Morgan and Doc played all night. Hand after hand were laid on the table and reshuffled. Players came and went. Luke quit his cards at two o' clock that morning. Four hours later only Doc and Morgan were remaining. With only two players left, the game ended quickly.

A cool breeze blew down the middle of Front Street. The sky changed to a deep midnight blue. In the distance, a flame of red was growing. The wind whispered as it blew across the prairie. The moon waited for the light's arrival and retired. The birds chattered. A deer walked down to the river in a relaxed manner. It sucked in the cool water. A door closed with a bang and disturbed the animal. It looked up. Its ears twitched.

At the Lady Gay Saloon, two men's souls were sealed together. The owner of the establishment was not impressed and screamed at the men.

Morgan dealt with the man in his usual relaxed manner. "Hey it's all right Henry. I'll take him home. Come on Doc." The door swung open for the second time. Doc and Morgan left the establishment in a drunken haze. A cold chill ran through Doc's body, causing him to shiver. He pulled his long gray overcoat over his shoulders and felt the warmth soak into his body. He walked with faltering drunken steps, clutching the half empty bottle of bourbon close to his chest. Morgan grasped the dentist's shoulders and supported his frame. From a distance it was difficult to know who needed the most support, but the men were past caring. It was a strange arrangement that two drunks should cling together. The men would have made more progress without one another, but in times like these it was companionship that defied logic. The gamblers strolled down the empty street. Morgan laughed and turned to face Doc, bashed into him and almost knocked him over.

"Well, that's five, ten, no. Fifteen hundred dollars you owe me Doc. Told you I'd whip you." Doc looked at Morgan for a long time with his bloodshot hooded eyes and laid a hand on his shoulder in a gentle manner. This caused him to wobble and he grabbed Morgan roughly by the jacket.

"You're a self-righteous bastard, Morg. You remind me of someone." Doc took time to think. "Wyatt. That's it you remind me of Wyatt." Doc smiled, let go of Morgan's arm and continued to make his way down the street.

Morgan smiled. He looked at Doc and was overcome with laughter.

Doc pulled his coat collar up and took on an arrogant, strut. "At least you have some fire in your guts. I'm sick of Wyatt Earp and all his lawman friends following me around. I'm pleased to finally acquaint with a gambling man like yourself."

Morgan stopped laughing thought for a second and started to laugh again. Doc watched Morgan and grabbed hold of his arm. The young gambler swung to a halt. The dentist's eyes were full of worry and mild paranoia, accentuated by the effects of alcohol.

"Oh God Morgan. You don't know Wyatt do you?"

"He's my brother."

"Oh Lord no! Don't tell me, you police too right?"

"Part time deputy of Dodge." Morgan replied.

Doc could do nothing but look off into the distance, bewildered. "Son of a bitch."

CHAPTER FOUR

A scream came from the Lady Gay Saloon.
Wyatt checked his pistol and rushed inside. The
bar was quiet when he entered. Everyone's eyes
were focused on the far corner of the room. Wyatt
cautiously made his way across towards the back
corner. At the far table two men sat arguing, one
was Bat Masterson, the other, Doc Holliday. Doc
grasped Bat's collar and pressed his pocket,
derringer against Bat's forehead.

"Well friend are you going to sit there all night or
do I have to shoot you for the money?"

Bat looked Doc straight in the eye, "I don't have
any money Doc. I spent the last of it on a whiskey,
half an hour ago. So why don't you go ahead and
shoot me? We've plenty of room in the jail tonight.
Once I'm dead, Wyatt will arrest you and find you
a cell."

"All right." Doc dug the barrels of the derringer
into Bat's head and pulled the trigger. Wyatt
moved forward to grab the gun.

"Don't Doc."

Doc looked up at Wyatt with flared nostrils and misty eyes. He pulled the trigger and aimed the gun badly on purpose. The bullet whizzed past Bat's ear as planned. It bounced off the wall behind them and smashed a glass. The tumbler splintered into pieces with a satisfying tinkle. Bat smiled at Doc and was rewarded by an affectionately skeletal grin from the dentist. "You are a lucky devil Bat. I think I love you too much."

The men erupted into fits of laughter. The only one who missed the joke was Wyatt. He looked at the two men with annoyance. "Wyatt please don't arrest me we was only playing," said Doc.He tried to stay serious but Bat's gleaming dark eyes sent Doc back into a state of hysterics. He laughed until the strain on his lungs made him cough. The more he coughed, the more he laughed. He leaned forward, clutching his side in a strange mixture of pain and happiness. The derringer slipped out of his hand and fell on to the floor with a clunk.

Wyatt picked up the gun. "How are you Doc?"

Doc stopped coughing and laughing and lifted his head upwards, his eyes smarting and watering in the light.

"Things are fine Wyatt and how are you being my most favorite marshal in Dodge an' all if you're not including Bat here?" His face creased as a devilish grin appeared and disappeared along the lines of his face.

Bat pulled a face at Doc and despite Doc's best efforts, he roared with laughter. Bat laughed until his sides hurt. Wyatt wondered if he had lost himself in a sadistic dream. He couldn't understand why Bat was suffering Doc's company or why he found that he was also sitting beside Doc.

"That's better Wyatt. Bat and I have just decided that you're gonna join the game. Let me buy you a drink of something. I think you'll find I know a lot more about you than you give me credit for."

"Well, you got me wrong, for a start, I don't drink."

"Oh and what makes you think I was offering something alcoholic? All things considered, if you're as fast with a gun as people say, it shouldn't matter if people laugh at you for drinking soda pops. I respect a man who stands up for his principles."

Doc smiled and winked at Wyatt, "Mark my words. It's nothing to be ashamed of. I hear they come in four flavors now."

Wyatt's head jigged up and down as he laughed quietly. The pressure was released like a cork popping from a bottle of champagne and he found it hard to stop laughing.

"Now, what in the world brought that on?" said Doc.

Wyatt stopped laughing but had an unusual smirk on his face. Bat studied the two men in surprise. He gathered the cards from various ends of the table, shuffled them, split the deck and reshuffled. "Another game Doc? Wyatt come on and join the game. If one lawman won't stop Holliday cheatin' maybe two will."

Doc looked at Bat with disgust. Bat smiled back and dealt the cards. Holliday swallowed the indelicacy. Wyatt noticed and recorded the event with amusement.

A cowboy galloped passed the entrance to the saloon and fired his gun, releasing a spray of shot into the air. The candle on the piano in the corner of the saloon, splintered and cracked in to two pieces. Rows of glasses behind the bar were shot to needles and showered down over the cowering people. The galloping hooves and hooting faded into the distance and everyone got up.

Wyatt grabbed his hat and gun and ran to the door. He looked through the swirling dust onto the empty street. There were horses snorting but he couldn't see where the cowboys were. The dust drifted and dropped to the ground. Jim Masterson walked out of the jail with a loaded shotgun. He tipped his hat at Wyatt and winked a signal. Wyatt nodded a reply, settled the weapon in his hand and waited.

The cowboy turned his horse at the top of the street and galloped down past the Lady Gay Saloon. The lawmen lined up their guns and fired. The dust swirled up and wrapped around the cowboy. He galloped away without a scratch. The cowboy's friend was next to try. He turned his horse and spurred it in the flanks. He fired his shotgun into the air. The horse pulled back as buckshot sprayed around. His rider jabbed him hard in the mouth and pulled him up onto his haunches. The horse reared and walked on his hind legs for a couple of wavering steps. The long gray legs floundered in the air trying to balance. Buckshot hit the heavy pane of glass at the butcher's store. Fragments of glass flew everywhere. The man pivoted his horse and released it to the ground, letting it gallop to its heart's content.

Wyatt stepped off the boardwalk, into the street, lifted his gun and took a steady aim. The cowboy rode at a steady canter towards the end of town. Wyatt fired a shot and the cowboy folded in the saddle, clutching his shoulder. The cowboys saw their friend bleeding and grew scared. They turned and galloped to the edge of town, only slowing to trot on to the large wooden, toll bridge that led out of Dodge.

Jim Masterson crossed over Front Street and met Wyatt in the middle. The cowboys disappeared into the darkness but the noise of the horses persisted. Their hooves banged against the wooden bridge. The river reflected moonlight upwards from the water and illuminated the trotting cowboys. Wyatt and Jim took the chance open to them and aimed the guns in a synchronized fashion. The guns panned the cowboys, both men pulled the hammers back and both guns went off at the same time. One of the cowboys aimed his pistol from the bridge but he was too far away. His horse danced at the last moment, causing the shot to hit the water. Wyatt and Jim fired at the same time, the cowboy folded cleanly in the saddle. His horse scared at the impact and bolted across the bridge, its hooves sliding on the wood. The cowboy hung on for as long as he could and dropped with a loud thud on the other side.

The lawmen approached the bridge with caution. It was still lit up and neither man wanted to risk being shot by the wounded cowboy while making the arrest. The cowboy lay face down in the dust.

Jim pointed his shotgun over the man while Wyatt grabbed him by the scruff of his neck and rolled him over. The cowboy groaned and opened his eyes. Blood trickled down from a gunshot wound to his upper thigh. His jacket was covered in blood from a wound that had pierced his shoulder.

"He's still alive. Go on and get the doctor and a buckboard."

"You all right here alone Wyatt?"

"I'll be fine, he's not going anywhere."

Jim headed over the bridge into town. The cowboy gave out another groan and mumbled, his face contorting with pain. It was hard for Wyatt to watch. He had never killed anyone during an arrest and he had no intentions of his current prisoner dying under his watch. It was something that every policeman dreaded. He kicked the dirt trying to release his anger in a constructive manner but nothing he did helped. The cowboy lay moaning and whining. After several tedious minutes of listening to the man, Wyatt found his patience wearing thin. He grabbed the cowboy by the collar and pulled his body a couple of inches from the ground.

"What were you doing? Do you hear me? Talk to me."

The man mumbled incoherently and one eye drifted upwards in pain.

"Talk damn it! I know you can. Were you trying to kill me?"

"It weren't me. It weren't my idea. He did it. He did it."

The noise of the horse trotting across the bridge stopped Wyatt. He dropped the man to the ground and waited for Jim to drive up beside him in the buckboard. Jim dropped the reins and jumped out before the horse had halted. They lifted the cowboy and lowered him into the buckboard. Jim took the reins while Wyatt rode shotgun, back across the river and back onto Front Street.

By the time they made it to the doctor's office, the cowboy had lost a lot of blood. The doctor had a table ready for the patient. It took all Wyatt and Jim's strength to lift the cowboy up on to the table. The doctor cleaned his glasses and set them high on his nose, peering this way and that, poking and prodding at the wounded cowboy. He lifted the patient's wounded arm. The man's upper arm bone shot out at an angle and popped out through the blood soaked shirt. Wyatt turned as pale and backed off a couple of paces from the table. The doctor looked at the protruding bone with a raised eyebrow and nothing more.

"Oh dear me! As you can see for yourselves gentlemen, the bullet appears to have shattered the bone in two places. It's not looking good I'm afraid. He may die of blood poisoning if we're not careful. We'll have to amputate his arm and that leg of his doesn't look good either."

The cowboy whined and grabbed the doctor's hand.

"Hush now. You'll be all right. Don't worry, I'll give you morphine for the pain."

"Will it cost a whole lot to amputate? Unless the cowboy has some money in his wallet, the city office won't be too keen on paying his medical bills," said Jim.

The doctor stopped with a sigh and stood up. He

adjusted his spectacles and unintentionally smeared blood on one lens, "Well, normally I pay by the hour."

"How much would that be?"

"Well in this case, it shouldn't take that long. Perhaps a couple of minutes for the leg and his arm. I won't charge you for the full hour."

Jim smiled, "That's pretty fast."

The doctor smiled with a smug grin, "Amputations are my specialty. I was the fasted doctor in my regiment during the war."

The doctor prepared his surgical utensils, laying out a saw and a long knife. He gave an injection of morphine to the cowboy. The cowboy watched the doctor with wild eyes until the morphine closed each eye lid one by one. The doctor began the amputation, bringing the saw down and leaning his body hard over his hand. The noise of tendons snapping and bone hitting the saw made Wyatt retch. He slipped outside to get some fresh air. Jim followed and found him in the back alley, sitting on a barrel, smoking a cigarette and staring at the stars.

"What's up Wyatt?"

"Nothing."

"What's wrong?"

"That man in there tried to kill me. I doubt if he'll live."

"He'll recover Wyatt."

"I don't think so. He's weak. Once the doctor takes his arm he doesn't stand much of a chance."

The doctor appeared from the side door.

"How's it going?" said Jim.

"Not good. He's lost a lot of blood. I don't think

he's going to live much longer."

"Damn it!"

"Wyatt, wait. What about the rest of our work tonight? Shift doesn't finish for two hours."

"I don't give a shit. Tell Marshal Deger I took sick or something."

Wyatt stubbed out his cigarette, headed for the tracks and walked over past the saloons. The noise of wild laughter and music poured out on to the street. He walked from shadow to light, shadow to light with agitation. Bat Masterson chased after him and walked alongside.

"Jim told me what happened."

"Good for you."

"You want to talk?"

"Not particularly."

"Look I know what it feels like. You had to protect yourself."

"I know. That doesn't make it feel any better. What if it happens again?"

"It won't. They saw what happened tonight. Believe me they won't try it again. Come on into the bar and I'll buy you a drink."

The two men made their way through the crowd in the Long Branch Saloon. Wyatt could feel people staring at him as he walked past. Some of the men moved out of the way as they headed to the back of the bar.

"Come on, we'll go into the poker room, there isn't a game on right now. Go on and take a seat, I'll be back through in a minute."

After Bat left the room, the silence swamped Wyatt. He could hear the tick of the grandfather clock in the small corridor between the poker room and the main bar. He walked up and down staring at the walls and walking around the poker table. On the far side there was the skull of a stag hanging over the dealer's chair. Wyatt had never noticed it before. On most occasions he sat with his back turned against it. On the other wall was a painting of a centaur with a naked woman riding on his back. Wyatt's mind switched from the picture to the skull and back again. He was glad when Bat returned with a bottle of whiskey and two glasses.

Bat poured out the whiskey and pushed one glass to Wyatt. "I know that you're still on duty but you looked like you needed this."

"I'm not on duty. I quit."

"What? You can't quit."

"Why not?" Wyatt took a swallow of whiskey. His mustache twitched as the sharp taste warmed his throat. "I'm sick and tired of having to deal with all this shit. Tonight was the final straw. I can't handle the stress any more. There has to be easier ways to make such a poor living."

Bat smiled. "I'm sure there's better ways but this is what you're good at."

"Beating people up?"

Bat's grin grew. "Don't feel so bad. I'm so good they made me county Sheriff. How do you think I feel about that? Kind of a backward compliment don't you think?"

A vague smile hit Wyatt's lips. "You're teasing me now Bat. Please don't do that while I'm trying to get drunk."

"Oh I'm sorry. I didn't mean to break your concentration. Here you want me to pour you another?"

"Sure thing." Wyatt took the glass and emptied it.

Bat laughed. "Go steady now. I remember that last time you got drunk. All it took was two beers and you spent the rest of the night throwing up in a pail."

"When was that?"

"The Fourth of July. Don't you remember? Neither one of us was on duty that night."

"You're making that up."

"Oh I don't think so."

Wyatt sighed. "This has got to be one of the worst nights of my life."

"I'll bet there'll be nights worse than this. Now tell me you're going to stay working. Where else are you going to work?"

"Well, I don't want to gamble full time. I sure wouldn't want to deal full time either. That would be boring."

"Well stay at policing then Wyatt. It won't be long, the summer will be over and we can move someplace else."

"I don't know if I can. I think I'm losing it."

"Don't give me that bull. You're just a little messed up over what happened."

"No. I'm losing it. I can feel it. I've started to think that all the cowboys hate me. I start thinking about getting shot. I can't walk down the street at night any more without worrying that someone's going to try and take me out. I can't relax in the bars any more."

"You're relaxed now."

"That's because I'm half drunk."

"Look you just need to wait a while. It will be all right, believe me it will. After they killed my brother I thought about quitting. To go on working seemed unfair. Here I am a year later still working as if nothing happened."

"Everyone loved Ed. They'll never forget him."

"I know that but it doesn't make it any easier to live with."

"I don't know how you coped. If someone had killed my brother I don't think I'd be able to handle it as calmly as you did."

"Well it's tough sometimes, but I love my job."

"Pour me one more and then I'm going to quit for the night."

"Are you sure?"

"I wouldn't ask you if I wasn't."

"Well all right then." Bat poured a final glass and Wyatt knocked it back in one go.

He shook his head as the alcohol hit his blood stream. "I guess I can stay."

"Stay in the bar or stay working?"

"Stay working."

"Good. I'm glad Wyatt."

Wyatt got up from the table and walked unsteadily to the door at the back of the poker room. He pushed on the door but it wouldn't open. "Do they lock this door if there's not a game on?"

"Sometimes they do. Why?"

"I need it open."

"Push harder on it. It swells up when it rains."

Wyatt flung his shoulder against the door until it burst open. The sweet smell of the night air drifted in to the poker room. Wyatt walked uneasily outside and stood leaning against the frame of the door.

"Are you okay?"

Wyatt staggered out into the night and retched until he threw up the contents of his stomach.

Bat shook his head with a smile, "What am I going to do with you? You ain't got any right to be a man with a stomach like that."

"Leave me alone."

"I'm just jesting you know that. I hope you ain't making a mess out there, Chalkley will love you for that. I'm going to tell him it was you so he don't blame it all on some poor tramp."

"The hell you will! You won't tell a soul."

Bat got up from the table and walked out beside Wyatt. The marshal was still hovered over a pile of vegetable peelings and old crates and boxes. Bat removed a cigar from his jacket pocket, lit the end and took a puff. He leaned against one of the crates with one polished boot up on an old box and gazed up at the stars.

"My God but the stars are pretty tonight Wyatt. You can see nearly every one of those little twinklers."

"I don't rightly care Bat." Wyatt wiped his face on the back of his sleeve and removed himself from the pile of garbage.

"I'm a mess," he said as he looked sadly at his boots.

"You're telling me," said Bat. "Here have a puff of my cigar it'll take the bad taste away and settle your stomach some."

Wyatt reached over and took the cigar, puffed on it for a while and passed it back.

"Oh no you keep the damn thing. I've got others where that one came from," said Bat. He pulled another from his pocket, bit the end off and lit it in the same way as the first.

"Thanks. You're a good friend Bat."

"If you say so. I suspect that's the whiskey talking but thanks anyway."

"No seriously. You're a real, good friend."

Bat looked over at Wyatt and smirked at the marshal's stained shirt, tired eyes and bedraggled hair. The marshal pin shone in the midst of the mess reflecting the light from the moon above. He sat perched on an old crate, with his head hung low, his body huddled together and his long fingers still gripping the burning cigar.

"Come on Wyatt. Let's go home. If I leave you much longer you're going to fall asleep back here. I don't want that to happen. You're going to have to deal with enough shit in the morning without having people thinking you're a drunk."

Wyatt nodded in silence and then pulled himself up.

"Can you walk?"

"I think so."

"C'mon then." Bat grabbed Wyatt's arm and supported him until he got moving.

"What will people think Bat?"

"They won't think nothing Wyatt. It's three in the morning. Only others who are around are as drunk as you are. Now come on."

Bat led Wyatt out from the alley and onto Front Street. The hitching rails were almost empty. There were only a few sleepy horses, waiting for their owners to take them home. The music in most of the saloons had stopped for the evening, although the lights were still on and poker games were still well under way. The two men walked from saloon to saloon watching as the last straggling cowboys came and went. Wyatt continued the walk and watched as the faces drifted past him. He wished that the night air would sober him up. Although he was drunk and shouldn't have cared, he still felt vulnerable. He relaxed as he gazed at the quiet of Chestnut Street. It was a different world filled with quiet sleeping citizens. Only a few more streets and he would be home.

The lawmen walked towards the Alhambra saloon's carved doors. The scent of grease frying caught Wyatt's nostrils and caused him to heave. He leaned over the side of one of the water barrels that stood by the doors of the saloon and vomited down the side of it. Bat watched his friend and shook his head in disbelief.

Both men were too preoccupied to see the saloon doors swing open. Holliday stood up on the top step. He pulled his suit jacket on. A rolled cigarette hung from the corner of his lips. He strode down the two steps onto the dusty ground and walked up to the two lawmen.

"I didn't recognize y'all at first," he said. "What's going on?"

"Nothing at all that concerns you," said Bat.

"It doesn't look like nothing. Is he sick?"

"I guess."

Doc walked around to inspect the scene and to study Wyatt who still had his head down. "You all right?" he said.

Wyatt lifted his head to examine the inquirer. "I'm okay."

Doc studied Wyatt's wet muzzle and pale face."You sure don't look okay. I've seen slaughtered hogs look better."

The marshal retched and put his head back down beside the barrel."Look, why don't you just go Doc? Leave us alone."

"You sure?"

"Yes go!"

"Well all right." Doc left the men and walked past, turned and stopped. He thought about the situation for a while and returned to the men.

"I've got laudanum if he needs it."

"Just go Doc!" said Bat.

"I was just trying to help. If he don't do something about it, come tomorrow he's going to wish he were dead. If you'll let me get him some laudanum, at least he'll stop being poorly."

"Where is it?"

"It's back in my room."

"Well let's go then."

Wyatt pulled his head up and did his best to clean his mustache with his hand. "Where are we going?"

"Back to the Dodge House," said Doc.

Wyatt pulled himself up and walked coyly until he caught up with Bat and Doc. The three men walked down the street towards the hotel.

The light shone out on to the street from the front windows of the Dodge House. The building was quiet although it was clear that there were still plenty of people around. The front parlor had a poker game in progress. Bat helped Wyatt up the

steps. Doc opened the door for the men and they
all strolled into the wide, bright lobby of the hotel.
Wyatt was happy that the service desk was empty.
His shirt had grown pungent and he couldn't
handle the embarrassment of being caught in such
a state.

"Where's your room?" said Bat to Doc.

"It's up the stairs and down the hallway to the
right."

"I was hoping it was downstairs for Wyatt's
sake."

Doc smirked. "I don't sleep in the bar Bat. All
the rooms are upstairs."

"I never suggested you did. How's he going to
get up the stairs?"

Doc looked surprised. "I thought you said he
was sick not stupid."

"Well he is sick of sorts. He can't handle his
liquor."

"Oh dear Lord," said Doc with a coy grin, "He's
bought him a wild ride then. Didn't he know
better, before he got in this mess?"

"He knows well enough. It's a long story, he
forgets what liquor does to him."

"Lord knows he won't forget after tonight."

Bat grinned. "No, I'm sure he won't."

"Well I'll walk behind if you take his side. He'll
be all right if he leans in to the wall."

"How do you know?"

Doc's eyes gleamed. "Let's just say I've had
practice."

The men climbed the twenty steps up to the
hallway. Doc went forward to open the door to his
room. He entered and walked in the dark to the

nearest lamp. Bat helped Wyatt into the room and sat him down on the bed. There was a moment of vague light after the lamp was first lit and then the light spread until most of the room was illuminated.

The room was large for a standard lodging in the Dodge House. Most rooms had space for a bed and little else but Doc's room was bigger. He had pushed his bed over to the right hand wall to make extra space. On top of the bed sat two revolvers. One was a heavy angular, Navy model, ten or more years old. The other was a two-year-old single action colt with ivory grips. It shone golden brown in the lamplight. Bullets lay hidden beneath old editions of the Dodge City Times. On the other side of the room, beside the window there was a washbasin and a portable dental chair. A bedside table sat beside the basin and a thin box containing various implements of oral torture lay open on top of it.

Bat gazed over at the dental hooks and drill and felt a shiver run down his back. "You're a dentist? I thought the nickname was just a joke."

"I got my license in Philadelphia. It's there on the wall if you care to look at it. I'm the only dentist in Dodge right now. I'll be more than happy to assist you. I'll guarantee you that you'll find that I'm more than just a prosaic tooth puller."

Bat tried to clear his throat and turned towards the bed looking for an opportunity to change the subject.

"That's a nice colt you got Doc. You mind if I look her over?"

"Be my guest."

"The nickel plating, that was extra right?"

"Yes, about five dollars more but it was worth it don't you think?"

"Absolutely, I'll bet she fires good too?"

"She certainly does."

Doc bent his long frame down and opened a large brown dental bag that was sitting on a wooden chair and searched with both hands. He pulled out a handful of poker chips and a pack of playing cards and dropped them on the floor. Bat watched with surprise and fascination. After a little rummaging the dentist found the small bottle of laudanum towards the bottom of the bag and pulled it out.

"You want a spoon for this? It may be the cleaner way to go?" said Doc.

"I guess," said Wyatt. He was sobering up rapidly. Everything appeared quite strange to him and only got stranger as the whiskey wore off.

Bat watched with intrigue to see where Doc would find a spoon. It was like watching a conjurer during a magic act. Things were appearing and being pulled out of the strangest of places. In this instance Doc pulled polished leather saddlebags from behind a chair. He unbuckled the flaps and pulled out a small leather wallet containing a spoon, a fork and a knife as if by magic.

"There you go Wyatt," said Doc as he removed the spoon and handed it over.

Bat watched as Wyatt swallowed the substance back. His mustache twitched as he tasted the bitterness.

"It'll take a while to kick in," said Doc. He could see the marshal turn pale again and grew

53

concerned for the welfare of his bedclothes. He reached for the basin and put it down on Wyatt's knees. "Don't vomit on the bed or I'll kick your ass. I swear I will."

Bat smiled. "You're a real sentimentalist, I can only imagine how pleasant you must be with your patients?"

"I don't get paid to be compassionate Bat. My job is to doctor teeth. Sentimentality has no place in clinical practice. How do you propose I become more compassionate? Maybe I should craft jewelery from the extractions and turn them into dandy Christmas gifts?"

"Now there's an idea," said Bat with a shade of sarcasm, "I kind of like that."

Wyatt gagged and vomited into the basin.

"Well I guess you painted quite a picture for Wyatt there," said Bat, grinning.

Doc's eyes softened as he felt sympathy for Wyatt. "Lord if I threw up like that every time I took a drink of whiskey, I wouldn't be able to live with myself. Speaking of which, drink?"

"Sure thing," said Bat.

Doc poured whiskey into two tumblers and offered a glass to Masterson. Doc took the other glass and knocked the liquor down his throat as if he was drinking water. He coughed in a low deep bark and topped off the glass with more whiskey. The cough persisted until the dentist's wheezing sounded like a tortured horse. He sat down heavily on the dental chair, pulled his handkerchief from his top pocket and heaved and choked until the fit left him. Once he gained control, he sat gripping his chest, his nostrils flared and his eyes watering. He worked hard, breathing in one deep noisy lungful of air after another until he was able to sit in comparative silence. As soon as he finished, he lifted the tumbler to his lips and cleaned the glass. Bat sat sipping his whiskey with a look of disgust on his face. Doc saw the look.

"You think I drink too much or something?"

"No," said Bat "I'm just worried about your health."

"It doesn't trouble me. It sure as hell shouldn't bother you. It's been a long night that's all, it catches up on me after a while."

"You take anything for your cough?"

"I'd take a couple of bullets if someone would honor me with the pleasure. I'm just jesting of course." The corners of the dentist's mouth turned upwards in a sparkling grin. A wave of depression hid his lips beneath his blond mustache again. He rubbed his forehead with a bony hand and then stared at the wall.

Bat felt uncomfortable and got up to leave. "Are you ready Wyatt? We better go."

"Fine, I won't keep you," said Doc.

"C'mon Wyatt," said Bat.

Wyatt looked up at Bat with sleepy eyes. "You go on. I think I'll stay here a while."

"C'mon let's go."

"I don't want too. I'll see you at work tomorrow."

"Doc don't want you to stay here now come on. Let's go."

"Well, I don't want to go. I'm fine as is."

Doc laughed until he coughed again.

"Oh I'm sure you think this is funny Doc," said

Bat with exasperation. "You just drugged the town marshal. What am I supposed to tell people?"

"Oh hush Bat! At least he's quit being sick. He'll sleep it off and be good in the morning. I can give you my word. Let him sleep here if he wants. It surely doesn't bother me."

"Fine." Bat placed his bowler on his head and turned towards the door.

"Well, good evening. I'm sure I'll see you later today," said Doc.

"If you say so," said Bat.He pulled his woolen coat around him and left, the door banged behind him.

"What's eating him?" said Wyatt in a tired whisper.

"Lord knows. I'm just glad he's gone."

"I've never seen him that agitated before. You sure have a way of rubbing people the wrong way."

"Thanks Wyatt I'll take that as a compliment."

Doc busied himself in rolling a cigarette. He sealed the end with a little spit, struck a match and lit it. He took a puff and coughed as the smoke reached his lungs. He regained control and cleared his throat. The fit caught up with him again and started another round of coughing. He coughed over and over again, deep and hearty until he could barely catch his breath. There was a sharp rasping whistle as air seeped out the holes in his lungs. Doc sat down on the bed and pulled the handkerchief from his top pocket. He pressed it to his face. Minutes passed before the sputum finally surfaced from his lungs, to his lips and into the filthy material. He sat on the edge of the bed and placed his head in his hands. His fingers trembled under the weight. He could feel himself shaking although his skin was dripping with perspiration.

"Here take the bed. I'll sleep on the floor," said Wyatt.

"Stay where you are. I'll be fine in a second."

"Don't be a fool Doc. Take the bed. I'm happy to sleep on the floor."

"You'd be more comfortable in the chair."

Wyatt sat up slowly and studied the dental chair with a little angst. "I'd prefer not to. It makes me uneasy."

"It's not the chair you should be afraid of it's the drill that causes the pain. Here take this blanket."

Wyatt looked at the dentist.

"Please I insist."

Wyatt agreed to the dentist's arrangement and sat up on the dental chair. He wrapped the blanket over his suit trousers and pretended to be comfortable.

"Oh pity's sake Wyatt! You'd think I was sentencing you to hang or something! The chair adjusts a little if you push the handle."

The marshal obliged and pushed the chair back into a more natural position for lying down. The chair was softer than he expected. He found himself fighting to stay awake. Before long he was sleeping deeply.

Doc listened to the marshal snoring and felt a vague relief at not having to entertain his guest any longer. A soft burning pain had been growing in his back for the past hour. He had hoped to shake it off but time had only added to the intensity. He leaned over the gas lamp and blew out to extinguish the flame. To his dismay the flame guttered and burned brighter. Doc swore under his breath and tried again. This time the flame went out. He dropped himself on to the bed with relief and kicked his boots off onto the floor. He removed his vest and undid his silk cravat. He fluffed his pillow and slowly propped his back into a sitting position. He bit his lower lip as the pain caught him for a moment. He coughed heartily and wiped the spit on his sleeve. He moved again and removed the shirt from his back and lay back against the pillow. He sat in the darkness. The end of his cigarette glowed. A cough crept up on him and caused him to jerk forward. He reached for the bottle of laudanum and took a quick slug. He followed it quickly with another shot of whiskey and sat back against the headrest wishing both drugs to take effect. He sat back and waited for sleep to take him.

CHAPTER FIVE

The moon was on the rise when Doc rode back into Dodge City with a stolen horse trotting at each knee. The air was cool, the light was fading and Doc was glad to get the horses back to town without risking a dangerous ride in the dark. The warmth of the lantern light seeped into the streets and coated everything with a warm, honeyed glow. The clear cold air during the ride had cleaned Doc's lungs of cigarette smoke and made him tired.

The trip had been profitable. He had ridden out to a neighboring town to play poker and returned with a pocket full of money and two racehorses. He had played against a group of men who after a couple of rounds of whiskey and poker had staked the stolen horses in the game. Doc had not managed to catch the thieves but had managed to get them drunk enough to lose the horses during the poker match. Doc knew that Dan Tipton, the horses' owner, had a reward waiting for the return of his animals. Doc was more than happy to come home with the horses and pick up the money.

He rode across the tracks and stopped in front of the Marshal's office. He walked in with a happy strut and was disappointed when neither Bat or Wyatt was on duty. He remounted and trotted back across the tracks and down Front Street. He had to find Wyatt, even if it meant searching in every saloon in town. He tried the Lady Gay but found only a handful of people sitting talking to the bar tender. He intended to try the Long Branch Saloon, but was drawn to the Alhambra across the street. He found Wyatt in one of the pool rooms.

Doc peered through the smoky glass door into the dark room. He tried to make sense of the little that he could see. There seemed to be the long shape of an open casket, sitting on a pool table and standing to the side of the pool table was a group of men. Doc removed his hat, dipped his head in a pitiful manner and entered. The room was full of flickering candles and the musty smell of incense floated on the air. Wyatt was standing at the far corner of a large group of men. He was dressed in black and looked more somber than usual. It was hard for Doc to understand the emotions in Wyatt's face. The marshal's eyes glimmered in the candlelight but most of his face was hidden in the darkness.

Doc feared the worst and hoped that none of the Earps had been hurt. He chewed on his lip and choked his apology. "I'm so sorry, Wyatt."

Wyatt acknowledged the words with a nod. He motioned Doc over to the casket and as he moved closer the men's faces were illuminated and he found he was able to recognize faces. The

Masterson brothers stood side by side on the far side of the casket. Luke Short stood uttering a prayer. Doc bowed his head in embarrassment. His talk with Wyatt would have to wait. Wyatt nudged Doc in the ribs and pointed at the corpse. Doc leaned over the wooden casket to take a closer look. He viewed the body and crossed himself before bowing his head. Bat Masterson watched Doc's sudden burst of piousness with surprise, looked at Wyatt and smiled. Wyatt sighed and nudged Doc again, this time jabbing the dentist so hard that he was almost knocked forwards. He pointed to the casket. Doc glared at Wyatt but did as he asked and took another peek. He studied the body this time. Doc was surprised and relieved when he recognized the corpse as a lawyer who had been visiting Dodge over the past couple of days. He remembered him from one of the Faro games that he had been banking a couple of nights before. He wondered how the man had died and examined the body for any obvious wounds and scars.

Around the dead man's head lay a wreath of sunflowers. His face was pale and his cheeks were crudely colored with rouge and lipstick. He was dressed in a tailored suit, except for his boots which had an inch of mud and horse manure on the soles. Doc was curious about the boots but stood silent. Surely it was the undertaker's job to take care of such matters. Maybe things were done differently in Dodge City. Dirty boots or no boots at all, if you were dead it didn't matter.

The lawyer's chest rose and fell, the corpse was breathing. Doc squirmed and choked. He muffled a cough with his handkerchief, but the cough got stronger, until he choked and wheezed. The body in the casket sat bolt upright at the noise and stared at Doc with a dazed expression. Doc screamed, pulled his derringer from his burgundy vest and aimed it at the corpse. His hand shook and was still damp with saliva.

The dead man came alive, saw the gun pointed at his face and saw Doc's gray eyes penetrating his pale body. He screamed and panicked, squirmed and pulled free of the casket. The dentist kept his eyes on the man. He stood still, his skinny wrist held the derringer perpendicular to his body. Wyatt grabbed Doc from behind and hit the gun from his hand.

"He's dead. He's dead," screamed Doc.

"No he isn't. Drop the gun. I'll explain it to you."

Wyatt tightened his grip on Doc until the dentist could hardly breathe. Doc dropped the gun, his chest heaved up and down with wheezing gasps for breath. The lawyer broke free and ran through to the main saloon. A young barmaid squealed and dropped the tray of drinks that she was carrying. The glass tumblers crashed onto the floor. One broke into hundreds of pieces. Another glass rolled across the wooden floor and in behind a spittoon, causing the brass to resonate on the way past. A drunken old timer, who sat on a bar stool above the spittoon, woke up from his evening nap. He opened his eyes wide enough to catch sight of the panicked corpse dashing past him screaming.

"I'm not dead! I'm not dead! I just came in for a drink. Dear Lord, someone help me."

Each man watched the lawyer study his form in

one of the long mirrors that hung along the side of the room. The lawyer trembled and tears rolled down his face and into his mustache. He turned to the mirror and stared at his reflection in horror. He was unaware that his pallor was rubbing off underneath the teardrops. The lawyer saw the reflections of the laughing men behind him.

"Sweet Jesus! Get out while you can!" He gave a high pitched scream and ran out of the saloon leaving the wing doors flapping behind him.

The barroom filled with laughter. In the backroom, the men stood around the empty casket with tears of joy running down their faces. Doc stood in the middle of the group with a perplexed expression.

"Oh Doc, if only you could have seen your face," said Bat.

"I swear I thought he was going to shoot him," said Luke.

Doc got the joke and smiled. "Y'all set this up on purpose?"

"We didn't mean for you to come on in here in the middle of it, but apart from that. Yep we set it up."

Doc laughed. "Dear Lord, I swear I just about dropped to the floor when I saw him move."

Wyatt smiled. "You see Doc I was trying to explain but you just about near killed the poor fellow. You pick your moments. Lord knows you do."

"Oh, I'm sorry Wyatt, dear God." Doc shook his head with surprise and grinned.

"Next time we pull a prank on someone. Make sure that Doc's in on it will you?" Luke said.

"You fellows do this a lot?" Doc exclaimed. "This isn't the first trick y'all have pulled?"

"Well no. Let's see. This'll be the fourth one this summer. Am I right?"

"We're going to have to get Doc in on one of the huntin' jokes next time"

"What kind of hunting?"

"Well we get a town novice to go out and help us on a little snipe hunt. We'll tell them to sit out in the darkness, down by the river until a snipe comes along and then to grab it and put in a sack. Meanwhile, we all come back here for a laugh and a drink."

"Sounds like a good deal. I like all kinds of hunting except man hunts. I can't stand those." Doc laughed at his own joke and was surprised to find that he was the only one to find the joke amusing. The men grew silent and looked at Doc with disregard. Doc looked back at the men and wondered if he had gone too far. He smiled weekly and was relieved when everyone else, except Luke smiled with him.

"So Doc, what made you want to come on in here in the first place? I don't recall anyone inviting you along?" Luke said. "You just think to barge on in on us all?"

"Luke, leave it. It's not important."

"Oh what Wyatt? You taking his side?"

"Luke, I said leave it." Wyatt eyed Doc. "Why did you come?"

Doc looked around at the other men and could feel the pressure building up. He swallowed down on to his dry throat. "I"

"Yes?" Luke snapped.

"I wanted to see Wyatt. I've got something to tell him."

"What is it?"

"While I was out at the poker game, I came across Dan Tipton's stolen horses. I've got them tied outside. I figured that I'd let you know, get the horses back to where they belong and pick up my reward."

"Thanks Doc. I'll come out and check them."

There was a silence as Wyatt stood thinking the situation through. Luke grew red in the face with anger.

"Are you just going to stand here and take that crap from him?"

The men looked at each other.

"Hell, it's obvious he's lying. He probably stole the horses himself."

Doc contorted his face and sucked in his cheeks until his cheekbones made him look skeletal. "Is that what you really think? You think that's what I do? You son of a bitch, you don't even know me."

"You did it Doc. You're just a low down horse thief and you're a killer to boot."

"You don't even know me. I didn't do it. I would never steal anything."

"Now isn't that funny, considering I've heard different from nearly everyone I've talked too." Doc saw the look on Wyatt's face and swallowed his emotions down, for Wyatt's sake. "You're not worth taking the time."

"He ain't even as tough as they say he is, skinny Southern runt.'"

"Don't you think you've said enough Luke?" said Bat. "If Doc had stolen those horses then why

on earth would he come here to us and turn them
over to the police? You ever thought about that?"

"If you guys are all going to stand here and take
his side, I don't see why I have to stand around
and hear this shit."

Luke turned and pushed his way out of the
backroom and into the bar. The men watched him
go in silence. Doc's eyes blazed as anger and
frustration filled his face. His jaw twisted and
tightened as he tried to speak calmly over the top
of his anger.

"I guess I don't have a reason to stick around.
I've had just about enough for one evening. If
anyone else wants to take a swing at me tonight,
I'll be over dealing Faro."

Doc walked out and slammed the door behind
him.

The group dispersed until only Bat and Wyatt
were remaining. Wyatt slicked back his hair and
placed his hat back on his head.

"I guess I better go out and check out these
stolen horses of Doc's."

"Mind if I come along, Wyatt?"

"Sure, it wouldn't hurt to get a second opinion."

The two lawmen walked calmly out of the
saloon. Despite the argument that they had both
seen, both men were in good spirits that night. For
once, there were no urgent tasks that they needed
to rush back to and all the paperwork that week
had been filed days ago. The cold air sharpened
their senses and reddened their cheeks. Dodge was
calming down after the long summer. Fall had
made its presence felt and the long nights of
having to arrest unruly cowboys were coming to

an end.

"I guess these are the horses."

Wyatt inspected the animals in the light that spilled on to the boardwalk from the saloon. He could almost see the gambling tables in the soft reflection of the horses' brown eyes. He watched the intelligent faces of the animals as they listened to the noise inside. The two equine aristocrats stood awkwardly amongst the cow ponies tethered beside them. The taller of the two twitched its nose in disgust and stretched its long black leg up to kick a fly from its belly. The other horse rested a hind-leg and watched the scene with a relaxed countenance. Wyatt walked up to the smaller of the two and placed his hand on the horse's cream hindquarters. He watched as a shiver moved through the horse's skin. He coaxed and gentled the horse with a soft whisper. The horse turned his head around, as far as the tether would let him and eyed Wyatt from the whites in his eyes.

"Handsome looking thing aren't you? Good conformation."

The marshal moved along the horse's side and ran his hand down the dappled neck. The horse relaxed, stretched down and snorted with relief as the tension left his body.

"Well I'd say he has a bit of Thoroughbred in him. Not as bullish as those cow ponies."

Bat lit a cigar and puffed thoughtfully. "Yep. The black has more quality to him. He's definitely a pure-blood." He blew the smoke out over the horse's rear and smiled as the black horse tensed its back in disapproval. "That thing that Luke said tonight you don't suppose it's true do you?"

"What thing?"

"The thing about Doc stealing these horses."

Wyatt sighed, "Well. I don't think he'd do it. I trust him."

Bat laughed. "I never thought I'd hear that from you. You know his kind well enough. He's killed men up and down the West. Don't let his charm get the better of you."

"We're talking about returning horses here Bat, not killing people. Doc gave me his word and I trust him. I've been watching him all the time he's been in Dodge and he's been on his best behavior."

"Just like an unruly child avoiding a whippin'."

"If you put it that way."

The men looked at each other. Bat smiled with a lazy grin.

"You want a cigar?"

Wyatt smiled and shook his head.

"Either way, he deserves the reward. These are definitely the horses that Dan lost. I'd recognize that black Thoroughbred anywhere. He's beaten my horses more than a few times in the city races."

"Well all right. I guess we can put these horses up in the livery yard for the night and then we can settle with Dan and Doc tomorrow."

"Okay let's go with that."

Wyatt unhitched the horses from the post and gave the rein of the cream horse to Bat. They led the horses over the tracks to the livery yard in silence. Neither knew what the other was thinking although they were both thinking the same thing. Had Doc really paid the police force a favor? Was he only in it for the money? Or was it true that Doc had wanted to see the horses returned to their true owners and despite his past had been looking for justice. Wyatt hoped that Doc had been looking for justice. Bat didn't know what to believe. The whole concept of a killer doing good for the sake of the police force made him queasy and worried about the future.

CHAPTER SIX

Doc stood next to Dan Tipton and fidgeted with his hat as he waited in the street for Wyatt to return with his reward. The two strangers stood in silence, both embarrassed by the lack of conversation. Doc searched through his mind for something witty to say but came up with nothing more important than a remark about the weather. Beams of light from a fall sun reflected off Doc's cheekbones and caused the dentist to contort his face as he tried to see past the glare. He groaned and stood tolerating the inconvenience of having to stand for so long. He was tired from the long ride the day before. Today every movement he made seemed slower and every part of his body worked with less efficiency. He worked hard to try and remain alert but he could feel himself drifting to sleep. Deep down he longed to sneak back to his room and take a nap but he would have to wait for Wyatt to return before he could do so. He watched Wyatt talking. He was relieved when the conversation ended and Wyatt crossed the street and strolled towards him.

"Sorry about that boys, I got distracted. So how are you getting on with one another?"

Both men mumbled and made vague comments to please Earp.

"All right Doc. One hundred dollars I believe it was."

Doc's eyes lit up. "That's a high reward for a couple of horses."

"They mean a lot to me," Dan interrupted. "I make a lot of money racing them. Wyatt here's the same way. I bet if he had his best horse stolen, he'd give an arm and a leg to get him back too."

"Damn straight I would."

"I'm just glad to do you a favor. I hate to see good horses get wasted."

Wyatt chuckled and dished the wad of money out into Doc's palm. Dan reached his hand out to Doc and shook his skinny wrist vigorously. "I won't forget this Doc. Next time there's racin' be sure and lay your money on one of my boys. I'll guarantee you'll triple it."

"Thank you Sir. I'll keep that in mind."

"Wyatt. I guess I'll have to leave you and Doc to it. Might go and take the horses down to the river for a bit."

"All right Dan. Nice seeing you."

Doc turned to leave and was stopped by Wyatt.

"Just wanted to thank you for getting those horses back, Dan's a good friend of me and Bat. You've made Dan's day."

"I'm glad to help you out. It was worth it just to see the look on those bastards' faces when I collected the money and those horses. Only losers would be pathetic enough to bet their ride home on a poker game. I may be an outlaw to you, but I hate lawbreakers as much as anyone else in this town. Any time you need the help Wyatt, give me a shout. I enjoy the challenge."

Wyatt looked surprised. "Thanks Doc. I'll keep that in mind."

Wyatt removed his pocket watch and studied the time with a groan. "I better get going. I should have met Luke and Bat ten minutes ago."

"I guess I better find a way to spend this money," said Doc. He grinned with his eyes glowing.

"Thanks. Maybe see you about. I'll buy you a drink tonight if you're around."

"Well I never did refuse a free drink. I'll hold you to that."

Wyatt turned to go and left Doc standing in the street, dumbstruck. He was surprised to note how happy he had made Wyatt. To top it off, he was financially liquid. He could feel the dollar bills burning a hole in his pocket. He knew that he should save the notes, but deep down he also knew that he would find himself in a saloon before he ever made it back to his room.

He pulled the brim of his hat well over his face and walked in the shadows where he could. He could feel his bed in the Dodge House, pulling him home. He could think of nothing else now. Sleep was the only thing that would sort him out at that moment. Perhaps he would go the whole hog and pay for a soak in a tub while he was at it. Once he got a chance to rest, he'd be fine. His only goal was to get home and catch up on sleep before he started another long night of dealing in the saloons. God help anyone who stopped him or got in his way.

He was too preoccupied with his goal to imagine that anyone else might be sharing the same boardwalk as him. Doc walked into a woman who was walking in the other direction. He felt the silk petticoats of her dress ruffle up against his thighs. For a moment the pair embraced in an entanglement of material and embarrassment.

"Oh my God! Who do you think you are? You just go crashing into everyone on the street? Why don't you look where you're going? Maybe next time you'll be lucky and bash into a large man who give you a good beating up. Now excuse me. I've things to do." She turned to go but Doc grabbed her hand.

"I'm sorry, if there's anything I can do for you in way of an apology I would be more than happy to oblige."

"More than happy to oblige. Pretty talk from a skinny man. Who do you think I am? Let go of me or I'll go to the police."

"Now you wouldn't want to do that. Besides, Wyatt Earp is a good friend of mine."

The woman stopped. She looked at Doc in a curious manner and pulled back. "Now I'm thinking, what would a man like you have with a man like Wyatt Earp? You're not a police man. I know the men on the force quite personally. I don't think you could fight much. You look like you're going to blow over in the wind. You must be a pimp or a gambler, surely?"

Doc laughed.

"Now you're insulting me by laughing huh? If I am so stupid, you tell me just what you do for a living. Come on now, shock me."

"I'm a dentist by profession but I've taken a healthy interest in gambling. I sometimes work the Faro tables. You may know me. My name's Doc... Doc Holliday."

A cackling laugh erupted from the woman.

"You a dentist called Doc? Well, I'll be damned! This is some kind of practical joke huh? Well Doc Holliday. Do you make plenty money on these tables?"

"Sometimes I do. What's a lady like yourself wanting to inquire into a thing like that for?"

"Oh please, cut the crap you make me sick. Let's just say it's my business to know about men's money."

Doc choked and coughed.

"Oh God, you've a hell of a spirit. Is there anything I can do for you Miss?"

"Big Nose Kate, that's what you call me eh? Everyone calls me that. You come and drink with me that's what you do for me. I buy first round."

"Oh honey, saloons don't sell tea or coffee."

Big Nose Kate smiled and rubbed Doc's chin. "Don't worry buttercup. I only drink whiskey. You buy me a round huh? Ten dollars says you slide under the table first."

She made a clicking noise with her tongue and walked towards the nearest bar. Doc followed in a state of shock curious as to where this new lady friend would lead him. He took a deep breath and whispered to the sky, 'Dear Lord. If she kills me in the next few hours please forgive me.'

74

Doc followed the blond haired woman into one of the bars on Front Street. He watched with intrigue as she pulled the glass door open with her jeweled fingers. He expected the usual frontier scene. He waited to hear the loud voices and the noise of the roulette wheel whirring. He anticipated the cigarette smoke that would tighten his chest as he entered. The scene that greeted him came as quite a surprise. The sound of sweet classical music poured into the air. In the corner an elegantly attired quartet played Strauss waltzes. Doc listened and remembered. He stood transfixed as the music drifted around him. In an instant he was back at one of the old Georgian dances. He could smell perfume and see the satin and ribbons of the bustled dresses as they swam around the room. He could hear the excited giggles of laughter of the young Georgian girls. The chatter drifted and echoed around his head. Words that people had spoken, places that he had been, feelings that he had felt.

"Come sugar. Tell me what you're thinking huh?" Big Nose Kate's voice prodded Doc awake.

"It's the music."

"Ah yes the music is very sweet but as much as I like to stand here with you, I don't care for all these people pushing past. Come buttercup, lets get down to nitty-gritty, yes? "

"All right. May I buy you a drink?"

"I'm sure you could but I'll get them. The barman is a personal friend of mine. He'll do us a good deal. Now my friend, a whiskey, yes?"

"Oh Lord Kate, that would be fine."

Kate yelled over at the barman for some service.

"Charley, two whiskeys, pronto."

She waited for a reply. The bartender motioned and pointed at the selection. Kate shook her head.

"Nah, not the shitty stuff. No that one there."

The barman pointed again and smiled waiting for orders.

"That's right. Is that the bourbon?"

Doc listened and began to laugh at the ridiculous situation.

"Ah look, wait there I'm coming over."

Kate moved through the saloon with determination. She pushed forward to an empty spot at the bar. Doc walked after her. He smiled with admiration and embarrassment as heads turned in their direction. He could hear Kate's tinkling laughter as she finally got what she wanted.

"Ah yes, that one. No the bottle, there yes, excellent, excellent."

Kate removed a wad of notes from what appeared to be her corset and flicked through the dollars, licking her index finger as she went. She located a desirable amount and handed it over to the bartender. "There now, keep the change, huh." She smiled. Her blue eyes gleamed under her long eyelashes. Doc realized that he wouldn't need much persuasion or alcohol to see the best side of the woman before him. She took the bottle of bourbon and two shot glasses from the barman and floated back to Doc. Her face beamed with satisfaction. Doc smiled at Kate. Her cheerfulness was infectious.

"There darling. Drink now. Quickly, before it heats up."

Doc took the glass and nodded his thanks. He lifted his glass in toast to Kate and then knocked the liquid back in one go. He choked and growled.

"Oh Lord."

"It's good?"

Doc smiled. "It's better than good. It's nectar."

"Well good. Here have another."

Kate filled the glass again before sipping her first drink. Doc covered his glass.

"Now hold on a second. I don't know about you but I'm in no hurry. Let's take our time. We've got all night. How about some gambling?"

Her face grew serious. She chewed on her lip and smiled.

"Yes, you're right. We need to play some games, how about roulette?"

"All right, after you."

Doc wasn't pleased with the idea. He knew that the odds of winning a large amount of money were more limited than he was used to. He followed Kate to a side table anyway and resigned himself to losing some money. He knew it wasn't a wise move, but he was proud and if it meant he would curry favor with the lady, roulette would have to be the game to play.

Kate took him by the hand and led him through to the roulette game that was proceeding at the back of the room. Doc eyed the table, and for the first time in many years, felt awkward. The green felt beckoned him with an amorous glow but it was strange territory. It wasn't his beloved poker table. The dealer started the wheel and all the eyes around the table turned their attention to the little white ball. It jumped and dived and rested on the red, seven. A man in a top hat and tails threw his hands in the air and kissed the lady to his right. The croupier pushed chips in his direction. He counted them into a pile and gave his lady another kiss. Doc groaned with disgust. 'God save us from amateurs,' he thought.

"Isn't this wonderful?" Kate beamed.

"What is?"

"Roulette. Let's join the game buttercup."

She pulled Doc by the hand. His glass of whiskey splashed over his wrist and onto the cuff of his suit jacket. The couple moved around the table. Doc eyed the other players with suspicion as he went past. He studied the players' hips and top pockets for signs of hidden pistols and knives. Kate found a place and stopped. She dropped Doc's hand. Doc let her sit down on the chair and turned to pull a chair from another table. Behind him lay four pool tables. The fringed lamps shone a smoky light down on the players. A tall man stood at the side of the table chalking his cue. Another gentleman of similar stature and looks reached over to pot the four. Doc recognized him immediately, it was Morgan. Doc opened his mouth to call to him but didn't want to disturb the game. He brought the chair over and sat down. He shivered as a cowboy brushed past him. It felt strange and dangerous to sit at a game with his back exposed and without the protection of a wall. He felt lost and uncomfortable. All gamblers had their obsessive habits and techniques and Doc was no exception. There were ways of cajoling luck and making her behave to your own specifications. If that meant you wore a lucky tie pin or that you dealt cards a certain way or had a preference for a particular chair, then that was what you did. To an outsider it was all insane, obsessive behavior. To a gambler it was a way of life.

Kate grabbed Doc's glass and poured him another drink. She squeezed his thigh with her long fingers. Doc jumped at her touch and then relaxed.

"There now this is cozy. We can get to know one another better."

"So, while we're dealing with introductions. Where do you hail from?"

"Me? Where do I what?"

"Where you from?"

"Oh I'm from Iowa."

Doc laughed. "Iowa, really, are you sure? There's a hint of something else in your accent."

"Oh, yes, yes. I'm sorry, I come from Budapest. It's been so long, I forget some times."

"Talk to me in Hungarian."

Kate blushed.

"Ah no, I forget so much. It takes much time for me to remember."

"Say something. Say anything."

"No maybe later not now. Let's play now."

A new game began and Kate removed a small pile of notes and bought herself some chips to place on the black seventeen. "I always like the black. I find it alluring I think. Come buttercup you better place your bet."

Doc reached into his inside pocket and pulled his leather wallet out from beside his breast. He hesitated and squinted at Kate in concentration.

"How much are your chips?"

"I'm not sure. One dollar each I think."

Doc pursed his lips and eyed the notes. He removed two hundred dollars and threw it at the dealer. The dealer looked down at the sum of money, blinked and looked up at Doc.

"Careful Sir, two hundred dollars is our limit. Would you like to change the bet?"

Doc cleared his throat and growled at the man. "Nonsense, leave it as it is. My bet remains."

"Take the smaller bet honey. There's no need to play the house. We're in this for a little fun," Kate smiled at Doc and tapped his knee. Doc gave Kate a fiery glare.

"Don't tell me what to do. Just leave it as it is."

"All right leave it. Just relax huh. We're playing for fun, that's all."

The croupier eyed Doc and marked him as a troublemaker. He looked at the other players, realized their impatience to start and readied himself to begin. The wheel spun into action. The ball hovered before taking its route around the wheel. The faces at the table watched with anticipation. Doc felt hypnotized as the colors flashed past at speed and moved the ball into a white blur. He eyed the numbers with suspicion and calculated his odds. Kate smiled over at Doc but he was too lost in concentration to notice. The colors whirled faster until he lost himself to the blurred merry-go-round and the pounding in his brain. The thumping in his ears blocked the other noises in the saloon. His energy seeped away from his body. He gripped the table with one hand and watched as his palms filled with sweat and his hand slid. His body shook and buzzed. The

whirring of the wheel spinning grew muffled and
distant. The ground pulled Doc like a magnet. He
hit the floor with a thump, dispelling the air that
remained in his lungs. He lay in a warm daze, his
body emitted heat until beads of sweat ran down
his forehead to his nostrils. He tried to pull himself
away from the contortions that lulled him to sleep.
He strained his muscles but his body seemed too
heavy to allow himself back up. In the distance he
could hear the echoing yell of the winner taking his
prize. Doc closed his eyes.

The gamblers at the table grew quiet. Kate knelt
down on the floor and tried to wake Doc. She was
aware of the eyes watching her from the table.

"I don't know what's wrong. He's out cold.
Somebody help him?"

By now a small crowd had gathered. At the back
of the crowd Morgan and Virgil Earp pushed
forward. Morgan reached Doc, cursed and got to
work.

"I know this guy. Hey, this fella's knocked out.
Come on over here and give me a hand."

A couple of people in the bar came forward and
helped to lift Doc up.

"What do you think's wrong with him?"

"Don't know. He's probably just drunk or
somthin'. Help me get him through.

We'll take him 'round the back to one of the
cribs."

The men lifted Doc through the bustle of the
saloon and out to a couch in the back room. Kate
followed the entourage hoping that Morgan was
right.

The men eased Doc down on to the little sofa.

His bony legs hung over the arm rest and dangled down like a rag doll's. Morgan raised Doc's head up against a velvet cushion. He reached around his neck to unclip his tie-pin and loosen his cravat. His fingers fumbled with the button that held Doc's collar. The clip released and Morgan managed to get some air to Doc's neck.

"Is he going to be all right?" said Kate.

"Yes. I think he's just drunk that's all. It's kind of hot through the front."

"Do you mind if I sit with him for a while?"

"Sure. He'll probably sleep it off. It shouldn't take long."

"Are you sure he's all right?"

"Sure, he's just drunk."

"Thanks."

"Hey, I didn't do anything."

Kate waited and watched Doc breathing. She ran her hand down and along the side of his broad jaw. His skin was pale and cold. It was strange to be able to study Doc without him knowing. She checked to see that she was alone and reached her hand down the side of Doc's chest and slid her hand into the inside pocket of his jacket. She moved her hand until she could feel his wallet. She opened it up. Her fingers slipped between the flaps and wrapped around a pile of dollars. She pulled the money out and slipped the bills into her dress. Her index finger slid against something else. It was thicker than a dollar and there was a tear along one corner. She felt the rough edges for a minute and then pulled the object out into the light. In her hand was an old ripped photograph. The faded photograph had a crease down the middle but she make out the image of a tall man in a stovepipe hat. His face was intense and determined. A slender looking woman stood, almost hidden in the shadows. Her body had faded but her high cheekbones were clear and her eyes seemed to shine out of the picture and question Kate's morality. Kate shuddered as she looked at the women. The pose was so familiar. It brought back so many memories of her own mother, back when she had lived in Hungary. "Don't look at me like that. I have to make a living." Kate whispered to the photograph. The eyes remained the same. Kate felt stupid but reached back into her dress and removed a couple of dollars and placed them back in Doc's wallet. "All right you win. I'll leave a little for your son but I'm taking the rest. All right? All right.' Kate tidied herself and sat by Doc as if nothing had happened.

She wanted Doc to wake up, but she was nervous of what might happen if he did. She felt that in some way he would find out about her drugging his drink and stealing the money. Kate had seen Doc's piercing gray eyes, grow angry that night and she was scared of what might happen if all the anger was focused on her. She had suffered men turning on her before, and had been forced to fight to protect herself.

Her attention turned to his long delicate fingers. They twitched and pulsed, as he lay asleep. Kate's heart pounded, she feared the fate that awaited her if he woke up. 'Maybe I should leave now,' she thought to herself. It was starting to get late and she still had things to do before starting her evening work. She sat and considered her position.

Doc was not like the others. He wouldn't hurt her. There was an alluring magnetism about what she had seen in Doc that afternoon that compelled her to stay. 'Another ten minutes and then I'll leave him,' she decided.

Doc's eyelids flickered as he regained consciousness. He floated in and out of a strange dream. He could hear noises but he wasn't sure where they were coming from. His hearing was still muffled although the sounds came in a constant stream. He relaxed and tried to make sense of his surroundings. He dreamed that he was lying on the drawing room chaise-long in Georgia. He could feel a soft breeze on his face blowing in through the long white lace curtains that hung around bay windows. At the back porch a potted palm billowed its slender green leaves in the evening air. His grandmother's wind chimes whispered with a soft metallic voice. The scent of moon-flowers and honeysuckle absorbed Doc's senses. Everything was still in the house. He listened to the steady rhythmic ticking of the walnut Grandfather clock that stood in the hallway. In the distance he could hear a hound dog barking and baying. He half opened one eye and saw the piano sitting in the corner. He remembered long evenings listening to his mother and Aunts playing Mozart. He remembered the nerves that he had grappled with when it came close to his turn to play. 'I'm home,' he thought and felt relieved.

When Doc opened his eyes the room changed. The clock and wind-chimes were gone. He could still hear the dog barking outside and somewhere in the distance there was laughter and music playing. The air was heavier too. He could smell perfume, cigar smoke and sweat. He tried to focus on his surroundings. His eyesight remained blurred and the figures in the room seemed to blend into the background. He raised his head a couple of inches from the pillow. The room dived and pitched out of his control. Scared, he laid his head back into position. He shut his eyes and swallowed. He attempted to view his surroundings again with his head supported. He opened his eyes, his focus was still blurred but it regained clarity with every second that passed.

A pink and orange light drifted in through what Doc presumed to be the open lace curtains that he'd seen during the dream. He twitched as the ringed hand of a woman rubbed his chin and stroked his brown mustache. He caught the faint image of a blond haired woman. The scent of lavender perfume was overpowering and caused his nostrils to quiver.

"Sweet Jesus, I'm in heaven," he whispered, watching the finger move.

"How are you feeling buttercup? I think you owe me some money."

Doc looked puzzled and tried to sit up. "I can't even remember who you are."

Kate laughed, "It's all right honey. You didn't do nothing. You passed out on the floor."

Doc swallowed with difficulty and tried to maintain the clear image that he now had of his surroundings. "If I didn't do anything, why do I owe you money? Who are you?"

"Mr. Holliday. It's very simple, I explain. I am

Big Nose Kate. I bump into you in street, I make
bet to drink you under table, you wager ten
dollars, we start to drink, you slide under the table.
Here we are, you owe me ten dollars?"

"Look I'm so sorry. What ever happened if
there's anything I can do?"

"Oh Doc. All you do is apologize to me huh?
You didn't do nothing. You obviously still don't
remember. Look I have to go now. Don't worry
about the money. You pay me when you're ready."

"Wait. Where can I find you?"

"I'm staying in the Long Branch for most of
tonight. Any time you're ready just come through
to the front and we'll talk okay?"

Kate smiled down at her new victim and turned
to leave. Doc watched her go in a trance. His head
ached from thinking. There were too many
questions that needed answers. He took a sigh and
laid his head back on the cushion.

CHAPTER SEVEN

A pale hand reached forward in the darkness and grasped at the air. It retreated back to the bedclothes and then felt its way across the lace edged pillows. It rubbed against the billows of blond hair that lay strewn across the covers. The hand stopped. A long bony arm pressed against the mattress. Doc sat up. He strained his eyes trying to make sense of the fuzzy images in the darkness. It all began to make sense to him.

Big Nose Kate lay naked beside him, her body stretched over the bed and the covers nestled over her form. Doc's gaze floated across the room. A couple of empty bottles of whiskey lay on the floor. Two glasses sat on a table by the wash basin, his clothes lay in a heap and stacks of dollars sat on the dresser. He watched Kate sleeping peacefully in a drunken daze. Minute by minute, he could feel the evening's events catch up with him. He sat and considered his situation. He was still tired and drunk and found it difficult to place his thoughts. It was obvious what he had done. In a way, he was happy that he had. In other ways, he wished he hadn't. There were questions that needed answering and he didn't feel in a fit state to answer them.

His nostrils and upper lip were itchy. He reached a finger to his face and felt the first drip of blood as it fell from his nostrils, to his chin and into the palm of his hand. The drips came steadier and pulsed down until he could see a small pool of blood forming in his palm. He got up and moved unsteadily over to the dresser and released the liquid into the washbasin. He poured some water from the jug and let the blood run off his hands. He watched in a stupor as one after one, the droplets of red tainted the water and swirled as the two liquids combined.

The unsteady feeling came slowly at first until it swam up his body and caused him to retch. He spat out a little phlegm but could still feel the nausea crawling in the pit of his stomach. Every second passed slowly and every retch that Doc endured was unproductive. He leant against the dresser with his head against the basin and waited for the feeling to subside. The sweat oozed from his body and unbearable heat engulfed him. The drops slowed. He reached a shaking hand to his face. His fingers felt the red crystals of drying blood forming around his nostrils. He sniffed and wiped his face with the back of his hand. He dried his hands and groaned as he wiped some of the blood onto the towel.

He reached to the floor and gathered his clothes. He dressed as quickly as he could. He wanted to sit back down but he knew that he had to leave, it didn't feel right to stay. He needed to be back in his own room. He needed to be vulnerable in his own privacy. One last look at the room told him that he had everything and was ready to leave. The door closed with an echoing bang. Doc stood by the door for a second listening, hoping that Kate was still asleep. The sound of her snoring told him that she was.

A cold draft blew down the corridor and caused an uncomfortable shiver to run down Doc's back. He made his way down the stairs with hesitant strides and clutched the banister to steady him. Luck was with him and despite the time, the front door was still open. He stepped out into Front Street and pulled his jacket across his shoulders. There was enough light to see but a great deal of the streets and alleys were still in darkness. In the distance a lonely horse stood hitched outside one of the saloons. It shifted weight from one hind-leg to the other seeking a comfortable sleeping position. Across the street, the small glow of a light shone from inside of the bakery as the baker slid the first trays of roll dough into the hot oven. A cold breeze rustled through the bare dogwoods and blew dust devils across the ground.

Doc walked down the center of the empty street, paranoid at what might be waiting for him in the shadows. He chided himself for being afraid. An old slave had told him stories of one-eyed monsters, ghosts and devils when he was a child. He had loved the stories but had reasoned never to lurk alone in the darkness unless he had a good reason too. He laughed at his own insecurity and choked. A spasm of pain caught him in the chest.

He folded at the waist, clutched his ribs and retched. He stood with his head down. His body trembled. He clenched his teeth against the pain until it subsided and he was able to walk again. He made hesitant progress forward.

There was a loud thud as a water barrel fell over. Doc swung around in fright and gazed out into the darkness. A shadow moved up the alley and then stopped. Doc watched over his shoulder and continued up the street. The shadow moved again. In the darkness eyes were watching. Doc pulled his pistol and cocked the hammer.

"Come on out. I'll fix a hole in your head."

Doc walked across the side of the street to get a better aim. He could feel the pain rising back up through his stomach and across his back. He smarted and choked over his left hand but kept the pistol straight. "Come on out and fight." Doc moved with caution into the dark of the alley. Another spasm hit him until he felt he would vomit if he continued. He walked a few steps and stopped in the darkness, half bent over with his head hung down.

Doc's eyes adjusted to the darkness until he could see the yellow eyes of a starved stray dog in front of him. The dog growled and crawled forward with its head low and its legs coiled underneath it. Doc watched the hackles rise on the dog's stark coat. The growl was a low rumble. The dog rolled his eyes and spit dropped from its teeth. Doc spoke to the animal but gained little reaction. There was no doubt that the dog was rabid. The animal jumped up and ran towards him. Doc pulled the trigger and shot the dog in the chest.

The dog yelped and fell. Its legs flinched and pulled as the bullet inflicted its damage. It growled and snarled and tried to raise its body. Doc took aim a second time. His hands trembled. The bullet made another hole in the dog. It twitched as the life left its body, then lay dead amongst the garbage and mud.

Doc lowered his gun. His heart raced from the incident. He placed the colt back in the holster and stood shaking in the darkness. He walked back towards Front Street and the growing light, but the pain was unbearable. Blood trickled from his nostrils. He choked and gargled, feeling streams of blood run down the back of his throat and into his mouth. His chest tightened, his muscles contracted in his chest and seized up completely. He coughed until the urgency to clear his lungs compounded and increased the momentum. He spat out a line of blood-covered spit into the dirt. A new flow of blood replaced it and filled his mouth. He had almost reached the end of the alley when his knees gave out on him. He struggled to pull himself up but the pain over came him. He lay choking in the darkness until the draining of blood knocked away any life that remained in his body.

CHAPTER EIGHT

Wyatt left the bakery store and strolled on to
Front Street. He opened the brown paper bag and
reached for a freshly baked roll. The sweet aroma
wafted up into his nostrils. He felt a wet nose
nuzzle his leg and looked down into the soft
brown eyes of his dog. Prospector walked
alongside of him, its long jaws open in a toothy
smile and a drool forming on its lips. Wyatt
reached down and rubbed the dog's furry brown
neck. He broke a piece of roll in his fingers and
gave his dog a crumb or two.

"There you go son. Don't say I don't treat you
right."

The dog ate with appreciation and licked the
flour from the marshal's hand. Wyatt ate the rest of
the roll as a quick breakfast and then closed the
bag. He walked on in the sunshine with his jacket
slung over one shoulder. The air felt cold and fresh
on his face. The dog trotted alongside, its long
sickle tail swinging and brushing against Wyatt's
leg. It cocked its ears to the side, stopped and then

raised its head to sniff the air.

"You smell that old buffalo hide?"

The dog jumped forward and loped off down the street.

"Hey come back here."

The dog eyed Wyatt over one shoulder and moved across the street and turned down an alley, out of the marshal's sight.

Wyatt whistled and broke into a long striding walk, "Prospector!" The dog ignored its owner. Wyatt chased his dog down the street and around the corner into an alley. Prospector stood with his head down, sniffing and pulling at the garbage. Wyatt walked up to his dog. He checked his gun and placed a finger over the trigger. As he drew closer he could see a dead dog lying in the dirt and the outline of a body. He whistled to his dog and was relieved when the greyhound pulled away from the corpse and ran towards him. Wyatt bent down over the dead dog and studied the wild eyes and the dried blood of the gunshot wounds. He got up, sighed and ruffled the fur on Prospector's neck.

"You always find the disgusting stuff, don't you son? Why can't you find me something nice for a change?"

Wyatt smiled, pulled a pair of gloves out of his pockets and pulled them on over his long fingers. He crouched down again and turned his attention to the body.

"Drunken cowboys! We'll identify this fellow and then head back home, that sound good to you?" The dog wagged his tail and waited.

Wyatt pushed the body and rolled it over onto its

back. He choked and felt his breakfast make a break for his throat. He swallowed and took a deep breath. The jacket of the man was splattered in blood. The clothes stunk of rotting flesh. The face and hands were coated in dried blood, the skin that was exposed was grey and void of circulation. Despite the bloody scene, Wyatt knew who the man was.

"Doc?"

He shook his friend and checked to see if he was still breathing.

"Doc?" he yelled.

The corpse inhaled and its lips mouthed the air. Wyatt tried to make sense of the words but they were too soft to hear. He got up and ran back out on to the street towards the Doctor's office. The door was open but the doctor was out on a call. Without thinking, Wyatt ran across the street to his brother's house and banged on the door. Morgan took a few minutes to answer. He opened the door; half naked with bleary eyes and his hair standing up on end.

"Morg, you've got to help me, it's Doc. I don't know what's wrong. He's collapsed or something."

His brother watched with sleepy eyes.

"What do you mean collapsed?"

Wyatt grabbed Morgan by the shoulder.

"Hell, it doesn't matter. Put a pair of pants on and get out here."

Morg struggled to fasten his belt and eyed up a shirt but Wyatt grabbed him before he could finish dressing.

"C'mon, let's go."

The two brothers ran across the street and back

down the alley. Prospector looked up at Morgan and whined. Wyatt pushed the dog out of the way.

"Jesus, what a mess, Wyatt I didn't..."

"Help me grab his legs."

"On three."

"Okay one, two, three."

"All right I got him."

They carried the dentist out into the daylight. The dog trotted after them. A small crowd gathered to watch as Doc was carried through the streets. Wyatt and Morgan listened to the whispers and comments, some of which were far from sympathetic or kind towards Doc. Wyatt rammed open the door to Morgan's room, and laid Doc down on the bed. A young woman stood in a nightgown, embarrassed and alarmed at the intrusion. The men worked around her and tried their best to make Doc comfortable. They peeled off the blood soaked jacket and fetched water to clean his face up.

"Did you get the doctor?"

"He was out. I left a note. He shouldn't be long."

Wyatt rinsed the cloth in the basin of water and began the job of cleaning up his friend. He smarted as he washed the congealed blood from around Doc's mouth and nostrils. He could hear Doc breathing. His lungs rasped against the material that congested his airways. Was he aware of the commotion that he was causing? Wyatt wasn't sure. He would cough and choke, from time to time but his eyes remained closed throughout. Morgan unlaced Doc's shoes. He smiled as he watched his brother make faces at the stench of stale blood and rotting flesh.

"He ain't pretty. I'll give you that."

Wyatt gave Morgan a critical look and continued to rinse the cloth and wipe the blood free of the dentist's upper body. He watched the water add substance to the dried blood and cause rivers of red to stream over the surface of Doc's skin.

Morgan smiled and watched his brother's face pale. "It's been so long I forgot. You never could stomach the sight of blood could you?"

Wyatt choked and closed his eyes. "Hell no!"

"Reminds me of when we was boys and Virge got his foot tore up in one of them traps that was laid out on the farm. We ran to get Mama and when she come she didn't know who to nurse first. Virge was sitting quiet with his foot bleeding and you were washed out like you'd faint, throwing up and sick as a dog. My God, things haven't changed so much."

The doctor knocked on the door and let himself in, making his way across to where Wyatt and Morgan were sitting. He recognized his patient with a groan, but put on a good face and got on with his work.

"How long has he been like this?"

"I'm not sure entirely. He was out cold when I found him. He's come around since then although he's still not talking."

The doctor grumbled as he checked Holliday's eyes and measured his pulse. He opened up his medical bag and removed a syringe and a small brown bottle. He took out a long needle, attached it to the end and proceeded to withdraw the liquid, into the tube. He pulled the dentist's long, skinny arm out, placed pressure on his vein and injected the substance deep into his skin. A tiny drop of blood surfaced at the point of the needle and was swiftly removed and cleaned down with a drop of iodine. He lifted the blankets and pulled them high over Doc's body.

"He's quite a mess. You did a good job cleaning him up. It's a disgrace to see a man get himself in such a state."

"Now surely you're not blaming this on his drinking? He can't help his condition."

"Oh it's easy of course to blame everything on the consumption, but quite frankly in my opinion, any man that squanders his life on whiskey has no one to blame but himself for the implications. There's nothing here that a few years of clean living and religion couldn't cure. Do you intent to keep Dr. Holliday here?"

There was a moment of silence as the two brothers thought over the matter. Wyatt fumed quietly but hid his emotion behind a calm exterior.

"He shouldn't be moved in his condition," the doctor continued.

Morgan's jaw dropped. "We didn't realize that he..."

"He stays here. We'll look after him," Wyatt interrupted.

Morgan looked to his brother with annoyance. "You can't just say that, this ain't even your cabin no more Wyatt."

"It's settled. Doc will stay here. You can move out and stay with me for a while if you need to."

"You'll need to look after him. He'll require continuous supervision."

The brothers looked at one another, looked at

Doc and then back at the doctor.

Wyatt sighed, "We'll work something out. It's not exactly busy in Dodge right now. I'm sure I can get a couple of days off to come and make sure he's all right."

"Well gentlemen. It appears you have everything in hand. The morphine should help his pain and coughing a great deal. If you have any more blankets, put them on the bed. Let him sweat it out and let him sleep. We can deal with him once he wakes."

"Will you check him again tonight?"

The doctor sighed. "It shouldn't be necessary. Not in Dr. Holliday's case. If you come later to my office, I'll give you a cough tincture. You can give it to him yourself."

"That would just be too much of an effort now, wouldn't it? If it was anyone else you'd be 'round here like a shot."

"Marshal Earp. I don't wish to get in a fight with you but I'm the doctor and I'll determine whether Holliday needs attention or not. There are other patients of mine, who are more careful with their health. I'm not about to waste time and energy, saving a malodorous drunk."

"Kind of quick to judge now aren't you? I'm going to pay good money for your services and I damn well except you to show up tonight and every other night until Doc here is well enough to thank you. Do you understand?"

"I think you're being very unreasonable. I was only..."

"Do you understand?" Wyatt glared at the man.

The doctor nodded.

"Good. I'll see you tonight at eight o'clock."

The doctor gave Wyatt a final glance, closed his medical case with a loud bang and left the room.

Wyatt stared at the floor, his mind was lost in contemplation. Morgan knew that it was best to wait until his brother was ready to talk. Wyatt walked a little way across the floor and stopped by the bed. He watched Doc sleeping. The noise of the dentist's breathing had softened although there was still a wheezing, rasping tone that made Wyatt uncomfortable.

"I'm sorry Morg. I pushed you into this."

Morgan shrugged and smiled. "It don't bother me one little bit. I kinda like Doc. You're just doin' what's right."

"Look why don't you go on and stay at my house tonight? I'll tend to Doc here."

"No Wyatt. We can take it in turns. I don't want you putting yourself out like that."

"Go on. I'll be fine."

"Please let me help. I'd feel bad if I didn't."

Wyatt smiled. "You remind me of Pa you're so stubborn. I guess we can take it in shifts. I'll tell you what. I'll buy breakfast if you'll pick it up from the Long Branch?"

"It's a deal. What do you want?"

"What ever they have pancakes or ham and eggs, it doesn't matter."

You want me to bring anything else?"

"Get me some blankets. Oh and bring a couple of my books and the newspaper."

Wyatt's attention turned to the woman who stood in the corner, leaning awkwardly against the wall. The woman raised her head and pulled the one sheet that she had, higher above her person to hide her translucent nightgown. Her eyes wandered the room with embarrassment. Wyatt's eyes ran up and down the woman.

"I didn't realize you had company."

Morgan swiveled around. His face lit up in a beaming grin. "Heck with all the commotion I nearly forgot. Come on over here honey."

The woman shook her head. "I ain't dressed or nothing."

"Hey that don't matter darlin.' I want you to meet my brother."

"Morgan?"

Morgan smiled, stood up, and walked over in front to hide the woman. "Here honey. Here's my overcoat. Slip that on for a while. It's good and long."

"Can't we wait a bit? I didn't want it to be like this," the woman whispered.

"Oh darling it's okay." Morg hugged her and gave her a kiss on the cheek. "It's only my brother." He smiled at Wyatt with a devilish grin. "Now come on out here."

He led the woman forward. She shuffled towards Wyatt. Morgan beamed with pride.

"Wyatt. This is Louisa. She's my woman. We got engaged a few months back. We're hoping on getting married some time early next spring."

"Pleased to meet you Louisa."

She smiled. "It's a pleasure to meet you Mister Earp."

Morgan laughed, "Hey what's with the airs and graces? Call him Wyatt. He ain't used to bein' called anything else."

Wyatt eyed his brother.

"Well it's true. You should have heard what we'd call him when we was kids."

"No need to trouble your lady with that. Congratulations. I can't believe my little brother's getting hitched."

"Neither can I."

"You sure it's all right about tonight?"

"Oh don't worry about it Wyatt."

"I'm sorry about this Louisa it's not normally as chaotic around here."

"Oh no it's fine, really. I want to help too. Let me bring you some coffee tonight. I bake real good too. Maybe I should bake something."

Morgan grinned and wrapped his arms around her.

"Oh honey, that would be just wonderful. She's an angel Wyatt. I swear she is."

"Louisa, anything you could do in way of coffee would be fine for me but please don't go to any more trouble."

"Oh it's no trouble. I hate to think of the pair of you going hungry over all this."

The brothers exchanged devilish glances.

"What ever you want to do honey. C'mon get dressed and we'll go and get Wyatt some of the things he needs."

Morgan stopped and turned "What about Mattie? Do you want me to ask her to come down?"

"Sure if she wants to. I'm not sure if this is her kind of thing. She may be busy sewing. Go on and ask her anyway."

"All right."

Morgan waited for Louisa to pull on some clothes before taking her by the hand and leading her out into the sunshine. Wyatt watched as the last trace of sunlight faded from the closing door and settled down to nurse Doc.

CHAPTER NINE

Beams of sunlight danced in the rippling water of the river. A breeze blew through the Georgian pines, murmuring as it caught the branches. The long grass swayed in elegant seas of green and set the lacy limbs of a weeping willow swaying over the water.

Doc opened his eyes and observed the hazy glow of the summer afternoon. The grass sparkled with moisture and caressed his face with a gentle touch. Something told him to sleep and he did. He woke to the touch of a young woman with golden hair. He reached out to touch her face. A strange light glowed around her face. It gave her skin an ethereal quality and softened her outline against the warm blue sky.

Doc shook his hair free of the grass and sat up. He smiled and stretched the muscles in his back and arms. He stroked the girl's cheek. She asked for his hand and Doc gave it to her. She stroked his knuckles and observed the worn bitten fingernails. Doc leaned forward to whisper. The girl obeyed

and leaned forward to hear. "I love you," he said.
He kissed her on the neck before she had time to
reply. The girl blushed and pulled back in
surprise. Doc watched. The woman turned to go
and with quick steps made her way into the
distance and disappeared.

Doc felt warm and moved to loosen his collar.
The cotton tightened around his neck. His skin
seemed to wedge around his throat as if someone
was pulling it from either side. The heat seeped
into his body. He unbuttoned the top two buttons
of the shirt. The sun burnt his face and hurt his
eyes. He leaned down to the creek's edge and
scooped a handful of water, splashing it over his
cheeks and down around his neck. This brought
little relief and he lay down in the grass to try and
sleep. He woke to warmth around his neck. He
opened one eye expecting the girl's return, but he
could see no one. He felt the warmth tighten
around him and begin to choke the breath from his
lungs. He sat up and opened his eyes. A snake
coiled itself around his body. Its eyes were
unforgiving and it appeared to enjoy the
maneuver, wrapping itself around and around
Doc's neck. He tried to scream but couldn't speak.
It tightened its grip and sucked his Adams apple,
moving higher to his throat and pulling hard
across his chest. Doc choked and swallowed
reaching a hand out to grab the snake. The reptile
swung its neck away and bit the dentist. It sunk its
fangs deep into Doc's throat until his blood ran
with poison and he lay back on the grass, pale but
devoid of any pain.

Doc sat up in bed shaking. He shivered as a line

of cold sweat slid down the crease of his spine. He choked but couldn't clear the lump in his throat. He tried to cough but could not. He swallowed hard and was greeted by coughing. His chest pumped like bellows to a fire as he went through the sequence of breathing in and coughing out. His side ached as it coped with the hard work and exercise involved. He could feel a break coming, as the substance worked its way closer to his mouth. He leaned down into the pillow for extra support to his chest and coughed most of the offending substance up. The relief was instant.

Wheezing, he sat back cold and exhausted. As he caught his breath he reflected on the dream. He reassured himself but he was inconsolable. He bit his lip and wiped the tears from his face with the back of his hand. His chest tightened with pain as he remembered. The emotions within him bubbled to the surface. He swallowed his feelings down into his stomach, huddled and shivered in a pathetic heap on the bed. His eyes burned and swelled, his chest heaved as he let go in an agony filled fit of sobbing.

The crying woke Wyatt from his sleep. His book fell from his lap, to the floor with a dull thud. He was surprised to see that Doc was awake. He got up from the wooden chair in the corner of the room, stretched his back and neck and walked to the bed. He watched Doc with a tired quizzical expression.

"You okay?" he said.

Doc looked at Wyatt with embarrassment and tried to stopper his emotions. It took all his efforts to pull himself together and stop crying. He sat in silence, his face still stained with tears. He took a deep breath and tried to talk. His lips moved but without sound. He tried again and was able to make a soft squeaking noise. Wyatt waited. He could see that Doc was frustrated. After several attempts at speech Doc succeeded in making enough noise to whisper.

"What you doing here Wyatt?" he said. The effort of speaking caused him to cough and it was a while before he could regain control of himself.

"Save your voice. Go on back to sleep."

The dentist tried to mouth words again but any hint of a voice had been lost in the last coughing fit. He grew mad and picked up the glass by the bed and threw it at the wall. Wyatt moved out of the way and looked around for a scrap of paper and a pen. He found some writing paper in a drawer and the stub of an old pencil. He took out his pocketknife and whittled away the end, until it was sharp enough to write with. He gave the pencil and paper to Doc and then looked for something for Doc to lean on. He picked up his book, a worn edition of Edgar Alan Poe's 'Tales of Mystery' and handed it to the dentist. Doc took the book, choked a surprised, silent laugh and then started to write. He handed the paper back to Wyatt.

It took Wyatt a moment to read Doc's curly writing.

'I love this book. I had a copy back in Georgia but it got lost after I left Texas.'

Wyatt's eyes lit up and a vague smile tweaked his mustache.

"Go on and keep it. I've read it too many times anyway. Now that you're getting better you'll need something to occupy your time."

The dentist mouthed a thank you and wrote on the paper.

'You look like shit. What have you been doing?'

Wyatt smiled. "I've been looking after you. Morgan's been in too. Jim even stayed for a while."

Doc wrote another message and handed the page to Wyatt. He sat for a while trying to decipher the letters.

"Your hand writing's awful. I can't work out what you're trying to say."

Doc's eyes grew intense and with a bony finger, he beckoned Wyatt to drop the paper again. He scribbled on the page and handed it back. He had printed in capitals and this time the page was easy to read. Wyatt read the note.

'I'm a dentist. What do you expect? Writing illegibly is part and parcel of the medical profession.'

Wyatt laughed. A slow grin ran across Doc's face. He wheezed as if he was laughing until the spasm took him and his chest reverberated. The coughing was slow at first and gradually picked up momentum until the dentist could not free himself of the rhythm. He tried to control his breathing but it was difficult to control. The result was a disconcerting whistling noise. The coughing slowed like the hooves of a galloping horse breaking down to a walk.

Wyatt looked on with concern. He picked up a bottle of laudanum and a tin medicine cup and took it over to Doc.

"Here take this."

Doc eyed him while coughing and refused. The marshal remained persistent and with a stern glance, he convinced Doc to change his mind. Wyatt poured the substance into the cup and helped Doc drink back the liquid. The dentist shivered as the bitter taste hit his throat.

"Persistent devil aren't you? You're worse than my mother," he whispered.

"Since when has your mother been a police officer?"

Doc smiled, tried to laugh and coughed again. He leaned into the pillow and pressed his chest down to stop his ribs from hurting. He rested a moment and pulled at the piece of paper, found an empty space and began writing again. He passed the paper to Wyatt and sat staring at the door.

'I can't bear it any more.'

"What?"

Doc took back the page, flipped it over and wrote a couple more lines.

'I can't stand living like this. Why are you doing this for me? I don't want to burden anyone.'

"I wanted to help. I couldn't just leave you in the street."

'Why do you care? I'm not worth a shit to anyone.'

"You're my friend. You could have let me get killed a year ago but you didn't."

"That was luck Wyatt." Doc whispered.

"That's bull and you know it. You wanted to help and you did."

Doc flinched as a pain caught him in the back. He tensed against the pressure. His eyes watered. He choked, coughed and leaned down on one shoulder.

Wyatt watched his friend with a troubled expression. Doc wiped the spit from his mouth, choked and swallowed. He scribbled on the paper and handed it to Wyatt. He watched the marshal's reaction.

'I hate that you get to see me like this. Promise me you won't tell anyone about the state I'm in. If it gets out, my reputation will be shredded. They'll jump me one night if they know how easy I'd be to kick the shit out of.'

"That's just the medicine talking Doc. I doubt if they'd do that."

"Please?" Doc whispered.

"I won't let anyone touch you till you get your strength back."

'That means a lot to me.' Doc wrote.

"Don't worry about it. I'm sure if you got the chance you'd do the same for me."

"Yes," said Doc. His voice was barely audible. The laudanum had its affect and within seconds the situation became too tiring for the dentist to stand. He tried to remain alert but the tonic lulled him to sleep. His head slid down into the bedclothes and the paper fell from his grasp. Wyatt removed the book from the bed and placed it on the bedside table. He turned down the light of the lamp, pulled his jacket on and headed out into the street. Morgan saw his brother waiting and met him at the door.

"How is he?"

"He's awake, or at least he was. Will you sit with him while I go talk to the doctor?"

"Sure thing Wyatt." A slow smile ran across

Morgan's face. He looked up at Wyatt.

"What you grinnin' about Morg?"

"I'm just glad Doc's okay. I knew that surly ol' cus wouldn't give up the fight that easily."

Wyatt smiled "Well he's pretty weak. It will be a while before he can play pool again."

"Dang Wyatt. I didn't mean it that way."

Wyatt shook his head, placed a hand on Morgan's shoulder and then walked away.

CHAPTER TEN

Morgan's hat flipped up and backwards and nearly blew away in the wind. He grabbed it and opened the door to the Dodge House. The attendant was at the check-in desk filing papers and returning keys to the correct hooks. The gust of wind blew his papers sideways. He grabbed at a few of the papers and watched the rest scatter. His attention turned to Morgan who was leaning on the door trying to shut it against the wind.

"Evening Morg. What you up to?"

"I've come to get Doc."

The attendant laughed. "Good luck."

Morgan ran up the stairs. The climb was steep but he lost no breath. He grabbed hold of the polished banister and climbed two steps at a time. At the top he walked up and down the dark corridor looking for Doc's room. He paused at number twenty-four and rapped his knuckles against the door but there was no answer.

"Doc, you ready?"

There was no reply, Morgan rapped again."Hey

Doc you ready?" He listened for a while,
wondering whether he should leave and come
back later or stay and wait. He banged on the door
until he could hear Doc cursing and the noise of
creaking floorboards.

"What do you want?"

"It's Morg."

There was a frantic rattling as the door was
opened. Doc stood in a pair of long-johns. His hair
was spiked up in a cowlick, his eyes were
bloodshot and his chin bristled. Morgan grinned
and choked in an effort to suppress a laugh.

"I take it you're not ready?"

"Would it surprise you if I told you that I was?
This is my disguise for Halloween. C'mon in and
sit down."

Morgan edged his way into the room and picked
his feet between the garments that were strewn
over the floor. The room was dark and it was hard
to see where the floorboards were, let alone what
he was standing on. Every corner of the room was
a disaster.

"You really need to get yourself a woman Doc. I
don't know how you can live here with it like
this?"

"I don't. Last night was the first time I'd slept
here in three days."

The dentist rolled a cigarette between his bony
fingers, lit the end and sucked the smoke as if it
was a gift from heaven. He walked over to the
window and pulled the drapes back enough to let
a strand of light seep into the room. The extra light
gave Morgan a better view of his friend than he
wanted. He was paler than usual, the only color in

his eyes were the red patches around them. A
black bruise colored the bridge of his nose and
highlighted one of his cheeks. It made his eye
socket appear skeletal in appearance. The other
side of his face was so pale it blended with the
light.

"What time is it anyway?"

"Three in the afternoon. What happened to your
face? What you been up to?"

"Chalkley Beeson had a high stakes poker game
last night. It went on until about four in the
morning. I was doing well, until the last go round.
The pot was higher than a Fargo bankroll, I was
breezing. I'd seen better cards but my hand was
good enough."

"So what happened?"

"It came down to me, the fellow who runs the
saddlery store and a Baptist preacher man come
up from Mississippi. We all took turns and the guy
from the store says he's out. I was expecting the
preacher to fold but he just keeps holding them
cards and staring at me. Well next thing I know
he's upped the ante. I'm thinking how nice it
would be to talk about back South and religion
and how sweet that pot will taste once I've got it
home with me. He calls my hand. I drop the cards
nice and pretty. I smile at him. He smiles back and
rakes in the pot. I ask him to show what he's got in
his grubby paws. He lays them out for me one by
one. The son of a bitch had a royal flush."

"You got beat by a preacher?"

"Yes Sir I did. Well about this time I notice that
his accent is slipping some. I give him a little of the
old talk and he looked bewildered he looked like

he didn't know what I was talkin' about. I can spot a liar from a couple of miles away. His eyes were blinking like a whole wash of sand was in them. I knew then that he had pulled a trick on me. He just got up from the table and left. He weren't no religious man he was a good for nothin' trickster."

"Didn't you say something while he was at the table?"

"I didn't have the heart too. I couldn't believe what had happened. I wasn't broke or nothing but I sure wasn't rolling either. I went and found a bottle of bourbon and got drunk until I couldn't walk straight. Next thing I know Jim Masterson is moving me on for being drunk and loaded. He buffaloed me and threw me in a cell. I have never been so drunk or so embarrassed in my whole entire life."

Morgan laughed until his face grew red.

"I've got to tell Wyatt this."

"He all ready knows. He was working at the jail last night. He charged me ten dollars and let me go early this afternoon. Wyatt told me the entire police force, are going to be going to this thing tonight. I'm a little embarrassed about the situation to say the least."

"Are you still going?"

"Yes Sir. Just as soon as I get my stuff together."

"You're going to be all right?"

"Surely. If I can lay my paws on a little sulphuric acid I will be."

"What?"

"I take some laudanum and mix it with a glass of whiskey and swig it down." He took the top off the laudanum bottle and poured it drop for drop into a water tumbler. Morgan counted more than twenty drops.

"Are you mad, that's enough to floor a horse?"

"Since when were you my mother? You don't know what you're talking about." Doc placed the laudanum bottle back down and reached for the bottle of whiskey. He poured liquor in until it came half way up the glass and then swirled the potion around.

"Don't Doc it's only going to make you worse. I'll tell Wyatt your sick and we'll leave it at that."

Doc grinned. "After a while it's like a dog chasing its tail, believe me it doesn't make a difference in the long run. It helps me though. I'll be all right. Trust me."

He took a swig of the mixture. His lip pulled back over his teeth as the taste hit him. He downed the rest in one go and started to wheeze and choke. He pulled himself over to the washbasin retching and straining, half choking and half wheezing. After a lot of effort the dentist vomited the mixture into the basin. The whole process looked to be excruciatingly painful. Morgan turned away, unable to watch.

"If you're going to mutilate yourself, you can stay here."

The dentist was too preoccupied to answer. Morgan could hear him retching. He wished he were somewhere else. He was thankful when it was over.

Doc pulled himself up from the basin, breathing heavily and choking. He reached for the jug, his skinny wrist shaking under the weight, he poured water into his hand and splashed it over his face.

He smarted as the cold water hit him. He blinked trying to remove any excess water from his eyelashes. He reached for a towel, dried his eyes and then dried his hands like a surgeon cleaning up after an operation.

"I can't believe you would do this to yourself."

"Oh hush up! I'm a doctor I know what I'm doing."

"Doctor my ass you know your just a dentist."

"Oh just a dentist? I don't recall seeing a diploma on your wall."

Morgan turned and was surprised by the marked improvement in the dentist. Any other man would have shown some after effects of the medication, but Doc was quite sober. He combed his hair with brilliantine, attempting to flatten the cowlick sticking up at the front.

"I can't believe that you're okay after drinking that?"

"It's when it wears off that it bothers me. If you don't see me for a couple of days don't be surprised. I'll be out of action for a while, most probably sleeping it off. It's the night terrors that almost kill me. I'll be dreaming I'm fighting man eating dragons somewhere in far Asia if I'm lucky."

"Sounds interesting."

"Believe me Dante's inferno is more alluring."

"We're going to be late. I said to Wyatt fifteen minutes."

"Well quit bellyaching and pass me my jacket and pants."

Doc flicked his razor in the cold water and took two swift swipes of the blade, shaving enough to

clean his chin but not enough to look tidy. Morgan
passed him his clothes. He pulled a pair of
crumpled pin stripes over his long johns and slid
his suspenders high over his bony shoulders. He
placed his suit jacket over the top, buttoned the top
button and put his grey overcoat on over the top.

"Pass me my guns."

Morgan looked at Doc with disapproval. "No
guns."

Doc sighed. "All right. No guns."

"Are you ready now?"

Doc picked up the cigarette butt and resumed
smoking. He picked up his walking stick.

"Yes, I'm ready."

Front Street was busy when they arrived.
Horseman rode up and down. The noise of horse
hooves filled the air. People crossed back and forth
chattering and laughing. Deep blue clouds drifted
and blackened the sky. The vague starlight of the
constellations became illuminated in the dark. The
cheerful sound of a piano rolled out into the night.
Further down the street a fiddler played 'Turkey in
the straw.' Doc sat in the buckboard and placed his
hands under his jacket to keep them warm. He
hunched his shoulders over and shook as a gust of
cold air caught him.

"You cold or something?" said Morgan.

Doc smiled. "I'm always cold. Don't have much
to keep warm with."

"I heard from Virge that it's warm in Arizona
most of the year around. Maybe you should go
there."

"Virge is your brother?"

"Yeah."

"Where is he located?"

"Prescott at the moment."

"Is there much gaming there?"

Morgan smiled. "I'm not sure, most probably not. Virge was saying that everyone in Prescott is into forestry."

Doc flicked his dead cigarette butt out into the street. "Oh Lord that sounds like so much fun."

"Well it's always a place to consider moving to."

"If it keeps me from dying of boredom than yes it is something to consider. I got my fill of forestry down in Valdosta. Nothing like watching trees growing to fill a boy's spirit and spark his head full of adventure."

Morgan laughed. "Your father ran a forestry plantation?"

"Oh he did lots of things. He still does. He likes to get involved in everything and anything that will make him some money. I hear he's selling buggies now. Lord knows what's next."

"Sounds like my family."

"Does policing run in your family?"

"Well I guess it does in a way. Our father was a lawyer back when we lived in Iowa… He works partly in law enforcement and other things out in California now. I think the farm is still up and running, I'm not too sure. It's been about six months or so since I was back home."

I would just about give my eyeteeth to be home right now. I'm so tired of Kansas."

"I think we all are."

Morgan slapped the reins at the pony and guided him through the crowds of other horses and up to the boardwalk. He jumped out with great athleticism and tended to the horse. Doc eased his long legs down to the ground. He leaned against the wagon, steadied himself and grabbed his cane from the wooden seat. Morgan finished tethering the horse and strode up onto the boardwalk. Doc followed steadily leaning a little on the cane.

There was already a large crowd of people at the Long Branch Saloon when they entered. It was hard to tell where Wyatt was from the door. Doc and Morgan edged their way in through the doorway. The cigar and cigarette smoke drifted on the air in a heavy mist. Doc caught sight of Wyatt sitting up beside the fire. He pushed past the people with Morgan following as best as he could.

"I wasn't sure if you'd make it after last night," said Wyatt.

"I'll never trust a preacher again as long as I live."

"C'mon and get heated up some."

Wyatt moved out of the way and let Doc in beside the fireplace. A greyhound mongrel and a pointer lay stretched out on the floor, enjoying the heat. Doc sat down and slid his legs in behind the pointer's back. He moved his cane in and balanced it against the wall. The dog looked up at Doc and tapped his tail against the floor. The dentist looked into the greyhound's brown eyes and remembered the incident in the alley. He wondered if he could trust the dog. The mongrel sniffed the dentist's fingers. Doc hesitated before he dropped his bony hand onto the dog's head and stroked it. The dog groaned with boredom and dropped his drooling muzzle onto the dentist's boots. Doc watched in disgust as wet drool dropped into the polished leather.

"What you drinking Doc?" said Morgan.

"Well what are you letting me drink?"

"Whatever you want. If you make a fool of yourself again Wyatt and I are dropping you. Ain't that right Wyatt?"

Wyatt looked up at his brother with a knowing look. "If he makes a fool of himself again, I'll arrest him."

"I appreciate that Wyatt. Get me a cup of coffee."

"Make that two cups. So, you Okay?"

"As well as can be expected. My finances are burnt up. I need to build up my bankroll again. If you know of any easy games I could make some money from, I'd appreciate it."

"I wasn't asking about your finances I was inquiring into your health."

"I'm still here if that's what you're implying."

"What's with the cane?"

"What do you think?"

"Why don't you tell me?"

"A couple of years ago I got shot in the leg. The bullet tore through some muscle tissue. It took a long time to heal. Normally I don't get any trouble from it, but after that long spell in bed last month my muscles are all wasted. I can feel the old wounds starting to fester again."

"It hurts?"

"When it's cold out it stings like I'm being burned with a hot poker. It brings back a lot of memories for me that I'd rather forget. Is that a good enough explanation Mister Earp?"

"I'd say that's a little more information than I

was looking for. Do you mind if I look at the cane for a while?"

Doc gave Wyatt a strange look and passed the walking stick over. "Go ahead be my guest. It's just a normal cane."

Wyatt studied the walking stick from handle to tip. He felt his hand along the edges, smiled and pulled a clip out from the side. The bottom of the cane sank into the mechanism and opened to show the barrel of a gun.

"I thought you said this was just a plain old walking stick?"

"I saw it in a Remington catalog. I couldn't resist it. It was a good price; hell it was beautiful. It's sort of an early Christmas present to myself."

"Have you fired her?"

"Not yet. She just fires one shot."

"Wouldn't it be a little awkward to shoot?" said Wyatt.

"Well it would just be for emergencies. I prefer my pistols, you know that."

"You do know that I should confiscate this? It still counts as a firearm."

"I understand. I'd prefer it if you didn't. I really can't walk too far without it. If you take it Morg's going to have to carry me home tonight."

"How come you never told me about this injury before?"

"Do you want to take a look to prove I'm not lying?"

"That won't be necessary. Go on and keep the cane for now."

Doc's eyes gleamed. "Thank you Wyatt."

Morgan returned with the coffee and sat two

sturdy mugs down on the table, along with a small metal coffee pot.

"There you go girls. Don't drink it all at once now."

Doc took one of the mugs of coffee with gratitude and wrapped his fingers around it. He pulled it in towards his chest to try and warm as much of his body as he could. He blew some of the steam off the top of the cup, the effort of which caused him to wheeze. He choked inside his throat and repressed the urge to cough. The whole effect made the dentist sound as if he was laughing quietly at something.

"What's so funny?" said Wyatt.

Doc shook his head. He removed his handkerchief, placed the cup of coffee down on the table and started to choke and spit into the fabric.

"I wouldn't put it that way. You're right though there should be a great deal of money floating around in Tombstone."

"You're going to police over their Wyatt?" said Bat.

"No. I doubt it. I'm going to start a stage line."

"Don't you think they may all ready have one?"

"I doubt it. If so I can always do something else."

"Like police work?"

"Nope I hope not."

"Well it's always an option. I'm sure they need someone to keep people from stealing the silver," said Bat with a grin.

Wyatt didn't laugh.

"I'm sure they've got enough lawmen all ready."

"You can never have enough policeman in a boom town,"

"So do you think you'll join us in Tombstone?"

"To tell the truth Wyatt, I'm not all together sure."

The crude noise of a piano being played interrupted the men's conversation. The pianist put all his heart into the music and swung backwards and forward as the carnival style music poured out into the air. Doc watched with vague curiosity. The crowd grew quiet until all conversation had halted completely. As the music rolled on the people lost interest and got back to their drinking. The bartender took orders by instinct rather than spoken words. The clicking and whirring of the many gambling devices got under way again. The pianist finished the piece by sliding his right hand up the keys and then there was relative quiet.

Mayor Kelley climbed the stairs to the small stage at the back of the bar and did his best to grab everyone's attention. He cleared his throat and grunted. People continued to chat, happy that the pianist had quit playing for a while.

"Gentleman please, if I can have your attention for a moment."

Kelley appealed to Bat for help. He grinned and shook his head. He climbed up onto the stage and positioned himself beside Kelley.

"Quiet everyone," said Bat. He barely raised his voice but the effect was ten-fold. The crowd stopped talking and gave Bat all their attention.

Kelley smiled.

"Now that I have your attention. I have a little announcement to make. You may or may not be aware that our busy season here in Dodge is drawing to a close. It's men like Wyatt Earp and Bat Masterson who help to keep this town and county quiet and law abiding during the summer months. Well this week Wyatt announced his retirement from the position Deputy Marshal respectively. Well I couldn't let our boy go without showing him some of the appreciation that we have for him here in town."

Kelly looked into the crowd but could not see what he was looking for.

"Wyatt? Where are you? Come on up here."

Wyatt pushed his way through the crowd and made his way through the crowd, up onto the stage. He was embarrassed with the situation and didn't know how to deal with it. Bat smiled at Wyatt, enjoying every minute.

"That's better. Now we can all see you. A few people in town thought that it was wrong that we let you go without something to remind you of Dodge, so the Republican faction in town threw some dollars together and got you this. Bat here ordered it so you can blame him for the glitzy trimmings."

An assistant beside the stage picked up a polished wooden box and passed it over to Kelley. The Mayor opened the box and lifted it up for everyone to see. "I don't know if you folks can see this from the back of the bar there but this is a special Colt we got made. It's bronze barrel measures over seven inches long and as you can see it's nickel-plated. We even got the back engraved so there is no doubt as to who the gun belongs to. I wish you many happy hours with this gun Wyatt and I hope that It'll help to remind you of Dodge when you're out on your travels. Out of curiosity, where are you going?"

"Tombstone, Arizona," said Wyatt.

"Tombstone! Well I know that everyone here wishes you the best of luck in your new destination. Let's hope the trip is a happy one. Everyone put your hands together and applaud this gentleman."

Clapping broke from the crowd. Wyatt felt his chest swell with pride as he recognized the people in the crowd. He could see Bat's brother Jim. Charlie Bassett stood by one of the tables, Bill Tilghman stood clapping, and even Luke Short had risen to his feet. Wyatt stood rock steady and let the moment wash over him. Kelley waved his hands in the hope of quieting everyone down again.

Wyatt and Bat said their thanks and left the stage. They walked back over to the table talking. Everyone shook hands with the men and showed their appreciation. Wyatt sat down beside Doc. The dentist tapped the retired marshal's shoulder.

"Congratulations Wyatt. You deserve every minute."

Wyatt nodded. "Thanks Doc." His chin wobbled as he spoke. He raised his face to the dentist. Doc could see that the marshal was close to tears. It was not something that any eye would have noticed but to a professional poker player it was obvious.

"I believe your gun is viable for confiscating Wyatt. Seeing how you ain't the law around here any more. You wouldn't want to break your own ordinance," said Doc.

Wyatt smiled until the arches of his handlebar

mustache twitched exposing a few teeth.

"I'm sure going to miss this place Doc. Some of my best years have been here."

"There are always other places Wyatt. Lord knows it doesn't take much more than dust to make a boomtown."

CHAPTER ELEVEN

Doc stepped out of Cornelius Fly's boarding house, pulled a match from his pocket and lit a cigarette. He waved the flame out and dropped the match to the ground. He held the door open for Big Nose Kate. She pulled her stole across her shoulders and took a deep breath of evening air. Doc let the door close behind her and placed his arm up around her shoulders. She smiled up at him.

"My God I think I'm going to burst."

"If I stay here long enough I'm gonna get fatter than a hog."

Kate laughed, "You're so funny. I can't imagine you fat." She pulled a cigar from her purse and placed it in her mouth. "Light me up darling."

Doc obliged. Kate sucked the end of the cigar and choked on the smoke.

The town had boomed over the past four months. Horses packed the street tied to hitching posts and corral fences. Saloons advertised their wares with billboards. Future businessmen eyed vacant plots of ground and etched their dreams on paper. A drunken cowboy leaned his head down into a water trough and drank his fill of dirty water. His horse waited second in line to take a sip. A loud siren blared from one of the mines, signaling the end of the second shift. Tired miners walked back through the town with dirty shovels and soiled clothes. The sun sank in the sky, orange light spilled across the streets. The clouds changed constantly, sometimes they were purple and sometimes pink. Kate and Doc narrowed their eyes against the brightness of the light.

"This is beautiful buttercup, so nice, not as nice as Las Vegas but still nice."

Doc gazed out over the back of Fremont Street to the gray mountains in the distance watching the light cast shadows across the surface. He felt hypnotized by his surroundings.

"Hey hallo! I don't think you hear me. What you think of all this? Isn't this nice? I'm sure we'll be happy here. I know it, yes."

"I heard you honey."

Kate watched as lines of people moved past the boarding house, along the side of the photographic studio and out past the stable offices. Behind the boarding house the noise of a rooster crowing rose up into the evening air.

"Doc darling," she said. "There's something going on, maybe a chicken fight."

"Cock fight honey, chickens don't fight, they lay eggs."

"Oh Doc you know what I mean. It's all the same."

"Most roosters would disagree with you."

Kate cackled. She nudged Doc in the ribs, "You're so funny buttercup."

Doc finished his cigarette, threw it on the ground and stubbed it out with the toe of his boot.

"Come on let's go."

They opened the picket gate and let themselves out into the alley. They joined the crowd and walked slowly into the courtyard of offices and stables that made up the OK livery stables. In a vacant lot a crude rope arena had been constructed. The crowd huddled around the ropes. A buckboard had drawn up to one side of the arena and two mischievous women stood up on the back, trying to get the best view they could. On the corral side, a man dressed in striped pants sat bareback astride a blinkered mining mule. The rider stretched his long legs down against its sides.

Doc and Kate squeezed through the crowd until the sway of bodies was too thick for them to get any further forward. A tall cowboy moved to the side giving them a full view of the fight that was about to take place.

In the center of the arena there were two men clutching a rooster each. One of the men was bent over with one hand on his rooster's back. He stroked and slicked the black silky feathers and said a silent prayer, his eyes closed, one hand clutching the rooster, the other playing with the silver cross that hung loosely from his neck. The other man adjusted the spurs on the back of his rooster's legs, watched the crowd from the corner of his eyes and waited.

The signal to begin was given and both men let go and stepped back. The black rooster growled in a deep voice and then rose to the air, flapping his wings, his feet outstretched. The red rooster lunched forward and jumped up to meet his opponent. The dust flew in little clouds of light, illuminating the feathers of green, black and red. The birds danced and strutted, circling, lunging and circling. Growling and crowing filled the air. The roosters attacked viciously, their beaks neck to neck, a rolling bundle of feathers, spilling across the ground. They jumped to the sky and back to the ground again. There was a scream from the crowd as the red and green rooster beat a retreat, his rainbow colors dashed with blood. The scene was blocked before Doc was able to see the fight to its inevitable conclusion. He turned with Kate and walked away. They headed through the back of the lot, past the corral stables and out onto Allen Street. There was a cry and cheer that went up from the crowd, as the fight ended.

"It's a pity about that rooster," said Kate. "What will they do with him now he's dead?"

"My choice would be to fry him," said Doc with a devilish grin.

"Oh Doc, you're so mean. That poor chicken did nothing to nobody."

"More reason to eat him I say."

Kate's eyes gleamed. She smiled up at Doc, pulled his thin neck down gently towards her and kissed him with passionately. He grabbed his hands around her waist and pulled her towards him. A consumptive wheeze caused him to cough and the kiss ended.

"Let's go get a drink, maybe it will help your throat," she said.

Doc nodded in agreement and coughed into his hand until the fit subsided. The couple walked along the boardwalk in the fading light. As the darkness spread across the street, lanterns were lit and the orange glow of oil lamps poured out onto the boardwalks. The pair came to the corner of Allen Street and Fifth Street. Something made Doc stop and look up at the saloon that sat on the corner. Standing by the door in a brown plaid hunting jacket, eyes narrowed against the light, was a familiar face. The more Doc looked, the more the figure stood out from the crowd.

"Wyatt?"

The figure looked up. His face was half hidden in the shadows.

"Doc? By God it's so good to see you again. I almost didn't recognize you. How long has it been? Almost a year isn't it?"

"It feels much longer."

"Morg come on out here a second," said Wyatt.

Morgan stepped through the saloon doors and out to where Doc and Kate were standing.

"Well I'll be..."

"I can't believe it. When did you hit town?" said Doc.

"Oh about a week ago. Jim and Virge are here too. Have you met Virge?"

"No I haven't had the pleasure."

"You look so different. I don't know how to put it but you look..."

"Healthy?" said Doc.

Morgan smiled.

"I remember having to carry you out of an alley back in Dodge. You don't look like the same man."

"Well I'm not. I hate to say it but I almost feel good. Katie here's been taking good care of me."

Morgan tipped his hat in Kate's direction and gave her one of his beaming smiles.

"You should see some of the bars around here Doc. There's a new one opening nearly every month. I ain't been here much longer than you and I've seen two open all ready. Take the Oriental here. It only opened two weeks ago and it's doing great business."

"You should see the inside, it's really something special," said Wyatt.

"Well what are we standing here for?"

The friends walked through the swing doors and were greeted by the sound of a fiddle being played sweetly and the restrained fingers of a classical pianist. Red velvet drapes hung down from the windows to the floor. Crystal chandeliers hung down from the ceiling, casting sparkling beams of light across the room and across the horseshoe shaped mahogany bar. The bar ran from one half of the room, through a central door and out into the other side of the saloon and was trimmed with gilt bar surrounds.

Suited, sporting men of every caliber stood by the bar quietly discussing business. One gentleman was in the process of selling a mining claim, the deed clutched in his hands. Another sat at one of the tables consulting a Tombstone map detailing vacant lots on the other side of town.

"Lord, it feels so long I almost can't believe this is real."

"No one forced you to stay in New Mexico. What you been up to?" said Morgan.

"I've been trying to keep my paws clean. I was working as a dentist for a while in Vegas. I even had my own bar for a spell. I met up with a jeweler who was at the springs the same time I was. He's a real nice fellow called Bill Leonard, me and him got to talking. He said he was coming to Tombstone. I told him to come and introduce himself. I don't know that he ever did."

"No. I can't say I've met anyone by that name here," said Wyatt.

"Well that's too bad. You'd get along with him right well. So where are you working now?"

"I'm deputy sheriff under Charles Shibell. I do a little gambling too. We even got a couple of interests in some mines."

"I thought you said you wanted to quit policing?"

"Well I got suckered back into it again."

"Can't leave well enough alone!"

Doc laughed to himself. Kate clutched Doc's skinny wrist and patted him on the hand. She leaned in to his ear and whispered something that only the dentist could hear. Doc straightened up with a smile.

"Any good games going begging? I need the money."

"Well I heard the owner here saying that there's a job dealing Faro," said Wyatt.

"Sounds good to me. What does it pay?"

"You'll have to ask Milt about that, I reckon at least twenty percent of the takings."

There was a murmur in the crowd and a man in his twenties, stood up on the stage and asked everyone to give a round of applause to the

Oriental's musicians. There was polite applause. The violinist raised his bow into the air, nodded to the pianist and they began to play Mozart's 'Hungarian Dance.'

The crowd listened in appreciation. A few cowboys stomped their feet in time to the music but it was the course laughter that turned everyone around. A cowboy sat at the bar, eating strawberries and drinking champagne, swinging his hand in time to the music, sarcastically conducted the musicians and laughing insanely. Before long it was hard to listen to the music alone without hearing the cowboy laughing and shouting at the pianist with delight.

"Damned if I ever saw anyone's fingers move as fast as that before." He threw a strawberry stalk at the pianist and hit him square on the back of the head. The pianist jerked around trying to find the offender while still keeping his place in the music. Another stalk flew through the air and then another until the pianist was quite distracted by the flying of stalks and the spraying of juice on his hands.

"Faster boy, play faster, you're making my night, I tell you what."

Wyatt couldn't hold a conversation with Doc or his brothers over the noise. Behind him was a tall, weedy looking fellow with wire rimmed spectacles sat stiffly at a table with a pile of papers and a fountain pen. Beside him were three cowboys. The older of the three was losing his temper with the weedy clerk.

"Look Sir I don't want to make you angry, I just need these questions answered. What is your name?"

"I don't see why I need to answer that."

"It's for this year's census information. It's important."

"The hell it is," said the man. He sat with his arms behind his head, his chair rocked backwards on two legs. He was a man in his early thirties with a reddish beard and a graying mustache. He was dressed in a suit jacket with elbows padded in leather. His clothes were in good repair but looked like they needed washing. His younger brother sat next to him. His eyelids were heavy from alcohol and he rested his boots on the table.

"For God's sakes Ike, just tell him the truth and we can get out of here. This ain't fun no more," he said.

"I ain't telling him nothing. I don't see why he needs to know about us."

"Well if you ain't going to tell him I will." He took his feet down from the table and looked eye to eye with the interviewer, "His name is Ike Clanton. He's my older brother. I'm Billy. We live on a ranch just beyond Charleston. It's about seven miles from here."

"What's your occupation?"

"I told you. We're ranchers, farmers, what ever. Just write it down."

"Excellent. Tell me, how many people are residing at your location?"

"I've had it with this guy," said Ike interrupting, "what in hell does it matter how many people are living at the ranch?"

"It's just for practical purposes. Say for instance you have children and you want them to go to school. We have to ensure that we have enough teachers in Tombstone to teach your family."

Billy laughed. "Oh Ike don't have any kids. He ain't even married."

"So it's just you and you're brother?"

"Well kind of. We're still really living at home with Pa. There are others too."

"Family?"

"I suppose you could call them that. They all work with us."

"How many would you say?"

"Oh five, ten, heck sometimes the whole dang caboodle's there. Say twenty just to make sure. In fact one of the guy's is over there. Why don't you talk to him for a while?"

"Thank you I appreciate your cooperation."

"Yeah what ever," said Billy.

The census clerk got up from the table and walked across to the bar where the tall, dark haired, strawberry throwing cowboy was sitting, still chuckling to himself and watching the pianist carefully. He sat on a bar stool, his lower frame curled over the top of the bar. He had finished with the champagne and was chasing it with a shot of bourbon. He had a cigar pressed between two fingers, which were still pink from eating strawberries. His silver spurs brushed against the brass railing as he stretched his lower leg down behind himself and leant forward listening and watching his friends. He sat up and laughed heartily. He laughed so hard that his leg slid from beneath him and his boot slid off the railing and kicked the bar with a thump. The bartender looked up from drying glasses and gave the cowboy a surly glare.

The census clerk crept shyly up to the cowboy and cleared his throat to get the man's attention. The cowboy turned around and grinned at the man. He had curly collar length black hair that hung against his bristled chin. He was a strange looking devil, being neither ugly nor handsome. His features were dark and his eyes were almost black. His face was robust and heavy jawed, carrying, across one cheek, the faint line of a knife scar. His eyes were loveable but cunning.

"Can I help you?" said the cowboy in a deep, dusty drawl.

"I was talking to your friends over there, a Mr. Clanton. He said that you would answer a few questions for me, for the census."

"What?"

"It's just a few questions."

The cowboy leaned over and stared at the man with drunken self-confidence and gave him an affable smile. "Ah! That explains it. Go ahead."

"What's your name?"

"My name's Curly Bill."

"Your proper name?"

"Ain't the one I gave you good enough?"

The census man swallowed uncomfortably. "I suppose if it's your name it's your name, right?"

"Right," said Curly. A wicked thought occurred to the cowboy. His eyes sparkled. "You may want to talk to a friend of mine. He'll answer a few questions for you. He's more into details than I am. Hey, Mr. Spence, perhaps you by chance would like to partake in one of them Census things that this here city dude is doing," said Curly in his best attempt at being high class.

Spence walked slowly up to the man, his silver spurs rang against the wooden floor. He was of average height, his complexion was dark and his hair black and cropped short to the back of his head. He had the side trims of a mustache but the middle bar was missing. It made him look cat like. His eyes turned slowly to the census man, the pupils were dilated and inflicted by too much opium.

"Ah Mr. Spence, it's a pleasure to meet you," said the census man reaching his hand out to shake.

Spence looked the man up and down and ignored him. "What's this man want Curly?"

"Census information."

"Oh," said Spence quietly.

He looked at the man again and pawed the air with his hand as if he could reach out and grab it. He raised his forefinger and beckoned the man forward. "Come closer to the bar. I've something to show you."

The man looked nervously around and moved closer.

"Look at this!"

Spence reached into the top pocket of his coat and, moving very slowly, pulled out the biggest tarantula the census man had ever seen in his life.

"This is my pet, isn't she beautiful?"

"Really?" said the census man with a dry throat.

"Yes. Do you want to see what I do with my pet?"

The man shook his head, "No, I don't think that's really necessary."

"Oh come on, it will be fun." Spence smiled at Curly with gleaming eyes. "Watch this."

The census clerk watched with his eyes half closed. Spence took the spider and let it run along his hand. It wandered this way and that, across his palm, it seemed irritated by the noise of the music. A crowd had gathered to see the trick. Even Wyatt and Doc had walked over to watch the show. Spence laughed, pleased at the attention he was receiving. He took a quick swig of whiskey and raised the spider into the air, dropped it into his mouth and closed his lips around it. The census man grew pale, his face contorted and his eyes blinked. He walked backward at first, still looking at Spence. He turned, gripping his papers and walked quickly from the bar, the wing doors swinging at his back.

"Well what do you think of that?" said Wyatt.

"It's clearly just a trick. I would say that the whiskey has probably subdued the tarantula," said Doc.

"Well I don't know Doc. I think anyone would be a fool to try a stunt like that."

"Who is that guy Wyatt?" said Morg.

"That's Pete Spence. I haven't had the pleasure of meeting him yet and I don't really care to."

Spence spat the dead spider out on to the bar. He pulled his handkerchief from his suit jacket and wiped away the gooey pile. The bar tender looked at him firmly and pointed a finger at him.

"Get the hell out of my bar! You can do you're little side-show tricks over in one of the cheaper saloons."

Spence sniffed at the man, "Fine by me. You're

way overpriced in here any how. C'mon Curly let's leave this shit-hole."

"I ain't leaving Pete. You're on your own."

"Well hell Curly. You piece of chicken shit, you're no friend of mine."

"Too bad Pete. It's your loss."

CHAPTER TWELVE

Fred White sat in the Marshal's office, reading the newspaper and drinking coffee.

Wyatt sat across the table, cleaning the barrel of a shotgun.

"I'm glad that Pete Spence has finally been arrested, that's a relief for all of us. It's just a pity those mules were never recovered."

"Well Wyatt, Spence is in jail, that's the important thing. Now if we can just get Frank McLaury to cool down we'd both be able to sleep well. Have you read this letter in today's Nugget?"

"I haven't had a chance yet."

"Well, let's just say Frank's a little mad about being accused of stealing those mules. He wants his good name cleared."

"Good name? He was willing to have all of us shot. I almost wish he had, we would have had him behind bars by now too. Shit, if he had shot Lieutenant Hurst, they probably would have had him hanged."

The distant sound of gunshot echoed in the dark

street outside. Marshal White and Wyatt grabbed their guns and ran out the door. They could hear the noise of gunfire long before they reached the door of the Oriental. Wyatt entered the saloon in time to see Milt Joyce knock Doc in the face with his pistol. Holliday staggered backwards, grabbed the railing of the bar and slid to the ground. A pool of blood oozed from his face and dripped onto the floor. He lay as still as a corpse, blood running down from his head, to his body and down to his feet. There was an awkward silence, even Milt who was clutching his bleeding hand, looked across at where Doc lay.

"Is he dead?" he said, "I hope to hell he is." His face contorted, he took his handkerchief from his top pocket and wrapped it around his hand to stop the blood.

Dr. Goodfellow rushed over from across the street and hesitated as he viewed the scene from the door. Milt clutched his wounded hand, Doc lay on the floor covered in blood and the bar tender sat on the floor with a bleeding foot. The doctor made his way over to where Doc was lying and tapped him on the back. Doc didn't move.

"Someone help me to lift this man up. He could choke on his blood if he's left like this."

Wyatt rushed over to help the doctor and grabbed one of his friend's arms. The doctor and Wyatt dragged Doc across to a chair and lifted him on to the seat. Holliday's head wavered and dropped. His face was so badly beaten up it was hard to see his features for the blood dripping steadily from his head and face. Wyatt had to keep a hand against Doc's head to prevent him from falling to the ground.

"He's still breathing Wyatt. He's just out cold. Someone get me some warm water. It will look better once we clean things up a bit." The doctor took some smelling salts from his bag, opened the lid and ran it once or twice past Holliday's nostrils. Doc coughed heartily, spitting up some of the blood that had dripped down his throat. He breathed in a raspy lung full of air, opened one swollen eye, swallowed and closed his eyelid.

Holliday sat humiliated as the treatment took place. He was conscious enough to know that people were staring at him. He could see the local newspaper editor, interviewing people and taking notes. He knew he would be the talk of the town, none of which would be good talk. Milt Joyce walked past with his hand bandaged and glared at Holliday. Before he could start another argument, he was ushered from the bar by Marshal White.

After the doctor was finished, Wyatt encouraged Doc to stand and lean on his shoulders. Doc felt like he was being stabbed in the head with a knife, the pain made him feel unfocused and dizzy. He stood still, trying to focus and stay balanced. Virgil walked in to the bar and took Doc's other arm. The two brothers led Holliday from the saloon and out onto Allen Street, where a buckboard was waiting. They helped Doc up onto the seat and drove him over to Fly's boarding house.

Big Nose Kate opened the door and showed the two brothers the way to Holliday's room. Doc leaned against Wyatt and Virgil. Kate entered the room at the end of the corridor, and lit the lamp by the side of the bed.

The two men guided Holliday onto the bed.

"I'm sorry Wyatt," Doc whispered.

"Don't be. You can explain tomorrow."

"Aren't you going to arrest him? He's free then?" said Kate.

"The bail is three-hundred dollars. If you pay that now we can forget about riding to Tucson tomorrow."

Kate hesitated before reaching into her purse. She pulled out a wad of notes and handed them to Wyatt.

"Is it enough?"

Wyatt nodded.

Doc looked at Kate with a surprised smile and reached out to clutch her hand. She patted the back of Doc's hand in a motherly fashion which was both half-hearted and patronizing but Doc was hurting too much to care.

###

Wyatt cut his way through the back of the OK Livery Stables and walked down the alley towards Fly's boarding house. Doc looked to be asleep when Wyatt opened the door. Wyatt cleared his throat to get the dentist's attention.

"It's all right Wyatt, I'm awake. Come on in."

Wyatt walked over to the bed and pulled a chair across to sit. The dentist sat up slowly in bed. His face contorted as he felt pain ooze through his bruises. He brought his wrists up over the bed sheets, slowly and painfully. His face was bruised across the forehead and down across the bridge of his nose. His chin was dark purple. Doc opened

his mouth to talk, winced and closed his lips again.
He sighed. Wyatt looked at his friend in dismay.

"You're one hell of a mess!"

"No shit," said Doc, barely moving his lips.

"Does it hurt?"

"Only when I laugh and as you can well imagine
I'm been doing a lot of that today." The dentist
smiled painfully.

"I'm so glad to see you Wyatt. The first thing I
saw when I came too this morning was Kate. She's
been real sweet to me but Lord she never quits
talking. I pretended to be asleep in the hope that
she'd shut up but I got tired of laying still."

Wyatt smiled. "Kate has her qualities but she'd
also try the patience of a saint."

"You're damn right." Holliday reached for the
silver flask on the bedside table and took a
swallow. He coughed and smarted as the sour
taste affected his senses.

Wyatt watched with a strange sense of pity.

"Do you think you can tell me what happened
last night?"

A sad look washed across Doc's face. "I'm sure
you've read the newspaper all ready Wyatt."

"I want to hear it from you."

"Well, all right. I was dealing Faro and one of the
players started to get sore about losing. He
threatened me a couple of times until I finally got
up, pointed my gun and told him to get the hell
out of the saloon."

"Fair enough, then what happened."

"Milt Joyce, heard the argument and told me
that if I treat my players like that, I can find myself
another job. He fired me and threw me out. I asked

for my other gun from behind the bar. He wouldn't give it to me, in fact he took the one gun I had at the table. I wasn't going to lose my job and lose my guns to boot so I went back home and got my other pistol. By the time I came back the man I threw out was back in the saloon. Milt's partner grabbed me and threw a couple of punches at me. Milt threatened me. I shot him in the wrist and then he hit me over the head with his gun. I'm sorry Wyatt."

"Well, I guess it was fair. If it makes you feel any better, Milt's reputation is on the line. It looks like he may lose the Oriental as a result of this. If that happens, how would you like to become a co-owner?"

"What do you mean?"

"I'm hoping to buy it. James and Virgil are going to be partners. Morg can deal Faro, I was hoping that you wouldn't mind working as a dealer, then once Luke and Bat are in town, maybe they'll care to join us too."

Doc smiled, "It sounds just like old times. If everything goes through, be sure and count me in." He reached his hand over for Wyatt to shake. Wyatt reached over and shook the dentist's skinny wrist.

"So it's a deal?"

"Deal."

CHAPTER THIRTEEN

Fred White looked down at the signed papers in front of him and reached across the table to shake hands with Virgil.

"You're hired."

Virgil smiled.

"It'll be a pleasure to work with you Fred."

"I think you'll make a great partner. You had more good credits than I could be bothered reading."

Wyatt smiled, "His normal resume is longer than the constitution."

"Well, you can add another credit to the list. You can start tomorrow night," said Fred smiling. I better get back to work. I've business at the other end of Allen Street to see too."

"Sure, I won't keep you."

"Anything I can help with Fred?" said Wyatt.

"Nope, just town stuff. I'm going to check that those cowboys that rode in today ain't getting too rowdy, after that I'm going to call it a night and get some sleep."

"Let me know if I can be of help."

"Everything will be fine Wyatt."

Fred got up and placed his hat on his head, he smiled at Virgil and walked along the curving bar and out the door.

"Congratulations!" said Wyatt.

"Thank you. I appreciate it."

"What you say we buy a couple of bottles of champagne to celebrate?"

"Sounds good to me."

Morgan and Doc headed towards Wyatt's table laughing and joking. Doc looked surprisingly happy for a change, if not a little drunk.

"Hey Wyatt! You coming over to play a game of pool with me and Doc?" said Morgan.

"No, Sir."

Doc smiled, "C'mon Wyatt. I bet him a couple of hundred he couldn't clear the table in one go. He says he's got some trick shot or other he's been practicing. Personally I don't buy it. I think he's talking a load of bull."

"Damn it Doc. I meant what I said. I expect to collect that money," said Morgan.

"Well, I guess it won't hurt to come along. It would be kind of nice to see Doc humiliated."

"Thank you Wyatt. I appreciate that."

"My pleasure!"

"Come on Virge, we can buy a bottle of champagne and bring it over with us."

"Well, I guess I have to see this trick of Morgan's."

"You and Doc go on. We'll follow on in a minute or two."

They left the saloon and headed out into the

night. A young, crescent moon sailed high in the sky. Clouds moved perpetually across the surface, causing periods of light and darkness, casting ghostly shadows over Allen Street and the board walk. A dog barked in the distance as if it had been rudely disturbed. Morgan and Doc grew impatient waiting for Wyatt and walked on towards Campbell and Hatch's Billiard hall. Holliday walked on the outside and sometimes in the street, preferring the light from the street lamps to the shadows of the locked up storefronts. His position afforded him a wider view of the street and if he relaxed his eyes he almost had a one hundred and eighty degree view of his surroundings. He turned to Morgan and watched his reflection walk along in the glass of the storefront.

"So what are you going to do with all the money you're going to win from me after doing this trick shot of yours?"

A huge grin spread across Morgan's face. "You still don't believe I can do it do you?"

"I believe there's a better chance of either one of us getting hit by lightning."

"You want to place a bet on that?"

Holliday smirked, "No, I don't think that's necessary."

There was a strange, eerie noise in the distance. It stopped Morgan in his tracks. He stood to listen.

"What was that?"

"Probably just coyotes or something."

The howling came again and stopped abruptly.

"Kind of dark for it to be coyotes."

There was another howl and a drunken yell.

Several pistols fired in rapid succession and then there was a period of quietness. Whoops and cries echoed off the buildings. Morgan and Doc looked at one another and ran towards the noise. They got half way towards the gunfire when Wyatt almost overtook them at a run.

"Can you see them?" he said, "Can you see who it is?"

"Nope I ain't close enough Wyatt."

"Give me your pistol."

"I ain't heeled."

"Here take mine," said Doc quickly.

Wyatt ran forward towards the noise. He slowed to a walk as he approached the corner of Toughnut Street. He rounded the corner running into the back entrance of a vacant lot. As he turned he caught a glimpse of a band of cowboys running in the opposite direction. At the other end of the lot, walking towards him was Fred White. In between both lawmen was Curly Bill Brocius. Wyatt watched the cowboy holster his colt and try to ignore Fred White's approach. After a while, the cowboy stood still and acted nonchalant. Wyatt walked closely in behind the cowboy.

Fred smiled and coaxed the shooter like a wrangler with an unruly mount.

"C'mon now, give me your gun. Easy does it."

The cowboy reached for his holster.

"Give me the gun," said the Marshal with an impatient growl.

Fred White reached forward to grab the gun by the barrel in an attempt to pull it from Curly Bill's hands. Wyatt moved forward and grabbed Curly around the waist. Fred jerked at the barrel. The trigger pulled back easily. The gun released the lead and the bullet coursed through the marshal's lower stomach and groin, boring deep through the layers of flesh. Wyatt had a hold of Curly Bill and reached upwards and brought the gun in his hand down sharply at an angle. The barrel hit the back of the cowboy's head with such ferocity that he collapsed to his knees and flopped over unconscious.

Fred was unaware that the bullet had hit him. There was a slight stinging but nothing to be concerned about. He sucked in and gazed at the blood seeping from his gut as if he was dreaming. He was brought to the ground by the weight of the bullet. He tried to remain standing but felt the heaviness of exhaustion drag him down to the ground.

Morgan and Doc appeared like ghosts from out of the darkness. Fred fell and Doc and caught him by the shoulders, lowering his body gently to the ground. Wyatt watched his friend. The shooting commenced from the shadows. Shot after shot dropped from nowhere, hitting the ground and causing little clouds of yellow dust to rise beside Fred White. Wyatt bent down and squatted beside Curly Bill's unconscious body.

"Morg, put out the fire in Fred's clothes," he said, his voice was quiet and calm.

His brother bent forward to do as was requested. Fred watched Morgan work and then drifted out of consciousness.

"We can take Fred to the cabin. Help me grab a hold of his legs and we can carry him across the street."

"What about Curly Bill?"

Wyatt looked up and saw Virgil walking across with a group of men.

"Don't worry about that. Virge will help you lock him up. When you're done meet me over at the cabin. I'll send Morg over later with some others to help guard him. The way this crowd is warming up I think Curly Bill will be lucky to get out of town alive. All going well we can move him to the jail in Tucson tomorrow."

Doc did as was requested and returned to the cabin. A large crowd of men had gathered outside. Doc squeezed past to try and see what was going on. Wyatt left the cabin and stepped outside.

"Did you do as I asked?"

"It's done. Morgan's guarding Curly, right now. How's Fred?"

"Dr. Goodfellow's trying to remove the bullet. It's serious but Fred looks like he'll pull through. Doc I want you to meet some people. These fellows are going to help us get the rest of the cowboys. This here is Jack Johnson and Jack Vermillion."

"I believe we've all ready met," said Johnson, "I remember meeting Doc down in Texas a few years back."

"Well, that's good. We'll split into two groups. We'll search the town. Round up anyone who's drunk and armed."

"Things are getting a little spooky over at the jail Wyatt. How will Morg and them know that we're coming?"

"Whistle," said Wyatt.

Doc gave Wyatt a perplexed look.

"Any tune in particular?"

"Nope, I don't think they'd care if you whistled Dixie, just make sure you whistle loud so Morg don't shoot you in the ass."

Doc watched as Johnson and Vermillion disappeared into the darkness.

"Let's go," said Wyatt.

Doc and Wyatt walked back on to Allen Street. The noise of their boots on the boardwalk was alarmingly loud in the comparative quiet of the street. They watched every shadow carefully, sensitive to movement of any kind. The narrow alleyways bothered Doc immensely although he would never have shown his fear to Wyatt. The dentist's eyes grew wide as he peered between the buildings, into the darkness, waiting for something to jump out. He scolded himself for being so childish but he couldn't deny his fear. The noise of glass breaking sent a cold shiver down the back of his neck. He searched for the perpetrator of the noise but could find no accomplice. There was a loud crash as a pile of trash fell over.

Wyatt watched his friend flinch.

"Did you hear something?" he said.

Doc looked around. The tinkle of breaking glass and the hiss and cry of a frightened cat, calmed his nerves. He shrugged his shoulders and pretended not to care.

"It's just a cat," he said and strode on as if the matter had never concerned him.

They walked further down the street towards the Crystal Palace. Doc walked up onto the boardwalk and peered in through the swing doors. The sudden brightness of the light from the saloon after being in the dark was shocking.

"Do you see anyone?" said Wyatt.

"I'm not sure. There's quite a crowd in there."

"Let's go."

Wyatt walked into the saloon with confidence. Doc followed and prayed that his friend knew what he was doing. Wyatt's gaze moved from one cowboy to another. He saw Frank McLaury standing with his brother Tom. He could hear the men laughing and discussing the shooting as if the whole evening had been a joke. McLaury caught sight of Wyatt from the corner of one eye. He turned and as he did Wyatt saw the reflection of McLaury's pistol in the mirror behind the bar. Without any questions he pulled his gun from his coat pocket and brought it down heavily against the back of McLaury's head. The cowboy's knees sank towards the floor.

Tom McLaury leapt up and lunged towards Wyatt. Doc reached forward and grabbed him from behind. He struggled to hold the cowboy and was relieved when Wyatt moved around and helped to knock Tom to the floor. Earp and Holliday removed the prisoners from the saloon amidst jeers from the cowboys.

"You'll pay for this. You and your stinking friend," said Ike.

"Hey Doc," said Billy, "Catch this!" The young cowboy leaned forward and hocked and spat a mouthful of spit at Holliday's back. It missed the dentist's coat by inches. Doc spun around in anger to retaliate but the look that Wyatt gave him was enough to make him calm down and concentrate on removing Tom and walking him to the jail.

By the time Wyatt and Doc reached the jail the tiny building was all ready full with the two other cowboys that the two Jacks had brought in.

"We found Pete Spence down one of the alleyways," said Johnson, "He said he was on his way home but I didn't believe him. He pulled his gun on me."

Wyatt nodded, "Fair enough. We're going to have to fine him and release him. Once we drop the McLaury's in there, they'll be no more room."

"Are you sure Wyatt?"

"We don't have any other choice."

"Well, you're the boss," said Morg with a mischievous grin.

Wyatt locked up Frank.

"Where's Virge?" he said.

"He's back at the cabin. Johnson and Vermillion were here so there was no sense in him staying."

"Sure, any word on Fred?"

Morgan sighed and looked his brother sadly in the eyes.

"He's dead Wyatt."

"What?"

"He died around half an hour ago. Last thing he did was exonerate Curly Bill. He said it was all an accident. He lost consciousness after that. He never did say no more after that."

"Poor Fred," said Wyatt, "He was probably too far gone to know how much trouble that's going to cause. I'm going back to the cabin."

Wyatt walked quietly though the darkness, back up to his cabin. He passed the spot where Fred was shot, barely hours before. He gazed down at the ground and thought about everything that had happened that night. A soft wind blew the dust from the street into a gentle whirlwind until Wyatt was unsure where the exact spot of the shooting had occurred. Wyatt sighed and walked on.

The crowd of people had left the cabin by the time he arrived. The only people left were lawmen of one kind or another. Virgil stood silently by the side of the bed, not really looking down at Fred's body, but up and over at the opposite wall. Wyatt walked passed and acknowledged him with a strong, pitying hand on his shoulder. The two men stood silently. There was nothing to be said.

They watched as two men from the morgue walked in and carried Fred's body away on a stretcher.

"They made me the city marshal tonight Wyatt," Virgil said sadly, "It's just until they can organise an election early next year. Until then I have the position."

Wyatt looked at his brother but said nothing.

"I feel kind of sick about it all," Virgil continued.

"I know," said Wyatt.

Wyatt watched his brother and waited for him to react. Virgil looked up into his eyes and sighed heavily.

"C'mon Wyatt, let's go home."

CHAPTER FOURTEEN

Bat and Wyatt walked down Fremont Street towards Fly's Photographic. Prospector trotted by Wyatt's heels, his sickle tail wagged as he detected new smells in the air.

"I've been meaning to tell you, I'm going to be leaving town later today," said Bat.

"Why?"

"My brother Jim sent me a telegram from Dodge. There's some trouble going on over at the Long Branch. I'm going to head back to Dodge to help him out."

"Well, I'm going to miss you."

"No you won't. We'll see each other soon enough. Once Jim is taken care of I hope to head back to Denver."

"Well, I guess I can head that way at some point."

They passed a corral full of horses. Wyatt turned down the second line of stalls and up towards the far side where he and Virgil kept their racehorses. He could see Virgil's dapple gray mare and the

long, back of the tall chestnut horse, he had bought
in Prescott.

"Gonna take the old horse for a spin?" said Bat.

"Yep it's just been too stressful around here
lately. You're welcome to join me if you want."

"If I can rent a buggy I might just do that."

Wyatt expected the whinny of his horse and was
surprised not to hear it. The horse never failed to
call to him on hearing his voice but today was an
exception, everything was quiet. He walked over
to the neighboring stall and found it empty.

"Well, that's funny, he ain't even over here."

"You think maybe Morg or Virge took him out?"

"Nope, Virge is busy working in town today and
Morg's still in bed. You don't think they rented
him out do you?"

"Well, I don't know about that Wyatt."

Wyatt looked around the stables hoping to find
some kind of an explanation. A boy of fifteen years
was busy grooming one of the horses.

"You lost something?" he said.

"You see a tall, blood bay stud in here son?"

"Maybe yesterday, heck I don't know."

Wyatt stood in silence, puzzled by the situation.
Bat thought things through.

"Well, maybe Doc took him out last night. He
may have ridden over to Charleston for a poker
game or something."

"Doc wouldn't just take him."

"You got any better ideas?"

"Let's go and see if we can find Doc and ask."

Bat and Wyatt walked back across the courtyard
to Fly's. Wyatt banged on the door to Holliday's
room. There was a delay before the door opened. It

was clear from Doc's bleary eyes that he had been sleeping.

"Where's Kate?"

"She got real mad at me for helping you all the other night after Fred got shot. She left yesterday morning on the stage."

"I'm sorry," said Bat with a grin.

"I'm not," said Doc, "Getting down to business... what are you doing here any how? Kind of early for calls don't you think?"

Bat smiled.

"It's two in the afternoon, ain't that late enough?"

"Not if you've been drinking till sunrise."

"You're real warm today Doc."

"Aren't I always?" said Holliday.

Bat ignored the dentist and looked around the room, remembering his visit to Doc's room in Dodge.

"What happened to your dental chair?"

"I sold it after I left Las Vegas. I got tired of hauling it around."

"Don't you need it?"

"What do you think?" He poured a tumbler full of whiskey and drank it back like he was drinking an iced tea on a hot afternoon. He refilled the glass, drank a couple of swallows and took a deep breath.

"So, how can I help you? The faster we get this over with Bat, the faster I can get back to bed."

"I was looking for my horse," said Wyatt, "I wasn't sure if you'd borrowed him."

"I'd be sure to ask you first. I haven't ridden in over a week. I haven't even been down by the stables."

Wyatt sat down on the bed and put his head in his hands, "Oh God," he said, "I guess he must be stolen then."

"But who would take him?" said Bat.

"One of the cowboys I bet," said Doc.

"That's impossible we near enough jailed every one of them who was in town the other night."

Doc's eyes grew intense.

"We didn't jail the Clantons."

"What have the Clantons got against me?" said Wyatt.

"You hurt their friends."

"That ain't no excuse to steal a horse."

"They think it is. Frank McLaury was madder than hell when we arrested him and Tom spat on me. I reckon they felt like they didn't deserve the treatment they got. They want to get their money back for all the fines and the hassle you gave them."

"Are you sure?"

"I'd bet my life on it."

Wyatt stared off towards the window, with a dead look in his eyes. Bat offered him a cigar and he took it and lit it with a sigh. Doc tried to think of something that he could do to help. He walked up and down the room and saw his silver ring sitting on the bedside table.

"Leonard," he whispered.

"Who?"

"Bill Leonard. He's a jeweler that I met in Las Vegas. He's friends with some of the cowboy gang. I'm sure he'd know where the Clantons would be holding your horse."

Wyatt gave Holliday a puzzled look, "What makes you think he'll tell us where my horse is?"

"It's better than nothing. You told me what happened to the mules from Fort Rucker. The cowboys won't take it well when an outsider's making accusations. You have to do things from the inside out. Let Leonard do the talking, then once you're sure of the location, go in and get your horse back."

"What's a jeweler doing hanging out with the cowboy gang?"

Doc hesitated as if considering something and then he continued.

"Leonard is a stage robber Wyatt."

Wyatt was silent for a long while, his brow sat in peaks of anger and frustration. Doc knew that Wyatt was angry; he always grew silent when he became angry. Wyatt stared Holliday straight in the eyes.

"How exactly do you know this?"

"I ride over to Charleston sometimes and play poker with him and his friends."

"And he just blurts stuff out about robbing stages? If he's so loose jawed, why the hell didn't you think to tell me or Virge about it?"

"It's not like that Wyatt. He's my friend."

"Virgil's a U.S. Marshal, I'm the county sheriff, Morg rides shotgun on those stages and you'd risk either one of us losing our jobs or getting shot, just because Leonard is your friend?"

"Please. Try and understand. He's real sick with consumption. He takes opium to kill the pain. He had a fever one night, got drugged up and told me. He didn't realize what he was saying he was talking out of his head. I didn't figure on telling you, I didn't want to have him accused of something that might not be true."

"Okay, I believe you. But you've got to promise me to be more careful. You could land us all in the shit for this. The elections are going to be coming up soon. I heard this Johnny Behan guy is getting a big following with the Democrats in town. I don't want to lose votes to him, shit I don't want to lose my job to him neither."

"I'm sorry Wyatt. If you don't feel comfortable talking to Leonard I guess you could talk to one of the others. What about Texas Jack or Johnson, or one of the other cowboys that helped us with Fred?"

"No, if you say that Leonard is the man we need to talk to, then we need to ride out to Charleston and talk to him."

"Well, let's go then. I'll meet you both at the stables in twenty minutes."

"Good," said Wyatt, "I'll have horses ready."

CHAPTER FIFTEEN

It took an hour to ride out to Charleston in Wyatt's buggy and by the time they arrived the horses were sweating and flies were riding with the wagon as if they were part of the entourage.

The town was quiet and almost empty from the mid-afternoon heat. A pair of stray dogs ran down the street barking orders at one another. The horses danced at the sight but with a touch of the rein, returned to a steady trot. One mongrel stopped on the street corner and cocked its leg over a water barrel, before chasing its scrawny friend down an alley.

Wyatt drove down past the residential part of town and out towards the saloons. Chickens pecked in the middle of the street. A donkey stood, outside of a house, resting its muzzle against the latch of a door. Its owner saw it through the window, came out of the house yelling and grabbed it by the halter, pulling it back to its stable.

"Over there," said Doc, "That's Leonard's jewelery store."

The blinds were pulled down over the windows and the store looked dark on the inside.

"Is it open?"

"Yes," said Doc, "He's probably just asleep."

"Doesn't do much business if he's asleep at this hour then?" said Bat.

"Oh, he does some."

Doc pushed on the door and it opened ringing the bell high above. A carriage clock chimed the hour. A glass counter took up most of the space in the center of the floor, filled with rings and pocket watches. The room was dark and it was hard to adjust to the dramatic change in light after the brightness of the street outside.

Leonard walked out from a back room. He was tall and thin, his hair was dark but his eyes were almost translucent. They sat deep in the sockets, immersed in blackened shadows. He had a vacant stare. He grinned at the sight of Doc, opened his mouth to speak and coughed instead. Wyatt couldn't take his eyes off Leonard's arms, they were covered in bruises from entry points where the morphine needle had pierced his skin. His hands trembled and he shivered constantly.

"Good afternoon gentlemen," he said, his voice almost a whisper, "Doc, it's good to see you again. How can I help you?"

"I'm looking for a horse," said Wyatt, interrupting.

Leonard looked surprised, "Who is this?" he said. "You've never brought friends before."

Doc smiled, "I'm sorry Bill. I should introduce you, this is Wyatt Earp and Bat Masterson."

"What in hell possessed you to bring the law

here?"

"It's all right, Wyatt just wants to know where his horse is, he's not here on any business other than that."

"Just as well," said Leonard, leaning to cough over his hand. "Take a seat, and we'll talk."

Leonard pulled over two chairs and the men sat, leaning over the glass case. Bat looked at the watches.

"So what kind of horse are you looking for? Are you buying or selling because if you're selling, I'm not interested."

"It's neither. My horse was stolen."

"Lots of horses get stolen, that's life Mr. Earp. If I were you, I'd forget about the old one and buy a new one. There are plenty of places to get a horse around here."

"So I've heard. Plenty of stolen horses wandering through Charleston. I don't think you understand, this animal is special, he has papers."

"Oh! A pedigree?"

"Yes Sir, he's a Thoroughbred. He was my best racin' horse."

"Well that's too bad, really too bad."

"Look Mr. Leonard, are you going to help me find this horse or not?"

Leonard smiled until every decayed tooth in his mouth was showing.

"What's your price?" he said.

"What information do you have?"

"Depends on the kind of money you'll pay to know."

Wyatt looked the man square in the eyes, "I pay after getting the information and not before. If you're going to fool with me then that's fine I'd sooner not pay you a dime."

Leonard squirmed in his chair and coughed, he dropped his gaze to the table.

"There was two thoroughbreds, come to town last week. Billy Clanton had one of them."

"Was he a tall bay horse?"

"Yes, I think so."

"When did you see him last?"

"A couple of days ago. Billy might not have him any more. There's ranchers that come out to the Clanton's that buy the horses; sometimes once every two weeks, sometimes once a month."

"I need more useful information than that."

"Well, I ain't got it."

"Well, I guess we've wasted our time. Come on Doc, Bat, let's get the hell out of here."

"Wait, Billy sometimes eats lunch in Stillwell's old saloon. He might be there now."

"Well, let's go and see if that's so."

Wyatt and Doc got up and made their way in the dark to the door. Bat followed them out. Bill Leonard smiled and locked his store behind the men.

Wyatt screwed his eyes up against the sunlight, "So do you know the bar he's talking about Doc?"

"Yes, I've played poker there before. It should be over by The Eagle Hotel."

The men walked down the street and crossed over to a wooden shack with a crude wooden sign at the front of it advertising beer and cigarettes. There were two horses tied outside but neither one was Wyatt's.

"C'mon, let's go inside."

They opened the door and squinted in the darkness.

"Doesn't anywhere have lights in this town?" said Bat.

The bar tender frowned, "Are you complaining about the saloon, 'cause you don't need to be drinking here if you are?"

"Nope, I just like to be able to see what I'm doing that's all. Is this Stillwell's bar?"

"What the hell do you think? Do you see Stillwell's name on the storefront?"

"No."

"Well, what the hell gave you the impression this place was Stillwell's?"

"I'm sorry I asked."

"Well, you should be sorry. Back when Stillwell owned this place it was a dump. It's come along ways since then and no thanks to him."

A cowboy at the end of the bar got mad and reached for the bar tender, "That's a bunch of crap Stillwell's a good friend of mine, I'll tell him what you said and he'll come and fight it out with you."

The barman sighed, "What do I care Pete? I'll give him a fight any time of the day and night. That low down bastard dumped all his cronies to get wealthy in Tombstone kissing Johnny Behan's ass. He ain't welcome in this bar."

"So this was Stillwell's bar?" said Wyatt.

"Yeah, why are you asking?" said the cowboy.

"We were told that Billy Clanton might be in here eating lunch. Have you seen him?"

The cowboy shrugged, "I don't own him. He comes by here most days, sometimes he don't. What do you care?"

"I'm looking for my horse."

"Well, you've come to the wrong place mister.
We serve cowboys around here not horses."

Wyatt turned from the bar and walked out into
the street. Bat and Doc followed behind.

"I'm sorry Wyatt. I didn't realize that Charleston
was full of idiots."

Wyatt smiled and shook his head, "I'll find that
horse whether they like it or not."

"C'mon let's go get a bite to eat. I haven't ate yet
and I'm starved. I'll buy."

"I'd rather not eat just yet Doc."

"I'll take you up on the offer," said Bat.

Wyatt sighed and followed his friends across the
street to a small restaurant. Inside the tables were
covered in white linen and the chairs were padded.
They were soon seated at a table.

Bat turned and looked up at a cowboy that had
walked into the restaurant. The cowboy looked
around nervously. He saw Wyatt and gave him a
strange look, screwing his eyes up against the light
that was oozing in from the window. He finally
recognized Wyatt and turned to go but it was too
late, the waiter had seen the cowboy and was
walking over with a menu.

"Ah, Mr. Clanton, sit, please sit, don't go. Can I
get you some shrimp?"

Billy turned and looked around, he smiled, "Ah
no, not this time."

"No really, you must come eat."

Doc smiled and got up from the table, "Hey
Billy, C'mon over and eat with us."

"Uh, no thanks, Doc."

"No really, I still owe you after that poker game

the other night. C'mon over and I'll buy you a nice steak."

Billy stood with his jaw slightly open. His eyes rolled from the smiling waiter to Doc's skeletal grin, across to Wyatt's questioning eyes and back again. He tried his best to smile.

"Well sure, if you're buying?"

"Absolutely, it's the least I can do. Here, sit with me."

Billy took his hat off and sat down, trying hard not to make eye contact with Wyatt.

Doc smiled, "So Billy, how's that paint horse of yours?"

"I didn't ride the paint today Doc. Ike's got me riding all different horses, any more, I can't hardly keep up with them all."

Wyatt pulled his horse's papers out of his pocket and laid them on the table, "You wouldn't happen to have rode this animal would you?"

Billy looked meekly across at the papers and looked into Wyatt's eyes, "I've rode some Thoroughbreds, can't say I remember this one."

"If you don't remember I will set a warrant for you and Ike's arrest and then perhaps once you're in jail, you'll remember."

Billy shook his head, "I don't know where he is Wyatt. I swear if I knew, I would tell you."

"Well, remember, I'm looking and if I hear mention of you with that horse, I'll have you arrested."

The waiter returned with a sizzling, steaming steak and put it down on the table, beside Billy.

"Boy, this steak sure looks good."

Doc slapped a skinny hand, against Billy's fat

back, "Eat up son, unlike some, I don't like to be indebted to anyone."

CHAPTER SIXTEEN

Doc endured the pain of seeing the last drop of smooth malt whiskey run off his mustache and drip on to the polished table. He ordered another without hesitation. Doc took the whiskey with gratitude and scanned the rack of newspapers at the side of the bar. He selected the current issue of the Tombstone Epitaph and returned to his seat. He flicked lazily past the advertisements until a page caught his eye.

'Earps stop chaos on night of murder.'

Doc peered closely at the page and smiled in coy amusement. He continued to read...

'The Earp brothers walked fearlessly towards the scene of Fred White's murder and dealt with the criminals in a just and fair manner.'

Doc's smile broadened, he took a sip of whiskey. He was rudely interrupted by Frank Stillwell.

"Doc Holliday isn't it?"

The man pointed in a fashion that made Doc shudder. The dentist lifted a firm, parental eye of disapproval, glared at Stillwell and continued his reading. The deputy hesitated for a moment and then decided to continue.

"We got a fella badly in need of you're help. Sayin' his teeth are killin' him somethn' awful, he don't want you to fix him but there ain't another dentist in Tombstone. We figured you'd do."

Stillwell grinned nervously.

Doc removed his glance from the paper and ensured he gave the man a glare of complete disgust.

"I'm retired."

The deputy gawked at Doc in a bewildered fashion and cursed quietly. Doc sighed and looked back at the deputy.

"Does this gentleman have the means to pay for the work?"

The deputy nodded in agreement. Doc breathed out a deep sigh and threw his paper down. He took the last swallow from his whiskey.

"Oh all right."

With that, the odd couple walked out of the saloon together. They headed towards the other end of town. The deputy led Doc back home to Fly's boarding house. Doc left to go to his room to fetch his things. It took him a while to find his dental bag and this only added to the deputy's frustration.

"Can't you hurry up?"

Doc gave the man a glare and continued his search. On finding the utensils, Stillwell led Doc back up Fremont Street and across to the Grand Hotel. There in a far corner of the hotel bar room sat Johnny Behan. He was tall and balding, dressed like a true dandy with a hint of Irish blood in him. His face was flushed in the cheeks, either from drinking or from inflammation, Holliday was not able to determine which. The dentist sighed and walked forward, stretching his hand out to introduce himself. Behan looked at Holliday, smiled and then ignored him. He glared up at his deputy, "God Stillwell, I told you not to get Doc. He's a killer. I hate him. Couldn't you find someone else?"

"I did the best I could," said Stillwell with a smirk.

"Well damn it, your best wasn't good enough."

A dark haired beauty walked over to console her lover and was ignored by both men. She sat down beside Behan, clutching his hand tightly, ensuring he wouldn't move. Holliday studied her satin dress and her almost black, brown eyes and seemed to remember the woman but he couldn't remember from where.

"Do I know you?" said Doc gently.

Josie put her hand forward to shake, as if she was a business man.

"I'm Josie Marcus," she said, "Good to meet you!"

"It's my pleasure," said Doc. He took her long hand towards him and kissed it gently. Josie grinned and removed her hand.

Behan watched his fiance with irritation.

"Can we get the pleasantries over with and get down to business? This tooth ache ain't getting any more congenial."

"I need more space to work than this. Where's the poker room in here?" said Doc.

"It's through the back," said Stillwell.

"Well, let's go there."

Behan and Josie walked through to the poker room, arm in arm. Holliday followed behind with his dental case in one hand. As they reached the poker room Josie reached up to give her fiance a kiss on the cheek.

"I'll see you tonight," she said and turned and strutted away, her bustled dress flounced as she bounced along. Doc watched her with fascinated eyes.

"Let's get this over with," said Behan gruffly.

Holliday followed Behan through to the poker room and settled him into a chair. One by one he removed his dental utensils and laid them out on the table. He turned his face to his patient who wriggled in the chair, like a garden mole with his head caught in a trap. He could almost smell the sweat rise from Behan's skin. Doc knew that Johnny was aware of his murderous history. Johnny had heard the rumors. Doc sighed and pulled his mirror from his top pocket. He breathed a whiskey laden cloud on to the surface before wiping it clean against his shirt.

"All right, open up."

Johnny's blue eyes flashed backwards and forwards. The muscle in his cheekbone rippled violently as he swallowed before opening his mouth for Doc. The dentist's eyebrows floated upwards as he concentrated on the job. He placed the mirror to Johnny's mouth and leaned forward to get a better look. He growled, dissatisfied at what he saw and leaned further over Johnny until the chair rocked backwards. Behan cringed and swallowed hard, anticipating pain. Doc tried to be sociable.

"What's your name?"

"John Behan."

Doc paused and straightened up. He recognized the name but was unsure why. He dismissed his memory and pressed over Johnny again. He reached with his left hand for his pick and found it in his top pocket. He scraped around Behan's mouth then straightened up again with a sigh.

"Well, John," said Doc, "I can successfully congratulate you on your efforts. That tooth is cracked down to the nerve. It's gonna take a while to get that sucker out."

Doc grinned with a wide, raw edged smile and coughed politely.

John Behan leaned back and gazed over at the blood colored wall. Holliday tried to resist it but his politeness caught up and strangled him gently. He choked deep down in his throat, coughed up the sputum, twisted around and spat it out into the spittoon that was down beside the dealer's chair. He swore quietly and wiped his mouth dry with the back of his hand. Behan flinched.

"Oh, it's all right, I don't bite." Doc pulled a silver flask of whiskey from his pocket and a small blue bottle filled with laudanum. He packed the side of Behan's mouth with a wad of cotton that he had found in his dental bag. So, what's your occupation John? I could swear that I've heard your name some where before."

John Behan stared straight up into the dentist's blue-gray eyes with his cheeks padded with cotton, puffed out like a chipmunk.

"I'm the Marshal of Cochise County."

Doc's face paled so quickly that his skinny frame almost vanished. He straightened up and swallowed nervously. He pulled the pick out again and pushed it into Behan's mouth. The pick hooked itself around the problem tooth. Doc pulled hard. Johnny howled in protest as the pain pierced through the enamel, up to his skull and back. Doc let go his grasp and pulled away from Johnny's mouth coughing sarcastically. He picked up a pair of pliers in the other hand and got a grip of the tooth. He leaned back and heaved. Behan wriggled in the chair. There was a sharp crack and Holliday pulled away from Behan's mouth, a blood covered incisor sitting cleanly in the pliers. The dentist breathed a sigh of relief and dropped the tooth into a small ashtray beside him. He brought the pliers back to Behan's mouth and swabbed the excess blood with the cotton. Satisfied with his work, he removed the blood covered cotton and dropped it into the ashtray, beside the tooth. Doc poured a glass of whiskey for Behan and offered it to his patient.

"Here, rinse out with this. It will help to cauterize it."

Behan took the glass of whiskey and swilled it around his mouth. Holliday moved a basin over towards Behan and let the marshal spit out the concoction. Behan reached for his handkerchief from his top pocket and wiped a line of blood and spit from his lips.

Holliday poured another glass of whiskey, reached into his bag and pulled out a small bottle of pills. He gave one of the white, pills to Behan.

"Here put this in your mouth and bite down. It may take a while. You're welcome to drink some whiskey to wash it down if you think it's necessary."

Behan took the pill quietly and did as Doc said. He drank a great deal of whiskey and passed the half empty glass back. Doc took the glass and took out a piece of gauze. He folded it into a small pad and dipped it into the remaining whiskey, letting it soak up the remaining liquid. He picked the pad up and placed the whiskey laden pad into the back of Behan's mouth over the space.

"Close your mouth and bite." Behan sighed and did what was asked. His eyelids had become heavy, the drug taking effect.

Holliday cleaned the area, packing his instruments back into his bag.

"Wyatt told me you was going to make him deputy marshal of Cochise, is that right?"

"It was planned that way but sometimes plans don't come to fruition."

"Wyatt feels like he got screwed on the deal. The only reason he stepped down from his position as deputy in Pima was he thought Bob Paul had a chance of winning and that you would give him the deputy position for Cochise."

"It's not my fault he thought that."

"I'd have to disagree with you there. It seems nearly every lawman in Tombstone thought it would be that way. That was until you're cowboy com padres stuffed the ballot boxes and got Shibel elected in Paul's place. You know there ain't more than one hundred voters in Cochise, never mind a thousand."

"That had nothing to do with me. I don't keep the cowboys."

"No and they don't mind you neither. Kind of sad for a county marshal don't you think?"

Behan grew angry, "I don't think that's any of your business."

"Do you have any pain, or is that none of my business neither?"

"What do you think?"

"I can't rightly say. I don't know how you feel. I can give you some morphine if you think that will help."

"That won't be necessary," said Behan, getting up from the table. He grasped at the side of his face and made his way to the door. "I'll get my own." He threw a twenty dollar bill on the table. "I hope that's sufficient," he said and left the room, slamming the door behind him.

CHAPTER SEVENTEEN

Despite the late hour, the light from a lantern shone out on to the city streets, casting shadows on to back alley. Inside the Wells Fargo Office a meeting was under way. In a small, dark room a group of agents, lawmen and U.S. Marshals sat discussing business. The table included Bob Paul, Virge and Wyatt. The men concentrated their attention on the speaker.

"Regarding the cowboys, we have a very serious matter on our hands. The incidents of stage robbery have increased ten-fold in the territory. Wells Fargo will not tolerate the loss of bullion that these robberies are causing. Valentine is well aware of the incidents. News has even reached the President himself in Washington, news that the new county of Cochise and the old of Pima are magnets for ruffians and thieves. This is inevitably bad publicity for Tombstone and is not the impression that we wish to give to outsiders. Our very livelihood depends on money coming into the state. As a result of these circumstances, there has been talk that the railroad will bypass Tombstone completely. Without a railroad our only physical contact with the outside world is by the stages that we are paid to protect. If this is violated by gangs of cowboys, the town risks losing outside investments and funding, to keep it alive. As you are aware gentlemen, Wells Fargo's motto is 'What ever it takes' and I damn well hope that we can ensure this is done to the last letter. I therefore suggest that we stop these thieves by outwitting them, which judging by the amounts of alcohol the cowboy band consumes, should not be a difficult thing to do."

The men at the table laughed politely.

"We've tried subtle interrogation and posses, none of which has worked successfully; I suggest that we set a trap. We lure the cowboys into a robbery and catch them in the act."

A murmur rose from the group of men.

"Isn't that a bit dangerous?" said Virgil, "We could lose bullion that way and risk lives."

"Yes, that is true. But we would have the upper hand in the matter and we're going to plan against failure. I fully intend to use all of you to your best abilities. I intend to place Bob Paul on the stage on the night of the robbery. I'm sure that you will all agree that with Paul riding shotgun, the coo is sure to be a success. I will place one of our detectives on the stage itself as a passenger."

"How will we know that the cowboys are going to rob the stage?"

"We must play clever. Make mention of the bullion in conversation. Be cautious about your company but make it plain that the stage will be heavy with money."

"And will it be heavy with money? Isn't that not a great risk?"

"No, it won't. The money will be kept save in the cash box in another area. It won't be on the stage. I may pay one of you to guard the box here in Tombstone while the robbery is taking place."

"How will we know when the robbery will take place?"

"That's the tricky part. I want all of you to watch the cowboys carefully, try and play poker with them, buy them drinks that kind of thing, find out what they're up to."

"And that will be enough?"

"You're right, we do need someone who has inside information. I may call one of you to befriend the robbers perhaps more than one. We need to know for sure when the robbery is going to occur."

There was a long silence as each man considered the idea. Reluctantly Wyatt spoke.

"I have a friend. He has information about the robbers. He's friends with one of the robbers. I trust him indefinitely. We could use him to get the information."

"If you trust him then use him. We need all the help that we can get."

"Don't you think its risky using outsiders?" said Bob Paul.

"Yes, but in this case it's necessary. Well, if that's all that is to be said on the matter than I will leave you gentlemen to get to work. I will talk with each one of you individually as the need arises."

The men rose from the table mumbling and

considering the situation. Wyatt and Virgil rose
and walked out from the room and into the dark
streets. Wyatt lit a cigarette and took a nervous
puff. Virgil gave Wyatt a concerned look.

"Are you sure that bringing Doc into all of this is
a good idea?"

Wyatt nodded his head.

"Well, I hope you're right Wyatt," Virge
continued, "Because if you're wrong, we sure are
in one hell of a mess."

"I know," said Wyatt, "I know."

###

In the distance a coyote howled at the full moon.
The night was bright, the moon lit the sage brush
and cacti, casting strange shadows on to the desert
floor. Doc Holliday stood beside the
Thoroughbred that he had borrowed from Dan
Tipton. The horse's satin coat shone midnight blue
in the moonlight. It stepped sideways, and turned
its head towards the empty street. It chewed and
sucked the bit. Holliday placed his gloved hand on
the horse's neck and whispered words to quieten
the animal but he was as nervous as the horse was.
He looked back in the direction of the horse's
pricked ears, and saw the closed storefront of
Leonard's store. He knew that Leonard and the
rest of the gang were watching him. His hands
trembled as he tightened the saddle. He mounted
and placed his heels against the horse's side. The
horse hesitated, snorted and broke into a canter.

Doc rode down the center of the street and out of
Contention, out across the valley. Small clouds of
moonlight coated dust rose from the horse's

hooves. Doc's mouth was so dry his throat ached. He waited until he was out of view of Contention and spurred the horse into a wild gallop. The horse pulled the reins from his hands and he watched the dark ears bob out in front of him, the hooves pounding the ground. He weaved this way between scrub and brush, jumping small creosote bushes and stretching out to a faster gallop over open ground. He didn't dare look behind him and he tried not to think about what he had done, he just kept riding. Doc rode up a dusty slope and across the other side of the hill to Tombstone. He galloped up Front Street to the Oriental Saloon, shook his feet free of the stirrups, careered around the corner and flung his right leg down from the horse's back. The horse slid to a halt in front of the tying rail with a puff and a snort. Holliday jumped off the horse and hurried into the saloon.

Wyatt sat at a small wooden table dealing a game of Faro. Doc's eyes glowed intensely at him from behind the two players that were seated at the Faro table. He nodded in Doc's direction and continued with the game.

"Winner is the King, loser the eight of spades."

Money was dealt out to the winners and the losers walked away. Wyatt turned towards the bar and tipped his hat. Morgan leant against the bar with his arms folded, he saw Wyatt's signal and walked across.

"You need me?" he said.

"I need to talk to Doc. Take over dealing for me. I'll be back soon."

"Sure thing!"

Wyatt got up and put his long coat on over his

183

suit jacket. Morgan sat down and began a new game.

"Let's go out the back," said Wyatt pushing through the crowd, Doc followed closely behind. Wyatt reached the door and after some effort, pushed it open. He walked out into the courtyard. Moonlight shone brightly in the small walled area at the back of the saloon. Holliday leaned against a water barrel. His hair appeared silver in the intensity of the light. Wyatt removed his pipe from his pocket and stuffed it with tobacco. He lit the mouth and puffed gently on the stem to get his smoke started.

"What have you heard about the robbery?"

"They're coming...Wyatt it ain't good. They know."

"What do you mean they know?"

"How the hell should I know? They know what's going on. Someone must have leaked to them 'cause they know about Bob Paul riding shotgun, they know that we're after them."

"Oh my God," said Wyatt, "Did Leonard say what they're going to do?"

"They're mad at Paul. They want him dead."

"And they're definitely coming tonight?"

"Yes absolutely."

"Then there's still a chance we can get them. With Bob riding shotgun there's no way they'll get away."

"I'm not too sure of that Wyatt. They were pretty mad when I left. I was worried they'd shoot me in the back, least they found out I'm helping you."

The back door opened leaking lantern light out across the yard. Virge strode out towards Wyatt with a telegram in his hand.

"Read this," he said.

Wyatt unfolded the telegram.

"What is it Wyatt?"

"It's from Bob Paul. Bud Philpot. He was driving the stage tonight, he's been killed."

"Did they get the money?"

Wyatt shook his head, "No, Bob Paul's on his way back to Tombstone."

"We're riding out as soon as it's feasible Wyatt," said Virge. "Near enough the whole town's coming with us the way Marshal Williams put it. There's gonna be two maybe three posses. Saddle a fresh horse and meet me outside the Oriental."

"What do you want me to do?" said Doc

"Get a horse and be ready."

CHAPTER EIGHTEEN

The posse reached the ravine on the outskirts of Contention at midnight. Wyatt slowed his horse at the bottom of the rise. He leaned down from the saddle and looked down over his horse's leg.

"What is it?" said Behan riding over to Wyatt's side.

"Hoof prints. Look, beside the brush there."

Behan looked down to where Wyatt was pointing and snorted with a smug grin.

"Well, if you say so. It don't seem likely there'd be hoof prints around here, what with twenty horses on the posse. What's so different about these prints?"

"They're not real clear. It looks like the robbers tried to put feed sacks over the horses feet, but they weren't done real good. See the tracks there. That's where the sacks wore out."

Behan shrugged and rode off with a big smile, "Whatever you say Wyatt. If you ask me I think you're just grasping at straws."

Wyatt looked away and took a deep breath.

"Oh come on Wyatt! He's just fooling around," said Morgan.

"I ain't foolin'," snapped Behan. "We ain't got time to mess around like this. The robbers will be near enough in Mexico by the time we get going."

"We can't go running around without a game plan."

"Sure Virgil, me and the boys here have a hunch as to where King is hiding. We ain't got time to mess around in the desert. We're figuring on getting our man and heading back to Tombstone."

"Well, come on out and tell your secret, Behan. You can't justify keeping information about the robbers to yourself," said Wyatt.

"Oh I'm not keeping it a secret. All my men know what's going on. Isn't that right Stillwell?"

"Sure is. We've known about King for a while now."

"Damn it, if you boys are so smart, why don't you just go off and get King and get the hell out of our way, you sure as hell ain't doing us any favours."

"You think that's wise?" Bat said softly, "We need all the help we can get."

"If he can't work as part of a team then that's his own fault."

"I never said anything to get any of you guys riled up or anything. You're all reading me the wrong way."

"And what way is that?" said Doc, "I knew you were a useless bastard before I ever rode out here with you."

"Shut up Holliday. You're walking a thin line riding out here with us. You got an honorary star at best. Mind and keep your nose out of my business and I might let you keep it."

Doc reached for his holster. Morgan gave Holliday a questioning look. The dentist turned his horse away and lit a cigarette. He smoked moodily in the moonlight for a while, his back to the other riders, his cigarette burning in the darkness.

"Look, this ain't getting us anywhere," said Virgil, "There ain't no need to fight over something like this. You're both right. We need to get moving and we need to know where we're going. This quarreling ain't fixing anyone's problems."

"I understand," said Behan. "But, I can't stand this shit any more. I think it would be more productive if we split into two groups. There ain't no sense in us all going the same trail. It's obvious that we don't work well together."

Virgil considered Behan's proposal and after a moment of silence agreed, "Okay, it's a deal. If you all know where Frank King is, go on and arrest him. We'll keep after the other robbers and meet you back in Tombstone once this is done. We can talk then. Our main goal is to get those dogs in jail."

Behan smiled, "Absolutely. You're a fine man Virgil. I won't let you down I promise."

With that he tipped his hat and rode out of the ravine with his six men trailing behind him. Wyatt watched Behan canter away into the darkness and felt relief wash over him.

"Thank God he's gone," said Morgan, "I ain't never seen you so mad Wyatt."

"Well, he's just got a natural way of ticking me off."

"Well, I guess we better get going again," said Bat, "Ain't no sense in hanging around here. We've only got a few hours until sunrise. It won't be pretty once it starts heating up out here."

"Let's go," said Virgil kicking his horse into a canter.

Several hours later the posse arrived back into Tombstone. They found Behan waiting for them when they got back. He walked out to meet the men.

"I'm glad your back. I heard you were having it rough out there."

"Well, it seems like nobody would give us supplies or water."

"Is that right?" said Behan in mock surprise.

"You knew that nearly all the ranches out there are in cahoots with the cowboys. It seems strange that they took your posse in, lent you fresh horses, watered and fed you."

"Well, it's just too bad you don't have any friends out there Virgil."

"I don't have time to argue about this shit. Did you get King?"

"Oh yeah we got him all right."

"Fantastic! He's in the jail?"

Behan scratched the back of his neck and smiled, "Well you know what its like. He escaped."

"And you went after him and brought him back?"

"Nope, can't say I did. By the time we realized he was gone, he was probably out of my jurisdiction."

"Figures," he said. "C'mon Wyatt, lets go and get cleaned up."

CHAPTER NINETEEN

Wyatt sat out in the Oriental courtyard, drinking a cup of coffee and reading the Tombstone Epitaph. The back door opened and Ike Clanton walked out. He looked around at the bar door, as if he was considering going back inside.

"Ike, come over here and sit down. I was hoping that you would show up," said Wyatt, closing the paper and folding it neatly.

Ike walked over to the table and sat down as if he had no intention on staying. "We're alone right? You ain't got no sneaks listening in or nothing like that?"

"Relax. We're alone."

"You're sure of this?"

"I'd bet my life on it. You got any idea why I asked you out here?"

"It's about the stage robbers isn't it?" said Ike, looking around the yard, as if someone would jump out on him.

"That's right, you know that Wells Fargo has a substantial reward available for King's arrest?

Now I need your help in getting him back. I think
that you and the cowboys that work for you know
exactly where he is. Any information that you can
give me will be rewarded. Bring King back to me
and I'll give you the two thousand dollars that
Wells Fargo is offering. The money will be yours.
I'm not interested in it I just want the credit to help
me get elected for the next term."

"So you will give me the money right?"

"That's right."

"No one else will know?"

"It's just between you and me."

"And the reward is it for dead or alive?"

"Wells Fargo doesn't care. You'll get your money
either way. So shake?"

"You've got a deal Wyatt." Ike reached his hand
across the table and the two men shook hands.

In the distance there was a loud bang and
screaming.

"What in hell was that?" yelled Ike.

The answer came surely enough in the voices of
men from the saloon. "Everyone get out! Fire!
Fire!"

"Oh My God," said Wyatt running towards the
wooden gate to the side of the courtyard.

He ran out into the alley and around to Allen
Street, Ike followed him in bewilderment. As
Wyatt approached the front of the saloon, there
was another explosion. Flames leapt up the face of
the building, men poured out of the front of the
bar, into the street. Horses broke away from the
hitching rail and galloped lose in the street,
bucking and kicking. People searched for ways to
dose the flames. Wyatt lifted water from one of the

water barrels from the side walk and throw the
water on to the fire.

"Ike? C'mon and help me," said Wyatt, he
turned and realized that Ike had gone. The bar
tender from the Oriental ran over from the
opposite side of the street, "Here Wyatt, I got a
couple more buckets from the stables."

The two men scooped water into the buckets
from the filled barrel and threw it on the flames.
The water seemed to be of little help, the fire
ripped through the building, sending flames
shooting through the front door of the saloon. All
too soon the roof of the building was on fire and
burning with an unmanageable intensity. Wyatt
watched as a strong breeze blew some of the
flames over to the wooden fence that surrounded
the Oriental's back yard. There was another
explosion from the ground as the flames licked
over barrels of whiskey and split the wood into a
hundred pieces. A heated barrel hoop flew
through the air and fell to the ground with a clang.
The flames spread across the sandy ground and
quickly set the neighboring buildings alight.
People ran screaming along Allen Street. Buckets
were taken from every stable in town. The fire
gained momentum with every building it chewed
up. Within minutes the whole of the business
district was burning; flames leapt high in the air.
People struggled to save their belongings, trying to
gather books and money before the fire reached
their building. Drivers galloped their buckboards
up and down the street, trying to salvage what
ever they could. Wyatt and a group of men worked
steadily to save the Oriental and neighboring

buildings. It wasn't long before the two water barrels at the front of the saloon were completely drained of water.

"Where's the rest of the fire committee?"

"They're coming Wyatt."

"Get out of the way!"

The heavy-built gray fire horses galloped towards the fire. The rolled up water hose clattered on its cradle. The horses' ears flicked forwards and backwards listening to the driver's instructions, over the roar of the fire and the screams of the people, his voice urged them through the crowd. The horses pulled forwards without hesitation despite the heat of the blaze and the sight of other horses galloping in the opposite direction.

There was a thundering bang as the fire reached the gun shop and exploded cases of powder explosive and loud popping as lines of ammunition was set alight. One of the fire horses reared back in the traces, roaring and squealing, its ears flat on its head and its heavy hooves splayed out in front of its chest. The driver held the reins steady and gentled the animal and encouraged it back towards the fire.

Members of the fire committee grouped together to pull the fire hose into position and hook it up to the city's water supply. The men formed a long line, each taking a section of hose to pull. Wyatt found his position on the line and waited for orders. The order to pull was given and foot by foot the long hose was unfurled from the cradle.

"Ready and stand back!"

"The water pressure's dropping," said one man to another, "We'll have to use the buckets after this."

"There's no need," said Wyatt, "the fire's almost under control there's barely any flames any more."

The men stopped to get their breath and raised their faces upwards. Smoke billowed from the rooftops and balconies all along Allen Street. The smell of burnt wood was horrendous but the light and heat from the fire had gone. Wyatt was surprised at how dark everything was. Everyone had been too busy dousing the flames to notice the night drawing in. Now without the light from the flames and without any daylight, Allen Street was a surprisingly dark and cold place to be. Wyatt looked himself over in the darkness and for the first time noticed the burns on his arms and the stinging sensation in his eyes. He looked up at the burnt shell of the Oriental. There was nothing more that could be done. Quietly he turned and walked home.

CHAPTER TWENTY

The noise of banging, hammering and sawing filled the air. Long planks of wood lay in piles. The smell of fresh sawdust tickled Wyatt's nostrils. Even the Oriental had recovered some of its formal glory. It was scheduled to reopen in less than two weeks; quite a feat considering it had almost been burned to the ground less than a month before.

Virgil walked over to his brother and stood and watched the building work.

"It's something ain't it?" he said.

"It sure is. I never thought the town would recover so fast. Are you working right now? I was going to suggest we get breakfast."

"I'm going to be working a whole lot more than usual. Marshal Ben Sippy went off on two weeks leave. He never did come back. It's been two months now, I doubt he ever will. He just upped and left. Seems like he was running some crooked business around here. He heard that someone had word of his involvement and he ran. I'm working his position until we can elect someone else."

"You never can tell with people around here any more."

"That's not all, Doc's been arrested."

"What the hell for?"

"Stage robbery, they brought him in early this morning. Behan and Stillwell got Kate drunk last night and she told everything, even signed an affidavit stating it was fact. That ain't all neither, they're saying not only was Doc along for the ride but he killed Bud Philpot."

"Leave it to Behan to arrange something like this. He'd do anything to get in good with the cowboys. He knows it ain't true. He even had words with Doc while we was on the posse. Why would someone ride as a deputy knowing full well that they was guilty? That don't make an ounce of sense."

"What are we going to do? I'll bet they'll hang him good if they think they can get away with it."

"We got eye witnesses. Near enough the entire posse and crowd at the Oriental will be willing to help."

"Put my name down Wyatt. I'm not letting Behan away with this."

"Where's Behan anyhow?"

"Don't Wyatt it's not going to help anything."

"It will make me feel better."

"Don't."

"Trust me, I won't do anything stupid."

"He's over at the Alhambra."

"I appreciate it."

Wyatt turned and walked away and made his way around the bars, collecting names to prove Doc's innocence. After an hour of work he found

Behan dealing Faro at the Alhambra. He watched
from a corner of the bar, as Behan dealt the cards
and talked his line of talk to players persuading
them to part with their money. Wyatt felt anger
rise up inside of him but he swallowed it down
and took a deep breath, trying to maintain a
restrained demeanor. He walked over slowly to
Behan's table and waited for a seat to open. One of
the players got up to leave. Wyatt took his chance
and sat down.

"Hey Wyatt, you want a piece of the game?" said
Behan.

"Damn straight. My money's on the ace of
clubs." He laid down a small stack of gold dollars.
Behan smiled with a curious look on his face. He
played the game and picked the winning and
losing cards.

"Congratulations, you win." He passed over the
winnings to Wyatt and was surprised when the
money was placed back on the following game.

"Winner's the two of diamonds," said Wyatt.

Behan smiled and started the game. "You win
again Wyatt. Feeling Lucky tonight or
something?"

"You could say that. Put me in for the next
game."

The money was kept over and the cards were
picked. This time Behan wasn't smiling when he
drew the card. "Okay now you're making a fool of
me. Why don't we call it quits for now?"

"I ain't ready to quit yet. Put it all on the seven of
spades."

"If you say so."

The cards were picked and again Wyatt was the

winner.

"Okay now I'm serious. Why don't you go to hell and leave me alone?" said Behan.

"Are you saying you don't have the collateral?"

"Not exactly."

"Well then, bets down buddy, lets play. C'mon John, what are the odds?"

"Okay."

Behan started another game, studied the winning card and grew ashen. "Get the hell out," he said.

"I won fair and square. Where's my money?"

"All I have on the table is half a thousand the rest in the safe."

"Well why don't you get it? It's not like you need to watch the Faro table any more."

"You bastard! How dare you walk in here and bust up my game. I would never do that to another dealer."

"No but you would accuse a man of stage robbery and murder using a falsified affidavit."

"I don't know what you're talking about. Now take your money and get out."

"Thanks John. You really made my day."

"Get out!"

Wyatt took his money and walked over to the city jail. He passed Frank McLaury and Ike Clanton in the street on his way. Ike followed after him and greeted him like he was an old friend.

"Hey Wyatt, I heard about Doc, that's too bad,"

"Yeah I never thought you had it in you to hang with a no good stage robber. That really comes as a shock," said Frank, with a grin.

Wyatt gave the two cowboys an angry glare and then walked on. He was relieved when he reached the door of the jail. He nodded to the deputy on the way in and made his way over to the cell. Doc walked up to the cell door. His face half illuminated, half in shadow. He raised his eyes to Wyatt. He almost smiled and then was overcome with pain and remorse. "I'm sorry," he said.

"Don't be," said Wyatt, "It's not your fault. I got you into this."

"I'm the one who was friends with Leonard."

"Yeah so what? Being friends with someone ain't a crime!"

"What's it like out there? Are they hungry for my blood yet?"

Wyatt smiled, "Let's just say you're not the flavor of the month."

Doc laughed, "Isn't it always like that? Sounds about normal to me."

"Here I brought you this." He passed the bundle of papers through the door to the dentist and he slowly started to read them.

"I got names from near everyone I could think off. Nearly all of them are saying they saw you in the Oriental or around town. I near enough got Kate to sign the dang thing. She's sore after last night."

"Well, she deserves to be. She's gonna regret what she did," Doc's face softened, "Thank you Wyatt."

"I wasn't going to let Behan away with it. I've spoke to Judge Spicer. Kate's denying the affidavit, she says that she was drunk and didn't know what she was doing. Spicer thinks that it won't be long before you're released. They ain't got anything on you Doc. To top it all there was another stage robbed tonight."

"Do they know who did it?"

"Frank McLaury was in town today, he's allready acting strange and being overprotective. I dare say one of his buddies was put up to it.

CHAPTER TWENTY-ONE

Morgan walked through the crowds of drunken cowboys that had gathered in the streets of Tucson for the festival and passed the Mariachi band. He stopped by the side of the street and studied the faces of people. He spied Doc and Kate standing on the opposite side, pushed his way through the crowd and grabbed Doc roughly around the shoulders. Doc jumped.

"How the hell are you? You shacking up in Tucson now or something?"

"Morg what are you doing here?"

"Wyatt wants you back in Tombstone."

"Well, shit doesn't he have enough company or something?"

"It's important Doc," said Morgan with a mischievous grin, "He's summoned you, he'll be real mad if you don't show."

"Why? What's going on?"

"Ike Clanton's been running around saying he wants to shoot Wyatt, shoot me, shoot you, nearly anyone he can think of."

"This is some kind of joke isn't it?"

"Nope it's for real. He's real mad at you. He thinks you betrayed him or something."

"What for?"

"How the hell should I know? He's been drunk since him and Tom McLaury rolled into town. He's been real unstable since his father got killed at Guadalupe Canyon."

"And he wants to talk to me?"

"It's not just that Doc. Wyatt and Virge are worried about the way things are going. Behan's just standing back and letting the cowboys do what ever the hell they want. His deputies are just as bad. The vigilantes are getting jumpy about stuff. We need you back in town. Maybe we can get this all straightened out before it gets any worse."

"All right, let's go."

"What about me Doc?" Holliday turned his back on Kate and walked on with Morgan.

"Doc, I want to come. Take me with you."

Doc turned with irritation, "Why?"

"I want to."

"It's a long ride to Tombstone. This is none of your business, besides you hate Tombstone."

"I don't care."

Holliday sighed and wondered if Kate was just bullheaded or down right stupid.

"I don't want you with me Kate. It will be dangerous. We're going back on Morgan's buckboard. You want to bust your ass for twenty miles?"

"I don't care. I'm stronger than you anyhow. I can take it."

Doc turned his head back around. Morgan

laughed at the dentist's exasperated expression.

"Doc let me come with you,"

"Okay. All right."

Doc wished he could find a way to get Kate to stay in Tucson, without being blatantly cruel. He should just end it there, say goodbye and never speak to her again, but he knew in a sick, obsessive way that before too long he would need her company at some point down the line, when he was sick or down. He was too smart to jeopardize those moments. Kate followed behind cheerfully, making her presence well known, trying to prove her hardiness.

"I'll show you I can go the distance. I can ride a buckboard as well as any man."

Holliday walked on ignoring her. He pretended to start a conversation with Morgan.

"I can Doc. I know I can."

Doc shook his head. "I don't doubt that Kate. I think that you're missing the point."

"What? I don't know what you mean."

"I didn't expect you would."

By the time that Doc and Morgan got back to Tombstone, it was late at night. Doc left Kate at Fly's Boarding House and rode over to the Occidental in Morgan's buckboard.

"Wyatt said he'd be eating here tonight," said Morgan. He pushed the swing doors open into the lunch room and saw Wyatt and Virgil sitting in the far corner.

"Hey Doc c'mon and sit down. Did Morg tell you why I wanted to see you?"

"He said it was something about Ike Clanton wanting to kill me. He didn't say why."

"He thinks that I told you something that was a secret between me and him."

"The stage robber deal, you're using him as an informant?"

"Yes how do you know that?"

"Shit, everyone knows that. All the cowboys know, he got drunk last week out in Contention and told everyone."

"He's saying that you leaked the information and that his life has been put in jeopardy."

Holliday grew mad, "That son of a bitch. I'll put his life in jeopardy."

"Easy Doc," said Virgil, "there's no need to go after him its just going to cause more trouble than necessary."

"He's the one that's causing trouble. I can't sit around and wait for him to kill me."

Morgan smiled, "He's full of shit anyway Doc. You know that. I don't think he could shoot straight if he wanted to."

"Well, the way he's been drinking lately. I'd be surprised if he could. He ain't been sober since his father got killed," said Wyatt.

At that precise moment Ike walked in beside the bar at the other end of the Occidental. Wyatt saw Ike enter but didn't say anything. He hoped that no one would notice. Ike talked to Tom McLaury, with large hand gestures and exaggerated expressions. He leaned heavily on to the oak bar and ordered a beer, took a swallow and stood with his glass hanging from his hand at an angle. He paused and caught his reflection in the mirror at the back of the bar. He stared for a while and nudged McLaury in the shoulder, pointing at the reflection. McLaury looked at the image and started laughing. Ike grew angry.

It took a moment for Wyatt to realize that Ike had caught Doc's reflection behind his own.

"Holliday!" he screamed, "That's Holliday."

Doc heard his name and caught sight of Ike. Before Wyatt could get a hold of him the dentist had made his way across to the other side of the saloon and was standing at the bar with Ike.

"Oh Lord no," said Virge, "I wasn't wanting this tonight."

"Too late," said Wyatt.

"You son of a bitch, I heard you were looking to kill me."

"You don't know the shit I've gone through because of you're lies. First Pa got killed and now they're trying to get me. All of the robbers are dead, even your buddy Leonard. Everyone's dropping like flies and its all cause of your mouth."

"That's right I killed your pa. I enjoyed it too. You lyin' bastard you know I wasn't even there."

"Is that right? Well, some say different. I'm going to kill you anyway. I'm going to shoot you and the Earps like jack rabbits, then it'll be safe around here again."

"All right. If you're looking to die from lead poisoning, pull out your gun and commence."

Ike hesitated and looked nervous, "I ain't heeled."

"What the hell is that supposed to mean? C'mon jackass let's go."

Morgan reached behind Ike and grabbed him around the waist.

"Outside," he said.

He dragged Ike out into the street. Doc followed.

"Morgan, give this ass a gun. We intend to fight it out."

Morgan gave Doc a disapproving look from the corner of his eye and ignored his comment.

"Morgan c'mon get him a gun. I'm not going to take this shit from this coward any longer."

Wyatt grabbed Doc around the waist, pulled him off his feet and dragged him backwards.

"Let go of me Wyatt."

"C'mon Doc, let's go, it ain't worth it, you know that."

Doc struggled to get loose. Ike was similarly annoyed and tried to punch Morgan in the face.

"Y'all keep acting like that, I'll lock you both up."

Doc cooled down considerably, "You don't need to worry about that Virgil. I was leaving any how."

Wyatt let go of Doc and let him walk away. Ike relaxed as he watched the dentist go.

"He was the one who started it. Didn't you see him Wyatt? You saw him come after me, he's just a trouble maker."

"Shut up Ike," said Wyatt.

Virgil checked Ike for guns and found none, "It's all right Morg. You can let him go, he's clean."

Ike adjusted his jacket, "I could have told you that. I tried to tell Doc but he wouldn't believe me."

"Just the same Ike, step out of line and you're going to jail, understand?"

"I won't cause no trouble Virgil. I'm just drinking away some bad memories, they're ain't no law against that."

"I've given you my warning and I mean it. Cause any trouble and you'll hit that jail floor before you know what's happened."

Ike smirked at Wyatt and turned and headed back into the saloon and immediately began a trumped up conversation with Frank McLaury, playing himself up to be a big guy. He ordered a drink and slugged it down in one go. He wobbled and pulled himself up on to a stool. Wyatt could hardly bare to watch Ike, he turned away. Doc walked down the street with an angry gimp, his walking stick hit the ground so hard it send small sparks flying from the metal tip.

"Thank God that's over," said Virge, "C'mon lets go and finish eating."

"The food will be just about cold anyway. I'm going to go over to the Oriental and close up that Faro game."

"Well, stay around this night ain't over yet."

"I hear you."

Even from the street, both men could hear Ike yelling and cursing. McLaury egged him on and encouraged him, milking it for every cent.

"Those Earps made a fool of you Ike. You gonna let them away with that?"

"Hell no, I'm gonna get every one of them. They'll be pushin' up daisies before sun up."

"You going to be the one that does it?" said Tom with a grin.

"Sure am. I'm going to pay them back. I'm going to shoot them. That Doc Holliday will be deader than a door nail."

"How you going to do that without any guns

Ike?"

"I'll get guns."

McLaury laughed, "You're so full of shit. You couldn't bust a hole in a rabbit at two yards."

"You better shut up or I'll bust a hole in you too just for the hell of it."

"You don't have the guts! Frank's coming into town this morning. You lay a finger on me and he'll knock you senseless."

"I ain't scared of Frank. He ain't nothing, I'm the leader of the cowboys now that Pa's dead."

Tom laughed and slapped Ike on the back, "Drink up Ike. I want to hear more of your stories."

Virgil heard every word of Ike's conversation. His face looked worn and tired.

"We need to do something about this. We need to get everyone together and sort this thing out."

"Where's Behan tonight?" said Wyatt

"He's been out of town on business."

"I heard he's over at the Grand throwing a party," said Morgan.
"Why?"

"It's his birthday. Shibbel and all of his cronies were waiting till he got back in town. The way I heard they'll be champagne on the house there tonight."

"Wyatt you go on over and get him. I'm going to talk Ike into walking over with me. I'll meet you over there."

"What about Doc? Do you want him to be there?"

"Best not to. We'll never get Ike and him in a room together."

Wyatt, Virgil, Ike, John Behan and Tom McLaury sat down in what was publicly announced as a private game of poker. They sat in the poker room at the back cellar of the Grand Hotel. The central lantern hung over the table lighting the men's faces, some were illuminated more favorably than others. Behan was the most irritated of the group. He looked tired and slightly drunk and not in the mood to deal with the situation. He lit a cigar and sat down in one of the poker chairs; rocking it backwards until his long back leaned up against the wall.

"So what seems to be the problem boys?" he said, "I've been working hard on a county issue all week, I come home and decide to take the night off for my birthday and what happens? I get dragged back here to talk to you all. I hope this will be quick."

"I appreciate you takin' the time, Behan, sooner we cooperate and find a solution to this problem, the sooner we can get out of here."

"Well, I think that it's about time that you all are listening to me," said Ike, "I need for you to know that I will kill Doc at the first opportunity."

"Is this what this is all about?" said Behan, ignoring the cowboy, "If that's the problem, why not lock Ike up and forget about it."

"I ain't done nothing to deserve being locked up. Whose side are you on, anyhow?"

"Ike, it'll be for your own good."

Wyatt lit his pipe and took a couple of puffs from the stem, "Look gentlemen you're all getting this wrong. Ike you believe that Doc betrayed you is that right?"

210

"That's the truth he deserves to die."

"How do you know he betrayed you?"

"I just know it."

John Behan sighed and brought the front legs of his chair back to the floor.

"Ike, you're drunk. What the hell is all this about anyway? Wyatt are you saying you bribed him? Maybe this is all your fault."

"I didn't bribe Ike. I used him as an informant. I thought maybe he'd help us arrest the stage robbers."

Behan smiled, "Why don't you leave that kind of thing to me? I'm the county sheriff."

"Well, you sure ain't good at your job. I recall that King managed to break loose from that jail."

"That's my deputy's fault not mine. You know that jail ain't fit to hold a dog let alone a stage robber."

"He paid you didn't he?" said Wyatt.

"He might have."

"You son of a bitch, me and my brothers were dealing with a dying horse out in no wheres and you took money to let King go."

"C'mon everyone, settle a little, that ain't important no more. Kings dead, Leonard's dead, they're all dead. What's important is that the cowboys get brought under control."

"That's what I was trying to tell you Virgil. If Doc is dead, there'll be no more trouble." Ike looked sincere; his drunken eyes half shut.

"Are you threatening us?" said Wyatt.

"Now what do you think?" said the cowboy. "You boys owe me for all these inconveniences you've caused. Pa would still be alive if it weren't for Doc."

"Your pa was killed for stealing Mexican cattle. It was Mexican bandits that killed your pa. Doc wasn't even there."

Ike jumped up and flung the chair back against the wall, "Are you saying my father was a thief?"

"Settle down Ike. We can't help you if you go against us."

"Maybe I don't want to be helped."

Behan intervened, "What if Doc were to leave Arizona would that be enough?"

"It might be," said Ike, "but between you and me, I'd prefer to see him dead in a casket. That ways we'd know he ain't coming back."

"But if Doc were to leave Arizona?" Behan repeated.

"No, no bull now. I want him dead, him and Wyatt, all of the Earps."

"Well, then I can't help you." Behan got up from the table, "Gentlemen, it's clear that the situation is hopeless. Until Ike gets sober there's no good in talkin' about all this. If you don't mind I'm going back to my party."

"Behan, wait this ain't through. This needs to get sorted now or someone's gonna get hurt," said Virgil.

"So far as I can see this is a town matter. You're the town marshal Virgil. Why don't you deal with it?"

Behan left the room and closed the door behind him. Virgil sighed and stared at the back wall.

"I want Holliday dead," said Ike again, trying to regain everyone's attention.

"C'mon Ike let's take you home and get you

sobered up. I'm going to make it clear though, if I see you or Tom carrying guns, you're going to jail."

"I can take him home," said Tom with a grin.

"I don't trust you Tom. You'll probably take him to another bar. I'll walk you both to your rooms."

Ike continued his drunken ramblings, trying hard to get Virgil to understand him, despite the marshal pulling him out the room. Tom followed silently behind them.

Wyatt stretched his long legs and checked his pocket watch. He pulled his overcoat on and walked out on to Fremont Street, the night was cold with an icy breeze. The smoke from Wyatt's pipe spiraled upwards. He walked, tasting the smoke and thinking about everything that had happened. As he passed the Occidental, he met with Doc. The dentist stood by the door, flipping up the fur collar of his long gray overcoat and pulling on his leather gloves. He breathed in the cold air and coughed sharply. He had his head up and his nostrils flared, struggling to regain his breath. He walked unsteadily towards Wyatt, whiskey and tiredness leaving their mark. Wyatt took a puff of the pipe and blew the smoke out into swirling clouds, "How are you?"

"I'm all right. I guess you and Behan told that son of a bitch what for?"

"We couldn't get much sense out of Ike, he's too drunk."

"But he's locked up now, right?"

"He's not armed. He's with Virge and Tom McLaury right now. His brother is going to try and get him sober."

Doc's eyes grew intense, "I fully expect to see a flying dog before that happens Wyatt. The sooner that boy gets behind bars the sooner this town can get back to normality."

"He'll probably sleep it off. Perhaps he'll see his lack of judgment in the morning."

"The only thing Ike's going to see in the morning is his own vomit."

Wyatt sighed, "Well I wouldn't put it that way."

Doc smiled and suppressed a cough. He breathed in a line of cold air and shook as a cold breeze cut through him. He choked and wheezed, leaning to slow the coughing. As soon as he could get his breath he cleaned his lips with his handkerchief, "Damn it! I thought Arizona was meant to be warm." He cleared his throat in an attempt to make his voice clearer.

"Not tonight, it ain't. Way things are going I wouldn't be surprised if it starts snowing."

Holliday coughed again and let out a shrill, strangled bray as his lungs reverberated with the fit. He walked on with Wyatt, the cough still persisting. He stopped and leaned over and choked until a line of spit dripped from his mouth. He straightened up and spat out on to the street. Wyatt watched and waited.

"I didn't know you was sick."

Doc straightened up and rolled his eyes at his friend, "No shit!"

"I mean it's been a long time since I've seen you this bad."

"It's nothing Wyatt. It's probably just a chill. The way I've been freezing in this hell hole, it doesn't surprise me much neither."

"Well, maybe if you weren't carousing Allen Street at three o'clock in the morning you wouldn't have got yourself in this mess."

Doc smiled, "Maybe I like being in a mess. Who are you, my mother?"

Wyatt smiled, "I sure as hell hope not."

Doc laughed and coughed. The more he laughed, the more he coughed and the more he coughed the more he laughed.

"What the hell am I going to do with you?" said Wyatt, "What you say I buy you a drink? Warm you up before you head home."

Doc smiled, "All right Wyatt. I can be persuaded."

CHAPTER TWENTY-TWO

The air was bitterly cold with a sharp breeze blowing. Wyatt crossed Fremont Street and turned on to Allen Street and met Virgil and Morgan by the Oriental.

"You heard about Ike?" said Morgan.

"Yeah, where is he?"

"I all ready arrested him," said Virgil.

"Then why the hell did someone get me up about all of this?"

"It isn't just Ike," said Morgan, "he squealed to Tom and now half the cowboys are coming into town this morning to give us hell. He was downright hateful about you Wyatt. I don't know what you did but he's hungry for your blood."

"He's crazy. What does he hope to achieve by doing this? Frank and Tom won't fight, they haven't got any business to."

"If you touch one, you touch the others. They blame us for the stage robbers getting killed. They especially want Doc. They feel like he betrayed them."

"They know about us using him as an informant?"

"Like I said, touch one, touch them all."

"Where are they now?"

"Behan's dealing with it, well he says he is. I ain't seen him in over half an hour."

Morgan grinned, "You should see him Wyatt, he's all tore up, I ain't seen any one so shook up over a hangover in years. I reckon he must have kept drinking after you all broke up the meeting last night."

"Well, that figures," said Wyatt gruffly, "Where's Doc?"

"He's still in bed. You want me to wake him?"

"Let him sleep. There's no reason to drag him out so early."

"We better head over to the courthouse. Judge Spicer is going to deal with Ike."

The brothers walked across to the other side of the street and up the steps into the brick courthouse. The room was almost empty, Billy Clanton, Ike's younger brother, sat with Tom McLaury. Wyatt looked over at Billy and met his gaze. The cowboy grinned like he was at a picnic and snickered quietly. The Earps took a seat on the wooden bench and waited until Ike was called.

Ike walked to the stand, looking worse for wear, his head bandaged with a strong smell of liquor and sweat oozing from him. He was unsteady on his feet, and mumbled things under his breath.

"My God, he's still drunk," said Wyatt, "Does he even know where he is?"

"I don't suppose it matters," said Morgan. He's going to get fined any how.

Ike was slow to react but when he saw Wyatt he flew into a rage.

"You, I've been waiting all morning for you to show your face. You didn't even have the balls to show up. I've been hunting you down."

"Well, I'm here now," said Wyatt.

Ike looked around at the other cowboys, the judge and the Earps, "Give me four foot of ground and I'll have you buried you son of a bitch."

The judge intervened, "I object to your foul language Ike. You're only making things worse for yourself."

"Four foot of ground," Ike continued, "That's all I need. Hell I'll make a fight with you now if someone will give me my gun."

"Okay, let's step outside. I don't need a gun to whip you good. I'll use my bare fists if I have to."

"That's enough Wyatt, sit down," said Virgil.

The judge felt a need to bring the confrontation to a close. "Ike Clanton, I fine you five-hundred dollars for contempt of court, resisting arrest, and being drunk and disorderly. In the meantime your guns will be confiscated and held at The Grand Hotel, until you have sense enough to sober up and leave town."

Billy and Frank stepped forward and paid the fine. The Earps made their way out of the courthouse. Wyatt avoided Tom McLaury but reached the door at the same time as the cowboy did. Tom swung his fist towards Wyatt's face and barely missed. Wyatt spun around, removed his gun from his holster and struck McLaury over the nape of the neck. The cowboy collapsed on one knee and cursed as the pain oozed over the back of his head. He slid down until he was lying flat along one of the steps. His hands were cut and covered in blood from the fall. He attempted to stand but wavered as the dizziness hit him. Virgil took him by the shoulder, arrested him, and walked him back inside the courthouse.

Wyatt stood on the step in a daze, feeling lucky at escaping Tom's wrath. The cool air blew his blond hair sideways. The clouds high above grew a deeper gray and the first snowflakes fell. The wind moaned and blew the flakes in greater mass. Wyatt walked down the steps and out across the street, he was still riled up by Ike's behavior. He caught sight of a saddled horse standing up on the boardwalk, outside Spagenburg's Gun Shop. The animal stood with its front legs on the boards and its tail end on the ground. Wyatt watched with curiosity. The horse reached its neck forward to the door of the store; its lips reached to nibble on something that Wyatt couldn't see and its reins dangled. It pulled its front hoof forward and with a hop brought its hind quarters up on to the boardwalk. The horse raised its front leg and kicked the wood. The sight of the animal angered Wyatt and without much thought he walked up on to the board walk and grabbed the horse by the bit, backing it stride by stride until its hooves rested squarely on the ground. He laid the reins back over the hitching rail and noticed something strangely familiar about the horse's saddle. He looked back up at the gun store and met with Frank McLaury's irritated face.

"What in hell are you doing with my horse? You trying to steal it or something?"

"There ain't place for a horse on the boardwalk. It belongs on the ground. City can't afford to replace boards like that."

"Well, maybe I don't give a damn what the city thinks. If my horse wants up on the walk, so be it."

"It's against regulations, horses belong in the corrals."

Frank gave Wyatt a glare, "Well maybe I can move my horse myself. You don't need to go touching my property. If I didn't know any better I'd say you was trying to steal it."

"You've just about crossed the line Frank. I don't think I can stomach your talk much longer."

"So what you going to do about it? You ain't the town marshal. You ain't the county marshal neither. Last time I saw, Behan was tossing his breakfast in the shitter."

Wyatt wanted to say something but knew that he would regret it if he did. He simply gave Frank an angry glare, turned and walked away. Frank revelled in Wyatt's retreat.

"You ain't got no balls Wyatt. Face it, you're a loser, just like the rest of the law around here."

Billy Clanton emerged from the store with his mouth full of candy and a brand new Colt forty-five in his hands. He dwarfed Frank as he walked up to stand beside him. He giggled like a six-year-old kid and gazed down at the gun that lay in his hands, "Frank, look what I got. Real shiny and pretty, ain't it?" Billy almost spat some of the candy on to the boards. A line of pink, sugary spit fell on to the gun. Billy rubbed the sleeve of his flannel shirt against the barrel but the candy and spit had all ready made the gun sticky.

"Damn it Billy, watch what you're doing. That gun is worth more than two hundred dollars. I can't trust you with nothing."

"Shut up Frank," said Billy, "I ain't no kid any more. I can do what I likes."

"Oh yeah who told you that?"

"My brother, Ike, he should know too, he's the head of the cowboys now that Pa's dead."

Frank laughed.

"What's so funny chuckle-head? It's so that Ike's the boss. He tells me that all the time. You're gonna have to be nice to me some now that Ike's in charge."

Frank stopped laughing and pointed his long finger at Billy's fat face, "Call me chuckle-head again and my knife is going to parlay some with your gut. You understand fat boy?"

Billy swallowed nervously, "I ain't scared of you. I ain't scared of nobody, not you or Tom, not Holliday or the Earps neither."

Frank laughed again, "Not scared of the Earps huh? Where the hell were you when Wyatt was messing with my horse?"

"Buying this gun. If I'd known he was there I'd have shot him too."

"Yeah sure you would."

"I ain't scared of him Frank. Ike says Wyatt's got a fight coming at him and I'm gonna show that son of a bitch a trick or two when it happens. No, I ain't scared of him none."

"C'mon Billy," said Frank, "We've got some business to attend to."

Wyatt walked into Hafford's Saloon and found his brothers Virgil and Morgan talking with

221

Johnny Behan. He walked past the walls covered with stuffed birds, up to the bar and laid a couple of gold dollars on the surface. He waited for the bartender to return, feeling the eyes of eagles, hawks, buzzards and cranes watching him from all corners. He felt relief when Hafford himself arrived to take his order. He paid for the mug of coffee and the cigar and walked back across the narrow room to sit with his brothers.

Virgil sat with a stern look on his face. Heavy shadows shrouded his eyes. Wyatt supposed that his brother had probably gained little sleep in the past twenty-four hours. His attention turned to Behan. The county sheriff was paler than usual and looked to be suffering. He tried to keep his attention on Virgil, but from time to time fatigue and dehydration would get the better of him and his eyes would close, as if he wished he were somewhere else that didn't require him to think so much. He smiled feebly at Wyatt and offered him a drink of whiskey. Wyatt looked disagreeably at Behan.

"Hair of the dog Wyatt. It's helping my concentration. You sure you don't want me to lace your coffee?"

Wyatt shook his head, "I don't think that would be appropriate do you?"

Behan looked pained and wished he hadn't offered, "For God's sakes Wyatt. I was just trying to be polite. You don't have to make it harder than it all ready is. This hangover's about to kill me."

"That's your problem, not mine," said Wyatt.

"So where were we?" said Behan ignoring Wyatt, "I think that you mentioned that the cowboys are threatening your lives and something needs to be done about it." Behan closed his eyes again and rubbed the corners with his finger.

"It's not just our lives John, the whole reputation of the town is being dragged down by the fact that nobody's doing anything to stop the cowboys. If they think that they can go against the law and get away with it, we'll never get a moments peace in Tombstone. That's bad for you and me and for everyone who intends to make Cochise territory work."

Virgil wondered if Behan was even listening and was relieved when the Sheriff opened his eyes again. He looked at Virgil with blood shot eyes and took a mouthful of whiskey. He smarted as the taste hit the back of his throat, "I don't see it that way Virge the cowboys ain't so bad. Some things we can't do anything about. Some of it ain't our business to do about."

"How can you say that? It's our business to do something. They've robbed stages, killed people, stolen horses and cattle. We can't live with that in our territory."

"What's that to you? You're the town marshal not the county sheriff?"

Virgil looked at Behan with sad eyes, "I may be the town marshal but first and foremost I'm a U.S. Deputy Marshal. That's why I came here. I was assigned here damn it. If I let those cowboys get away with threatening me like they are everything I've worked at these past two years has been for nothing."

Behan snorted, "Well if you're so damn smart, go on and arrest them. I won't stop you. All I know is a bullet in the gut isn't going to help your career record none. I would rather sit a fight out than risk losing a limb or getting killed. No job is worth that."

"I wasn't talking about doing it alone. I need your help John. I had a band of miners yelling at me to do something this morning, the safety committee is willing to go against the cowboys. It wouldn't be one on one it would be a huge posse. If we could work together and corner the cowboys we could at least have them arrested, if they run, with all those men working against them they wouldn't stand a chance."

Behan laughed, "Are you serious? You're going to let a group of untrained vigilantes roam the streets of Tombstone hunting down the cowboys? It would be a mess. I'm sorry Virge I can't allow you to do that. It's too risky. There'd be a blood bath."

"Not necessarily, not if we plan it right."

"No," said Behan firmly, "Look, if you're serious about this. I'll go and talk to the cowboys some and try and get their guns for you but I'm not making any promises. I'm not going to go out of my way to piss them off just to get shot for nothing. This ain't really the county sheriff's job after all you're the town marshal. You're the one who should be working this thing out."

The brothers sat in silence. Wyatt puffed on his cigar and let the smoke engulf him. Virgil stared deep into the shot of whiskey that Behan had left him and thought about the situation. The saloon doors swung open and Doc Holliday walked over to the table, leaning heavily on his cane. Morgan was the only one to acknowledge the dentist. Holliday sat down in Behan's chair, poured himself a shot of whiskey from Behan's abandoned bottle and slugged it back in one go. The alcohol caused him to cough over and over, until he had to beat his chest to get the fit to end. He swallowed hard, his eyes watering. He sat and studied the group of men as if he was about to play a game of poker. He breathed noisily through his nose and mouth and coughed again.

"I heard what's going on with the cowboys. What's being done about it?"

"Behan's going to talk with them," said Morgan.

Doc laughed until he choked.

Wyatt watched his friend, "Why did you come out here today Doc? It's been snowing outside it's not going to help your condition none unless you want to catch pneumonia. I told them to let you sleep."

"Kate woke me. She told me Ike was looking to kill me."

"Damn it. If she'd had an ounce of sense she'd have let you alone."

"Where's Ike?"

"That's none of your business," said Wyatt sternly.

"That's a hell of a thing for you to say to me. The man's out there trying to hunt me down and have me killed."

"Listen Doc," Virgil interrupted, "I need us all to work together. If we get split up and work one on one, we're all likely to end up dead. Wyatt's right, you'd be doing yourself a favor if you'd go back to bed."

Doc smiled, "I'm sorry but I can't do that. The cowboys moved down there by the boarding house as I was walking up the street. I'm guessing they're fixing to stay. I can't go back there unless you want me to face them alone. Besides, where's the fun in staying in bed?"

"How many of them were down there?"

"There's around five or six, they were just hanging around when I saw them."

"Did you see Behan down there with them?"

"Nope, last I saw he was getting a shave."

"I should have known. Well, I guess you're right. You can't go back there. If you promise to do as I say, I'll swear you in and we can get this sorted out in a legal fashion. Behan ain't coming back so I guess we're going to have to sort this out ourselves, together. Are we all in agreement?"

"Count me in," said Doc. Wyatt and Morgan nodded.

"Just to even things out I'll give you my shotgun Doc. You give me your cane. I don't want them to see that we're wanting trouble."

Doc grinned, "There's one shot in there, if you need it Virge. I hope to hell you don't."

"What's he talking about?" said Virgil.

"That cane of his is a gun."

"And you let him go around here with it Wyatt?"

"It's a long story, he told me about it back in Dodge. He ain't never fired it and I don't suppose he ever will. He's right though. If there is a fight there's one good bullet in that sucker, it's better than nothing."

Virgil raised an eyebrow and studied the cane with a perplexed expression, "I'll keep that in mind. I hope to God it doesn't come down to a fight."

Doc grinned, "For your sake Virgil I hope not. That cane was never meant for that kind of action."

"Well, if everyone's ready, let's go," said Virgil.

The men got up from the table. Doc laid the shotgun under the crook of his right arm and wrapped his gray overcoat around it. The gun felt heavy and awkward. He could feel it nudge him in the ribs with every step he walked and it put more weight on his other leg. He tried not to swing his stride, not wanting the shotgun to move any more than it all ready was. He followed the Earps out into Allen Street and caught up with Morgan, walking along side him. They walked in silence. Doc studied his reflection in the shop window. He could see the butt of the shotgun sticking out into the back of his overcoat. He adjusted the gun under his arm until the shape of the gun was not as noticeable and walked on. As he turned the corner on to Fremont Street, a sharp, cold breeze blew past his cheek and against his side. The coat flapped open. He shivered and pulled the coat back over the gun.

Virgil, walked out in front with long confident strides. Wyatt walked along side him, the two brothers talked from time to time as they headed along the street. Holliday tried to listen but the slight breeze made it hard to figure out the words. Morgan was frustrated, there was something that he was thinking that he didn't feel right about.

"Stop, hold on what if they've got horses? Shouldn't we get some horses so we can chase them down?"

Wyatt stopped and turned around, "It'll be all right Morg. If that happens then I guess we'll have to shoot the horses. I hate for it to come to that, but if it does, then so be it."

"I guess your right."

"C'mon now," said Virgil, "let's get this over with."

The men headed down the street. Doc coughed sharply as he walked until his chest was clear. He looked out across the street and saw people watching from windows and from store doors. At Bauer's butcher store meat hung on hooks, swinging in the cold breeze. They approached Fly's Boarding House. To Doc's surprise he could hear Behan's voice. It wasn't until Wyatt and Virgil had stopped again that he could see Behan, walking forward with one hand in the air.

"Stop, wait," he said. "You don't have to go down there. I've all ready disarmed them."

"What?"

"There's no need they're unarmed. Go home."

Virgil gave Behan a stern look, "If you've disarmed them then where are their guns?"

"I left them at Fly's."

"I don't believe you."

Virgil pushed past Behan and made his way down the alley that led into the back of the corral. Doc and the others followed behind. Behan chased after Virgil, "No don't. Please for the love of God don't go down there. I lied, I admit I lied. They're armed. They're going to kill you. Please for God's sakes turn around. You don't know what you're getting yourself into."

"My mind's set John. I'm going to arrest them.

Now get the hell out of my way!"

Behan stepped aside and let Virgil past. The
county sheriff turned and walked away. Doc
watched him go in through the front door of Fly's
and close the door behind him.

"Well there goes Behan," said Wyatt.

"Obviously he has more important things to
attend to," said Doc.

Doc could see the cowboys waiting. They stood
leaning against one wall of the alley. Frank
McLaury stood with his horse blocking the
entrance to the corral. Before the men could meet,
Billy Claiborne lost his nerve and ran across the
alley and up towards Fly's Photographic. The door
to the studio opened and Behan's arms reached
out, grabbed the young cowboy by the coat pockets
and dragged him in. Billy's desertion acted as a
catalyst and both sides more determined. Doc
stopped at the mouth of the alley with his back to
Allen Street. Virgil walked forward with the
walking stick raised in the air.

"Throw up your arms!"

Doc watched the cowboys' reaction. There was
some hesitation. Doc's attention turned to Wyatt.
He looked serious and determined. His eyes were
almost colourless in the bright light.

Doc waited. An icy breeze cut across his face.
The course of the storm clouds changed in the
wind, the sunlight shone down illuminating the
cowboy group for a second and then another cloud
covered the sun and left Doc blinking as the scene
changed from bright to dark in seconds. The
shotgun was heavy against his arm. His shoulder
ached with the effort of keeping it hidden. The

metal of the barrel sucked the warmth from his body. Morgan watched Virgil, waiting for him to give the writ and make the arrest. His face was serious but he took the time to glance over at Doc before his attention returned to his brother. Doc shivered and pulled his arms into his sides, trying to retain as much warmth as possible.

On the opposite side of the narrow alley, Tom McLaury took his horse by the bit. The animal shifted its hindquarters out of the wind and pivoted around in a tight circle, reversed and backed its tail up against the wall. McLaury gagged the horse in the mouth with his left hand. It jerked its head upwards and backed up a couple of strides.

"You boys are under arrest. Throw up your hands," said Virgil.

Doc readjusted the gun. A gust of wind blew his coat open. He moved to wrap the fabric around the shotgun but it was obvious what he was hiding. Tom's horse snorted at the flapping coat. In the cowboy line, hands moved towards guns. One of the pistols clicked as it was pulled around to half cock. It clicked again as the bullet was brought around to the firing pin.

Virgil threw his hands up in the air with Doc's walking stick in his right hand, "Hold, I don't want that."

Doc knew that it was all over. There would be no arrest. The adrenalin pumped through the blood in his veins. His muscles tightened and his hands trembled as he pulled the shotgun out from beneath his overcoat. He brought the pin back. A bang echoed down the alley as the first shot was fired, sending clouds of blue-grey smoke up into the air. Doc hesitated and stopped. He looked to see who had fired the shot but couldn't see in the smoke. The second shot was fired and the small alleyway filled with smoke. It drifted this on the breeze, bringing faces into focus and then hiding them again. Wyatt and Morgan reached forward in unison, both guns engaged and both guns fired. The noise of three guns firing was deafening. Behind the layer of smoke, Billy Clanton cried out and collapsed on the ground. He touched his side, watching the blood ooze, amazed that he'd been hit.

Doc took courage in seeing the hit and brought the shotgun up to his shoulder. The smoke cleared and he looked directly across the lot into the eyes of Tom McLaury. Tom's horse squealed and humped its back. Tom remained motionless, his grasp was tight on the reins, he pulled down on the bit and the shanks forced the horse's mouth open. Doc cocked the shotgun and pressed into the trigger. The gun released a spray of hot metal and kicked Doc hard, almost knocking him off his feet. He looked for Tom wondering if he had been successful but the cowboy was hidden by his dancing horse. Another shot and the horse reared up on its haunches, roaring. Tom let out a yell and fell backwards, dropping the reins and letting the horse free. The animal plunged towards the dentist, bucking and kicking. A stray shot hit it in the haunches and sent it galloping on to Fremont Street.

Doc's muscles burned from taking the kick of the shotgun. He threw it down in disgust and reached for his pistol. There was a blinding ray of light as he drew the gun, a beam of sunlight breaking through a storm cloud high above and reflecting the gun's shiny surface. The gun glowed like it was on fire. Holliday stretched his long, skinny arm out towards Ike Clanton. He was surprised to see the drunken cowboy stare with wild eyes at him and stagger across the alley. Ike grabbed Wyatt and tried to pull the gun from his hand.

"Don't shoot. I ain't armed."

"Get to fighting or get the hell out my way," said Wyatt, trying his best to keep his eyes on the other cowboys and keep Ike from getting his gun at the same time.

The door to Fly's opened again and Ike needed no invitation. He ran as fast as he could and stumbled into the photographic studio. The door slammed behind him and as soon as he was out of sight, a gun was fired from the studio window.

"Look out Morg," said Wyatt.

Morgan spun around, his gun ready to fire but he tripped on the drainage channel at the side of the alley and fell heavily on his side.

Billy Clanton lay on the ground, riddled with bullets, watching the scene with one eye. He had at least four wounds but he had no intention of giving up. He reached a tired hand up towards Morgan, aimed his gun and fired. Doc rotated the chamber of his pistol and brought the gun to firing position. He drew back on the trigger and shot Billy cleanly across the wrist. The cowboy screamed out and dropped his gun, the bullet missing its target. Frank McLaury saw that Doc was distracted and took his chances, a stray bullet flew across the alley and hit the dentist across the hip, deflecting off his leather holster. Morgan saw the trouble Doc was in and reached out and shot Frank McLaury in the head. Holliday winced as the pain hit him. Morgan yelled as a bullet spliced his coat and went into his shoulder. Virgil was the next to fall with a bullet wound to the leg.

Doc fired another shot into Frank McLaury and watched the cowboy stagger towards him, blood dripping from his shirt, his eyes bugged out. The cowboy raised his gun to the dentist. Wyatt turned and fired his pistol. A bullet hit the cowboy square in the forehead, toppling Frank and tripping him. He dropped to one knee and slid on to his side.

There was a strange moment of silence. Doc felt his heart beating hard against his chest. There was a persistent ringing in his ears and his hearing was muffled as if he'd been punched in the face. He turned and looked around, paranoid that there would be another shot, but it was over. The gun smoke billowed in the wind. It had an acidic, sour taste that reminded Doc of other fights. It lingered in the alleyway and the cold air intensified it.

He swung around and turned back towards his friends. Wyatt stood still at a strange angle, leaning forward with his gun still hanging from his hand. He was gazing out into the lot. Outwardly, he looked all right but Doc knew differently. From where he was standing, he could see Wyatt's right hand trembling.

A hound dog bayed in the distance and one of the silver mine sirens wailed. Doc saw Morgan lying on the ground and felt a gut wrenching sense of disgust.

"My God Morg!"

Morgan lifted his head a couple of inches from the ground and then dropped it back again. He touched his shoulder and looked surprised at the blood running off his fingers.

"I've been shot Doc," he said, "I'm shot right through."

Virgil sat up slowly and tried to lift his leg from the ground. He gritted his teeth against it, holding his leg, rocking it to reduce the pain.

Wyatt turned and looked around. He placed his gun back in his coat pocket and bent down to Morg to study his shoulder. "I'm sorry," he said.

Morgan winced and half tried to smile. "What's there to be sorry about?"

The door to Fly's opened and Ike Clanton and Billy Claiborne stepped down on to the street. Ike brushed past the growing crowd and made his way to where Billy was lying. He bent over his brother. Billy gave out a pained yell and beat the dirt with his foot. Ike grasped his brother's bloody hand and held it tightly.

"They've killed me Ike. They've killed me."

"They're murderers!"

The crowd broke to let buckboards come through.

"Is Frank still alive?" said Ike, watching as his friend was lifted into the back of the buckboard.

Billy was loaded on to the same wagon as Frank and despite his pain, was able to gaze over at his friend. He could see Frank's lips and fingers twitching. He watched the blood soak through the grey flannel blanket that covered his legs. He watched the twitching slow and stop, snow flakes dropped silently on to Frank's nose and lips, but the cowboy was still. Billy watched with curiosity at first and then a strange concoction of fear, anxiety and anger grew deep inside him. He knew that Frank was dead. He screamed out and banged his boot against the wooden buggy bed. He yelled so loud that Ike came over to check that he was okay.

"It ain't fair Ike! It ain't fair!" He lay shaking his head from side to side with tears rolling down his round cheeks. His face was flushed. His eyes closed tightly and opened again and then there was nothing more. Billy twitched and lay as still as Frank, his mouth pursed open, the tears still rolled down his face.

Ike reached over and clutched his brother's hand. He called the doctor over to the buggy. "What's wrong Ike?"

"Check my brother's okay."

The man looked in at the two cowboys. "I'm sorry, he's dead."

"Are you sure?"

"He's dead Ike. You can check him yourself if you like. They're ain't no pulse."

The doctor pulled the blood stained blanket over the cowboy's faces, jumped back into the driver's seat and waited for Ike to sit beside him.

"You want me to take you back to the hotel?"

"Don't seem much point. Take them to the undertaker, best we get this over with."

Johnny Behan walked out to the buckboard, just as Morgan was being lifted up into the back. Holliday looked down at Morgan and then up at Behan. He pushed himself forwards and shoved

Behan backwards, grabbing the sheriff by the collar.

"You bastard, I should kill you right now, you're the cause of all this."

Behan looked the dentist in the eyes and smiled calmly.

"There's been enough bloodshed today don't you think Holliday?"

"Why didn't you help us?"

"I told you, this ain't my jurisdiction."

Wyatt grabbed Doc by the shoulders and pulled him away from Behan. "That's enough, best to leave it alone."

"Wyatt, you and Doc are under arrest."

Wyatt slapped his hat down against his legs.

"You can't do that."

"Yes I can."

"I won't let you. This ain't your jurisdiction Behan. Only my brother can have us arrested."

Behan swung his fist in the air. Wyatt caught the Sheriff's hand swiftly, and held it tightly. The two men looked each other in the eyes. Behan relaxed his hand and Wyatt in turn dropped his grip. Behan was more than aware of the crowd that was watching him. He quickly changed his attitude. He tightened his neck tie until it was touching the pearly buttons on his white shirt and did his best to smile. He strode proudly away from Wyatt, his walk full of swagger. He raised his hand to the crowd in a friendly wave.

"Okay people," he said, "the fight's over, time to go home. C'mon now."

He grinned as the crowd dispersed and made their way from Fremont Street, back to their homes and businesses. Behan spied one of the more prominent ladies of the town, tipped his hat at her and walked away with her, chatting happily.

Doc and Wyatt watched him go with disgust.

"I figured Behan would do something like that. Wouldn't do for people to get the wrong impression of him. He's all ready countin' the votes for the next election."

"I don't give a damn any more Doc. I don't want nothing more to do with town politics. All that matters now is my brothers."

Wyatt walked back to the buckboard that carried Virgil and Morgan. He jumped up into the driver's seat.

"You may as well come along, if you want."

The dentist climbed up on to the buckboard and sat down by Wyatt.

The pony eased forward, walking steadily along the road as if it were part of a funeral procession. Doc saw the looks of the people as they drove past. He wondered what was going on in people's minds. He wished he could hide from his feelings. He could hear Morgan groaning with every rut and stone that the wheels rolled over, he wished that he had been the one to get hit. At least the pain would have been a distraction. It would have been honorable to take Morgan's place. The thing that hurt him the most was knowing that it wasn't him that was bleeding and that it was one of his best friends who was suffering. He knew that if it had been the other way Morgan would have kept him cheerful, cracking jokes and taking his mind of the pain. The way it was, Morgan was lying wrapped in a blanket, the snow fluttered around his body and his face was full of pain. His brother lay beside him. The only sound was the blowing of the wind and the pony's hooves on the dirt. Doc wanted to be funny, to lighten Morgan's spirits but the sight of his friend filled him with so much agony that when he opened his mouth to speak, all he could do was cough and huddle in silence as they drove along, the cold breeze chilling him to the bone.

The buckboard pulled up outside the drugstore. The pharmacist came running out to where Morgan and Virgil were sitting.

"I heard the shooting."

"Do I need to get them down?" said Wyatt.

"Nope, rest easy. I'll bring everything outside. There's a place 'round the side, you can bring the buggy around if that will make it easier."

Wyatt nodded silently and skilfully asked the pony to turn, the buggy rolled down the side of the alley and stopped outside a glass framed side door. The door opened and the druggist emerged with a pan and an assortment of tools and medicines.

"Let's take a look at the damage."

"Do you need some help?" Doc said.

The man looked at Doc with surprise.

"What the hell would you know about medicine Doc? This ain't poker!"

"I'm a dentist."

"Dentist huh? I figured that your nickname was some kind of a joke."

"No sir, it most certainly is not. I take my profession very seriously. But if you see me as some kind of a bar fly, then I'll be more than happy to leave you to it."

"No, why don't you pitch in. Let me know if I

miss anything."

The men worked, the pharmacist searched for shrapnel while Holliday washed and dressed the wounds. Doc finished suturing one of Morgan's wounds and snipped the end of the thread. Morgan opened one sleepy eye to Doc.

"You feel all right?" said Doc.

Morgan smiled and nodded lazily. Doc chuckled and coughed to clear his throat.

"That morphine I gave you must be working good. It'll numb the pain for sure." A pained expression filled Doc's face he turned his head away from Morgan so that his friend couldn't see him and reached for the roll of bandages to his side.

"Are you okay?" said Morgan.

Doc snorted abruptly, his chin trembled, he forced a smile, "Hell, I'm as good as I'll ever be."

The smile faded and the pained look returned, tightening the dentist's jaw, causing ripples to flash across the surface of his cheek. Doc clenched his eyebrows together in concentration and worked on wrapping the wound.

"Can you hold this?" he said.

Morgan nodded and grasped the dressing with his blood stained hand.

"Hold it firm now."

The dentist worked the bandage skilfully, bringing it around Morgan's waist and then up over his shoulder. He gave the bandage one final wrap, ripped the ends and tied them in a double bow.

"The dressing will probably need changed. Early morning you may want to wash out the wound a little."

"Thanks Doc," said Wyatt.

Doc sighed, shrugged and cleared things away.

"Ready?" said the pharmacist.

Wyatt jumped up into the driver's seat. The pony turned back on to Fremont Street. Doc watched the buggy disappear down the street and turned back around to walk down through the alley, a cold breeze buffeting his back. He walked across the street towards Fly's. He paused at the site of the gunfight, now quiet and still. The wind blew dust through the alley. He was filled with a strange feeling of loneliness. The sudden quiet had crept up on him, the adrenalin stepping aside and leaving him with nothing. The coldness of the afternoon seeped into him, the wind blew icy cold. Doc trembled, sighed and walked on towards the door of Fly's. He thought of Behan and Ike and Billy Claiborne using the door as an exit from the fight and he felt anger seep deep within him. He wanted to be angry, just to feel anything other than emptiness. He saw the dusty boot prints on the hall carpet and allowed his anger to wash over him, to know that the cowboys had been close to his room, running from the fight, tainting his home. To think that Ike was still alive and that Wyatt had spared him. In spite of everything and all the trouble the fight had caused, the main perpetrators of the fight had been left unscathed. Doc wanted to break something just for the hell of it but he couldn't find anything worth breaking. He wanted to be angry and to let everyone know it.

A door creaked open and Mrs. Fly walked out

into the hallway. She was normally friendly to Doc but today she looked at him oddly, turned quickly and strode away down the hall, her skirts brushed against Doc's leg with a rustle as she passed. Doc saw her expression and felt hurt. He was surprised that he cared so much. He felt disgusted and exhausted. Beads of sweat dripped down his back. He hated himself. He wanted to forget everything and be alone to drink away the day's events. He hated to think of Kate waiting for him in his room. Kate was the last thing he wanted right at that moment, she loved it when he was helpless and crawled back to her in apology. This time there was no apologizing to be done but Doc knew that she would be delighted by his turn of circumstances, lapping up his emotional state, enjoying feeling more powerful than him. He promised himself that he would be strong and tough and would tell Kate to go. He opened the door and found her lying stretched out on the bed, eating from a box of chocolates. She sat up when she saw him and looked him straight in the eyes, her expression pitying.

"Are you okay?" she said.

"What the hell do you think?"

"I was worried about you."

"Did you go to breakfast?"

Kate nodded slowly.

"Pass me the bottle of bourbon."

She reached over beside the bed and passed across a half empty bottle of whiskey. He took the bottle from her, his hands shook. He uncorked the bottle and took a slug. The whiskey burned his stomach. He knocked the bottle back and drank deeply.

"Pass me the dish over there and the roll of cotton."

Kate obliged. Doc undid his gun belt and removed his pants. He sat down on the bed. There was a huge rip through his long johns around his upper thigh. He ripped the fabric enough until he could see the wound clearly. His hip and leg were badly bruised but there was no serious damage. He dipped a piece of cotton into the whiskey and washed down the wound. He twitched with pain, his skin stinging.

"What happened?" said Kate.

"What the hell do you think happened? That son of a bitch, McLaury shot me." He washed the wound rapidly, adding more whiskey to the surface, trying to make it hurt as much as possible.

"Where's McLaury now?"

"He's dead," said Doc, his voice wavered. "Didn't you see anything? Didn't you hear?"

Kate shook her head, "I couldn't watch. I tried but I couldn't do it. I heard the gunshots but that was it. Did Wyatt get shot too?"

"No but Morgan and Virgil are shot up real bad."

Doc took another slug from the bottle of whiskey.

His lips trembled, "Oh God Kate, it was awful, just awful." He sucked in a mouthful of air and wheezed sharply, his eyes burned as the first tears fell. He wiped them away with his sleeve. Kate touched a hand on Doc's shoulder. To Doc's surprise, he placed himself in Kate's arms and let her rock him like a baby. He sobbed deeply and dropped his head into Kate's lap. She grasped him and held him. They lay in silence. She stroked his hair, her hand stopped at the dentist's forehead.

"My God honey, you're sick."

"I know."

"Why didn't you tell me you were sick?"

"I had more important things to worry about this morning."

Kate smiled, "I wouldn't have let you out this morning if I had known."

Doc chocked a laugh, "So if I'd been healthy, you would have been happy to let me get shot."

"No buttercup I didn't mean it that way."

Doc smiled, "It sounded that way." He coughed sharply and wheezed, choking, and trying to clear the fluid from his lungs.

"Pass me the laudanum that's over there." Kate did as requested. Holliday poured a finger full into a shot glass and knocked it back. He pulled his face at the sourness of the medicine. He cleared his throat with a growl. He reached for one of Kate's chocolates and swallowed it whole.

Kate gave him a questioning look.

"I'm sorry honey I had to get the taste out of my mouth. Here's a dollar run on and get me a pot of coffee from Mrs. Fly."

"You want something to eat, you must be hungry?"

"No, but you can get yourself something if you're hungry."

Kate took Doc's money and left the room. Doc shivered and wrapped himself in the bed clothes. He stared at the wall, thinking about the day. The noise of gunfire echoed within him. His ears rang with the noise. He closed his eyes, wishing for sleep but all he could see was McLaury standing in front of him, his eyes intense and filled with hatred and anger. The cowboy lunged forward to the dentist, cursing and yelling. Doc opened his eyes, McLaury vanished and the wall became his replacement. Doc rubbed his forehead and felt lines of sweat drip down over his eyebrows. He felt overwhelmed by his emotions, he wanted to sleep but couldn't. His eyes filled with tears of frustration, he pounded his fist deep into the bed and punched the mattress over and over again until his knuckles ached.

CHAPTER TWENTY-THREE

"Is that the rain come?" said Morgan. He got up and walked unsteadily to the window, his shoulder heavily strapped, one arm gripping the other. His eyebrows were peaked in concentration, every ounce of energy going into each step. The closer he got to the window the more he smiled. He grabbed the window drape with satisfaction and pulled it aside to watch the water cascade down the glass.

Allie walked into the room and was surprised by what she saw.

"What are you doing out of bed? You're about as bone-headed as your brother moving around like that when you shouldn't be movin'. C'mon now and I'll help you sit down again."

"Leave me be Allie, I'm fine as is." A broad grin filled Morgan's face. Allie couldn't help but to smile back at him.

"If Wyatt comes back here and sees you walkin' around like nobody's business, he'll pin it on me."

"If Wyatt comes back here and causes a fuss I'll tell him to kiss my ass."

The front door opened and Wyatt walked in. Rain dripped from his oilskin and puddles of water dripped over the brim of his sombrero. He removed the hat and wiped the excess water from his long mustache. He reached for a small towel and wiped his face and hair dry.

"I'll take that jacket of yours and hang it over some newspaper to drip," said Allie.

"I can do that myself. What's Morg doing up? Did you walk to the window alone?"

Morgan smiled, "I got tired with laying around. I'm getting stronger Wyatt. Soon as this old shoulder is up to the action it's back to Campbell and Hatch's for a game of pool.

Wyatt walked to the window and took Morgan gently by the arm and helped him walk back to the couch. Morg sat down painfully, lifted his legs on to the couch and let his brother wrap the crocheted afghan around him.

"When that night comes, the champagne will be on the house. Till then, why don't you rest up some? I want to talk to you."

"What's wrong?"

"Ike Clanton's made murder charges against us for the gunfight."

"He's crazy. He wouldn't even stand and fight to save his brother. He's the one who run away."

"Well, I guess he'd rather fight with paper than guns."

"What we gonna do? I sure as hell don't want to hang for that spineless rat."

"They won't arrest us. I'll make sure they don't arrest you and Virge. It ain't right to jail an invalid. Besides," said Wyatt with a nervous laugh, "It's not as if you're going to raise hell around here or anything."

Morg's eyes sparkled, "Oh I don't know Wyatt. I could make Allie's life hell if I wanted."

There was a rap at the door.

Wyatt turned himself in the chair, trying to see the door from where he was sitting.

"That's probably Doc, he said he would come over and visit tonight. Go on and open the door Allie."

Allie walked through to the door, wiped the flour from her hands and worked the lock. The door swung open with a creek.

"C'mon on in Doc," Wyatt shouted.

There was no reply. The door closed with a bang.

Allie walked back through to the parlor, her face pale.

"What is it?"

There was a man.

"What did he want?" said Wyatt.

"He told me to beware. He cussed something awful and said that we'd get what we deserve."

"Did you see who it was?

"It was hard in the rain. He was dressed so dark."

Morgan smiled nervously, "Probably just some Halloween prank or something."

Whispering drifted into the room from outside. The whisper changed to laughter.

"There's someone by the window." Wyatt rushed over to peer through the drapes. He saw a shadow move from the side.

Someone running caused the windowpane to vibrate. There was a second of silence and the echoing bang of a pistol shot. Everyone in the little room folded flat on the floor. The bullet knocked a hole in the window pane and tiny fragments of glass sprayed into the room. Wyatt got to his feet as soon as he could and ran outside with his colt drawn. He saw the backs of two men running away from the front yard. They vaulted the white picket fence and ran out into the street. Wyatt fired a shot after them and jumped the gate. A horseman galloped up and hauled one of the men up to ride behind him and off they galloped into the darkness. The other man disappeared into the shadows, being drawn into a neighboring house. Wyatt ran out into the street with his gun raised, looking into the shadows for any clue to the identity of either man. There was nothing but the mud and the rain. The rain soaked his hair and his shirt was so drenched it showed the pink of his skin beneath.

Wyatt noticed the curtain move across the street at Stillwell's house. A shadowed face gazed from the window before it vanished from view. Wyatt wasted no time in getting indoors.

Allie was sitting on the sofa, her hands trembling. Virgil hugged her tightly and rocked her.

"Here now, drink this," he said. He gave her a shot of whiskey and she took the glass gladly and knocked the liquid back in one go. She scrunched up her face and stretched her jaw as the sharpness of the whiskey warmed her stomach.

"There you go old girl that's better now. I ain't going to let go of you until you're good and ready." Virgil hugged her tightly and rubbed her waist gently. She looked up at her husband and did her best to smile. "You're a wonderful man Virge."

"I'm just doing my job that's all."

Virgil looked up at Wyatt, "Did you see who it was?"

"Nope, I couldn't see a damn thing. I don't like it. I don't like it one little bit."

"Sit down Wyatt. They ain't coming back," said Morg.

"I'm not going to risk it. I can't have us all living in here like this. We're leaving tonight."

"What? Where will we go?"

"We can go to a Hotel."

"I ain't leaving my house. Me and Virge put too much into this house of ours. I ain't leaving," said Allie.

"We'll be safer in the hotel."

"Don't you think that you should think this over a bit Wyatt?" said Virge.

"I've done enough thinking all ready. I'm ready to leave tonight. I'm tired of watching my back. I'm going to ask Doc to come with us."

"Doc won't come along," said Morg, "He ain't scared of nothing. He won't like you bossing him around."

"Doc's not stupid. If he doesn't move then that's his decision. I know for one thing he doesn't like watching his back and he sure don't like getting woke by cowboys in a hurry."

Virgil smiled, "Ain't that the truth."

A gray horse shivered in the OK Corral. Its wet face reflected the warm light that shone across the back alley from Fly's photography studio and boarding house.

Mrs. Fly stood in the kitchen of the boarding house, ironing her husband's shirts and humming to herself. Two rooms along from the kitchen, a figure sat half in shadow at the window. The rain ran down the pain of glass in streams, casting strange shadows on Doc's sallow face. Doc gazed out of the window in a half trance. The reflections of the window became his own shadows and caused ghostly tears to fall over his cheeks. He pursed his lips in a thoughtful manner and sighed deeply. A warm glow came over him and he smiled. He sat by the window, his legs perched up on the ledge itself and his slender back leaned against the corner of the wall of his room. In his hands he clutched a letter from his cousin back in Georgia. He touched the pages gently and turned the cream paper in his hand. The letter had taken several weeks for it to arrive. The envelope was covered in black ink stamps, where the letter had been readdressed and sent on to Doc's most current destination. It was one of many letters.

Doc was not such a dependent correspondent. Sometimes, the words would reach the page but the letter would simply, never reach the mail and would finally find a home in the pocket of Doc's overcoat, the envelope, ripped and crumpled.

Doc continued to read. There was a paragraph inquiring to Doc's health, several pages devoted to the news in Atlanta, a few pages reserved for family news and then a couple of paragraphs that Martha kept open to fill with what ever she fancied. Any range of subjects from literature, music or fashion might fill this slot.

Doc turned his gaze to the rain falling outside. He remembered how he had felt the day that he had loaded his things on to the train that had carried him away from home and out to Dallas. His feelings had been divided; part of him ached to stay with his family, part of him buzzed with excitement at the life that lay out West. He had been assured by a good doctor that if he moved west that the change of climate may improve his condition. Perhaps, he had hoped, the Tuberculosis would retreat to remission and allow him to return back home after a year or so. The disease showed no signs of retreating and John Holliday, as a result, showed little sign of returning.

The wind blew in a different direction and the rain splattered the window with greater ferocity. It woke Doc from his recollections of Georgia, back to his room at Fly's. He shivered at the memories and gazed down at the letter. He coughed, soaking a segment of the paper. The spit hit the ink and caused it to run into a smeared blob. Doc finished reading and turned the room inside out, looking for a piece of paper to write with. He finally found a scrap and sat down to write a reply.

"Dear Mattie, How are you today?"

He scored it out and tried again.

"My Dear Mattie, I was overjoyed to hear..."

He scored it out again and sat thinking. He never knew how much to tell her. She knew about about the fights that he had got into. He never told her directly about them but she seemed to know anyway. Occasionally she would request a photograph to be sent and Doc would obligingly have an up to date picture taken and would send it east, but those were rare occasions. Doc was unsure how much Mattie already knew about his life and his situation. She was not naive and would surely have surmised the truth from what he wrote. He needed to confide in her but censored his stories, leaving out the reality of his physical condition, the seedy side of the saloons and the incidents that he had seen.

He preferred not to speak of the bad side at all. He would talk of the animals that he had seen out west, the colorful people and the magnificent landscapes. He would reflect on shows that he had attended and books that he had read.

'Did Mattie think that he was a killer?'

She obviously still cared or she would have given up writing a long time ago.

'How did his father feel?' Doc sighed. He knew how his father felt. 'He'd probably be willing to see me dangling,' thought Doc.

He turned back to look out of the window and tried to chase away the thoughts mingling in his head. He opened a fresh bottle of whiskey, filled a glass half full and took a drink. The cheap liquid sped quickly down his throat and settled with a warm glow deep in his stomach. He stretched his shoulders, shuffling his body into a position that was comfortable to write in. He dipped his pen in the ink and shook the excess free before starting the letter with another clean piece of paper.

"My Dear Mattie,

I enjoyed your letter greatly. You never fail to cheer me with your news of Atlanta and my family. I hope you are well. I am as well as can be expected. I'm glad my photograph pleased you.

I'm not sure how fast news travels to your end of the world but you read the newspapers so I imagine you've read about the Gunfight all ready. I am ashamed to tell you that I was a part of it and that some of my bullets helped kill the cowboys who were up against myself and the Earps. Please don't think badly of me Mattie. I swear to God, those men were evil and rightly deserved to die as they did. You may have read that I got shot in the fight, please don't be concerned. I am indeed very lucky and suffered little more than bruises. It's my pride that's injured. I feel that I have done my friends the Earps an injustice and have helped to dirty their reputation. It is a terrible thing that has occurred. I don't think that things will ever be the same. I don't believe that all of this is over just yet.

Today I watched the Clanton and McLaury funeral. It was quite an occasion, the likes I have never seen. The procession took the entirety of Allen Street and everyone was obliged to stop and watch. There was a silver trimmed hearse, with pitch black horses in black, netted trappings. There were at least thirty of the cowboy gang walking behind the hearse, a carryin' signs and looking mean. The signs said, "Murdered in the streets of Tombstone." They had some nerve, it sickened me to watch. They had hired the local brass band and a big old snare drum was being beat at the front of the procession; like they was going to bury the town heroes. They had two black Thoroughbreds pulling the hearse with the longest plumes on their heads you'd ever seen.'

Doc stopped writing, dropped the pen and pulled out the gold watch chain from his vest. He cursed, realizing the time, pulled his coat on over his shoulders, grabbed his hat and the bottle of whiskey and rushed out of the room.

He walked down the dark corridor of Fly's Boarding House and was passed by a man dressed as the devil and a woman dressed as a witch. He shook his head and questioned his sobriety and then remembering that it was Halloween, continued on his way. The devil grinned at him unnervingly as he passed by. It made him shiver.

Every corner of Fly's rung with laughter and excited voices. A door opened and a strikingly handsome woman, drunk on whiskey backed out into the corridor and crashed into Doc. He apologized and tipped his hat. She giggled and ran into the next room down, swinging her long, fake tail behind her.

'Of course,' thought Doc, 'she's dressed as a cat.' He reached the front door and pulled the fur collar of his gray overcoat around his neck, preparing for the heavy rain that awaited him. He stepped off the porch into the wet and watched a skeleton wave to him as he passed by in the alley way. Doc laughed and shook his head. He strode on through the rain and whistled casually into the darkness.

He didn't notice the shadowy figure turn down the alley behind him and raise a gun level to his head. A shot was fired and narrowly missed the dentist's overcoat. The whiskey bottle smashed around the neck and dripped bourbon over Doc's hand and on to the wet street.

Doc dropped the neck of the bottle, drew his gun and turned. A tall man dressed in a long black cloak stood before him. Doc lowered the gun, perplexed at what he saw. The man smiled at him and tipped his hat,

"Happy Halloween," he said.

He turned and slunk away until he was hidden in the darkness. Doc fired shot after shot, until the figure had completely disappeared. He peered into the darkness. His gun was empty and the rain had soaked his wool overcoat. He was surprised to see Behan's deputies appear from the shadows and grab him from behind, bending his arms behind his back.

"Well now, shooting at the shadows were you Doc? Come on, we've got a surprise waiting for you back at the calaboose."

Doc strained against the men and kicked the nearest of the two in the shins. The man yelled out and in his pain, reached for his gun. He slammed the barrel of the colt down hard against the back of Doc's head, knocking the dentist into the mud. The men dragged the dentist away, a stream of his blood dripped on to the wet ground.

CHAPTER TWENTY-FOUR

Doc was unsure of the thing that woke him, perhaps it was the intensity of the light that was shining on his face, or the pungent smell of sweat from the bunk mattress. He opened one eye and gazed at the worn, white wooden walls around him and the small metal barred window and needed no clue as to his location. He tried to move and felt the full impact of the blow to the head he had suffered. He heaved and reached for the slosh bucket on the floor, vomiting a trail of spit and what little else he had contained in his stomach.

"Oh God," he groaned, "what in hell in name was I drinking? I haven't felt this hungover since the Forth of July."

"It's not a hangover, you got buffaloed."

Doc opened both eyes and looked around the cell. In the far corner, sitting on the floor, was Wyatt, looking unshaven, unwashed and thoroughly bedraggled. His white shirt was stained with blood and mud splatters. One of the shoulder seams was ripped. His face was pale, his eyes circled in bruises and his lips cut and swollen.

"What happened to you?"

"McLaury's older brother rode in from Texas last night. He's madder than hell and wants revenge for us shooting his brothers. He fell in with Ike and the pair are charging us with murder. Behan was only too happy to lend the cowboys his deputies for the night, which I guess is why we're both sitting here."

"What about bail, can't they bail us?"

"Behan made sure there's no bail."

"I don't like this Wyatt. This jail couldn't hold a sedated dog. What if they lynch us tonight? I don't much like our chances, there won't be a police force to protect us."

"Don't worry about it. I've got friends to guard us. Dan Tipton is out there right now with Texas Jack. Virge has friends in the force. We'll be well enough protected."

Doc sighed and placed his head in his hands, "I'm sorry. I don't know how the hell we got in this mess but I'm certain that I'm to blame. I shouldn't have walked down the street that day. You told me not to and I came along anyway."

"You never do anything I say anyway. Virge made the decision. We needed all the help we could get."

"I'm a damn fool. My father always told me I'd amount to nothing. I guess he got what he wanted."

"Don't take it so hard. I've met plenty of fools and you sure ain't one of them."

Doc laid stiffly down on the bunk and pulled his cards from out of his top pocket.

"I appreciate that Wyatt, but you don't know the half of what I've been through."

"You've got a degree don't you? That's more than I've got. I dropped out of college."

"You was at college?" said Doc sitting up.

"Yeah, two of the worst months of my life. I was studying law, I fell in love and got lazy, next thing I know I was married, my wife was pregnant and I had dropped out to become a two-bit deputy in a small Missouri town."

Doc smiled a devilish smile, "Must have been awful busy to do all that in two months?"

"I was. I was so busy chasing my tail I could hardly tell if the sun was shining."

"So what happened?"

She got sick and died. She lost the baby and then shortly I lost her too."

"I'm sorry. What did you do?"

"I can't really remember but I know I got in a fight with her brothers one night. They said that her dying was all my fault. They said I didn't take care of her. I had been drinking and I didn't take that too easy. I beat the shit out of her youngest brother. Her family never spoke to me again after that. They made sure I lost my job, got me kicked out of town. I drifted south to Arkansas. I needed drinking money, so I stole a horse and sold it for as much as I could get.

"You stole a horse? Did you get caught?"

"Yep, I was stupid. I picked the finest Thoroughbred in the stable. He was a beauty and sorely missed. It wasn't long before they caught up with me and threw me in jail. Then my father rode from Missouri to pay my bail. I ran before they had a chance to hang me."

Doc smiled, "My God Wyatt. That is one hell of a story."

"So you see if anyone's the loser, it's me."

"Oh I appreciate your attempts at consoling me, but I'm still a loser."

"But you come from a good family."

"I did and I still do."

"And you're a doctor."

"I'm a dentist, not a doctor."

"Sorry."

"Don't be. I wouldn't want to be associated with that side of the medical profession anyway. They're a bunch of low grade, swindling, carpet baggers, except for my Uncle of course."

"He's the one that got you into dentistry?"

"Yes, he helped to pay part of my tuition. He was always good to me."

Doc lay back on the bunk and stared at the ceiling. A silence washed over the cell. It got quiet enough for Doc and Wyatt to hear Texas Jack and Dan Tipton talking outside of the jail.

"Dan's hands are cold. I can hear him rubbing them," said Doc.

"Yep I bet they are. I'm almost glad to be in here rather than out there. I'll guess it will drop below freezing again tonight."

"What's that? I thought I heard Ike."

"You're imagining things."

"Nope that's Ike's voice out there."

"My God you're right. What's he doing?"

The men listened intently. They could hear Ike talking to Texas Jack.

"He's trying to get in here."

"Don't worry Doc. Jack won't let him passed."

"Who the?"

"Shush. It sounds like Behan."

"What do you mean Ike can't go in there. It's not up to you who visits the prisoners."

The door swung open and Ike walked into the jail with Behan at his side.

Doc jumped to his feet and reached for his gun, realizing he was unarmed, his hand fell down by his side.

"What's he doing here?" he said.

Ike smiled, "I was just looking in on you boys. Making sure you're still where you belong, in jail doing time for murdering my brother and my best friend."

Behan gave Ike a look of disapproval.

"I'm just telling the truth. They can't get mad at the truth."

"You son of a bitch," Doc rushed towards the bars of the cell and reached his hand through the bars as far as he could, grasping for Ike. His long fingers reached for the cowboy but missed.

Ike laughed, "I wouldn't do that if I were you. Folks will be coming in to town to testify against you. Won't help your character none to be acting like some crazy rattler."

"How exactly do you expect me to act?"

"Like some honest citizen, which I know you ain't, Holliday."

"All right Ike, I've heard enough," said Behan, "I didn't bring you in here to antagonize the prisoners."

"I ain't doin' nothing that ain't legal Mr. Behan. I'm just an honest rancher."

"Well, you can be honest some place else. C'mon out and leave them boys be."

"Bye," said Ike, "see you at the hanging."

Doc glowered at the cowboy, with both his eyebrows level, his eyes as black as the barrel of a shotgun. Ike looked nervously at the dentist's face, turned away and walked out with Behan.

"Thank God that's over with," said Wyatt. He's got some nerve."

"I hate him so much. I swear I've never hated anyone so much in my entire life. I wished you had put him in the ground that afternoon. Of all the people at the fight, he was the one who should have died. He's the cause of all this."

"He wasn't armed. You can't shoot an unarmed man."

"I'm passed caring any more."

"You wait until the hearing. We'll get him then."

"And you think that will be enough to finish this?"

"I would hope it would."

"Well, I think you're a damned fool Wyatt. If you can't shoot an unarmed man you can't hang him either."

"But we can redeem our names."

"That won't be much good months from now when they're creeping around in the shadows trying to shoot us in the back."

"I'm sorry you feel that way."

"It's got nothing to do with the way I feel. Don't you see this is about survival? It's not some polite legal case like they have back East. I saw them last night, you saw them. Was that anything like any normal arrest that you've experienced? No. The

cowboy gang is devoted to none but themselves.
Nothing else matters to them Wyatt. They don't
care about the law they just care about repaying
debts and right now, in their minds we owe them
for the souls of Frank, Tom and Billy and they will
make damn sure that we pay them back."

"You're crazy. I don't believe you. We have
everything to play for in this hearing. I'm sure
we'll win. We'll be free men after that."

"And they'll be hiding in the shadows waiting for
us."

Wyatt turned his head away from his friend, not
wishing to show the anger that was seeping
through his body. The cell was unnervingly quiet.
Doc laid his head down on the bunk and stared at
the ceiling.

CHAPTER TWENTY-FIVE

A stuffed eagle hovered grimly over Wyatt's head, casting shadows over his face.

"I can't believe it's finally over," said Morgan. "A whole month, I never thought the hearing would last that long."

"It's over now, we're free men and it's all thanks to Judge Spicer. I say we drink to the Judge."

"To Judge Spicer!"

The group of men lifted their glasses full of sparkling champagne up until each man's wrist was touching, the glasses clinked together and each man drank the heavenly brew. Wyatt's mustache sparkled as the bubbles popped on his lips.

"By God, I've been waiting a long time for this."

Virge put an arm around his little brother and gave him a quick hug, "We all have Wyatt. We did it."

"We sure did," said Morg. "Did you see the look on Ike's face? I never seen him look so mad."

"Serve him right too," said Doc, "that lying cuss hasn't spoken one word of truth since last

October."

The men's joy was broken by galloping hooves and the clattering of a stagecoach. A woman screamed, "They've robbed the stage. They've robbed the stage."

The entire saloon emptied out on to the street to see the commotion. Wyatt left with Doc and his brothers, filing out into the darkness. The dust was still drifting. Four horses stood fidgeting and snorting, their necks and backs soaked in sweat. The gray lead horse had a wound to its upper chest and sweat tainted blood drizzled the gray coat and ran down over its knees. The horse panted heavy breaths, its nostrils flared and its ears cocked back in exhaustion and pain.

The armed guard held his wounded leg with his left hand, blood oozed between his fingers.

"They tried to kill me," he said, "they're crazy, they took the money and then they shot me. They tried to kill me."

"Someone get a doctor."

The gray horse roared and collapsed on to one knee. It struggled to get up on to its feet and unbalanced the rest of the team in its efforts. There was a gasp from the crowd as the horse fell over on to its side. A group of stage hands worked at unhitching and untangling the team. A doctor came over and helped the guard to walk away to a quieter place for treatment. The horse was led away from the street, staggering and limping with blood gushing from its chest. The horse disappeared from view of the crowd, but a single pistol shot determined the animal's fate and everyone flinched at the noise.

"We need to get these men. Who's willing to join me?"

There was shouts from the crowd as men volunteered.

Wyatt stepped forward, "Count me in."

Silence washed over the crowd.

"You ain't the law any more Wyatt, if it weren't for you Earps this would never have happened."

The crowd yelled in agreement.

"You need order. You can't just go running willy-nilly around the county, someone will get hurt," said Wyatt.

"What the hell do you care? You killed those men and didn't think nothing about it."

Behan stepped out in the street with his arms raised, "Okay people, look you'll have your posse if you want it but I need to deputize you all first, I expect you to follow the lead of my deputies here."

"Sure thing Marshal, we're ready. Let's get this thing going."

People from all around Tombstone mounted horses and passed guns and rifles. Wyatt cast an eye over Behan's posse, he watched Stillwell mount and check his guns. He booted his old nag in the ribs, the pony walked forward with reluctance. Behan stood like a king amongst his followers, giving orders and distributing ammunition.

"I don't believe this," said Wyatt, "half the town's leaving."

"I ain't never seen Behan so happy," said Morg.

Behan mounted his horse and beckoned his men forward with one hand raised. The posse left with galloping hooves and whoops and cries from the men.

"What the hell is Behan thinking? I hope those folks know what they're getting into."

"They'll be all right," said Virge, "If I know Behan, he won't lead them anywhere close to the gang, most likely they're riding in the opposite direction."

The men walked back into the saloon and found it almost empty. They sat back down to their champagne. Wyatt picked up his glass from the table, studied it and laid it back down.

"You know, it ain't right, us sitting here. None of this is right."

"I know Wyatt. But what are you going to do? I'm suspended; you're not legal any more."

The men sat without saying anything. The ticking of the Grandfather clock echoed in Wyatt's head. He gazed around the walls at the stuffed birds and felt their eyes bearing down on him.

Virgil broke the silence.

"You know, I don't suppose this is the right time to say this but the Editor of the Epitaph received a letter this morning. It seems that someone don't like the way he's been writing stuff in our favor."

"And how's that?" said Wyatt.

"Why don't you read it for yourself?" Virgil unfolded a piece of paper from the top pocket of his overcoat and passed it along the table.

Wyatt read the letter.

Doc saw the scrawled writing from over Wyatt's shoulder. "What does it say?" he said.

"Apparently they want to kill John Clum. They don't like his editorial style. It says to him to beware and that he's one of many that are going to behold the wrath of God. It says that there's a list of people they want dead but it doesn't say who's on the list."

Doc reached into his pocket and pulled out a brown envelope. He unwrapped a piece of paper and laid it on the table. A bullet fell out on to the sheet of paper and rattled as it rolled on the table.

"Is this the list they was talking about?" said Doc.

Virgil reached forward and took a hold of the piece of paper, pulling it from under the bullet. The first thing he noticed was that the letter was in large red, spidery letters.

"My God is that blood?" he said.

"Is what blood?" said Wyatt squeamishly.

"That's blood all right. The whole list is written in blood," said Doc. It says here they wrote it in blood, so that we'd know that it's not a hoax."

"Shit, why would anyone hoax something as sick as this?" said Wyatt, "I never could have imagined this in my life. I've come across some kooks before but this is just twisted."

"That's not all," said Doc, "read the list."

"Judge Spicer is on the list, no surprise there."

"Read further."

"We're on the list, all of us. Morg, Doc, Virge, me, we're all in here."

###

CHAPTER TWENTY-SIX

The air filled with happy chatter as people left the Bird Cage Theater. Cowboys pushed and shoved each other as they made their way outside, slamming the doors behind them. One of the cowboys lifted a Christmas wreath off the door and flung it into the center of the street, laughing and hollering. Wyatt watched the incident with disapproving eyes. He and Morgan took their time and waited until they had space to move before stepping into the street. The moon disappeared behind drifting gray clouds.

"I can't believe Virge didn't come and see the show. Where is he anyways?"

"He wanted to go over to his old office to clear out some of his stuff and say hello to the guys. It's the first time he's really been well enough to get out and do that."

"Well I don't blame him. It's hard being locked up in that hotel. I'm getting cabin fever Wyatt. Before long Allie will have me darning socks."

"I doubt it. Allie would have a fit if you messed

with her sewing."

"I love getting out. I've missed thinking about something else for a change, bar all this stuff with the cowboys. Let's go to Campbell and Hatch's and play some pool."

"No I don't think we should. We've been out a long spell all ready."

"Oh come on Wyatt. It won't hurt none. It's been months, you promised."

"No not tonight. Why don't we go to the Oriental and check the tables? I'll buy you a beer."

"Well I guess that would be all right."

The two brothers walked across the street and opened the door to the Oriental. A shotgun blast ripped the air. Pistol shots echoed and a woman screamed. Both brothers turned and rushed back out to the street.

Wyatt caught a glimpse of a cowboy's back running around the corner of the street and into the darkness. On the other side of the street a group of cowboys rushed a young woman away into the midst of a crowd of theater goers.

Wyatt wondered vaguely what the row had been about and was happy to see Virgil walk out of the crowd.

"What's with the commotion?"

"The cowboys were shooting."

"You okay?"

"I think so."

Virgil walked towards Wyatt and collapsed in his brother's arms. Wyatt caught hold of Virgil and held him. He could feel the wetness of his brother's blood soak through his coat.

"You're shot."

"I am?"

"Right through."

"I don't feel anything."

Virgil stopped talking and slipped through his brother's arms. Wyatt tightened his grip and reached around his brother's waist, to stop him from falling.

"Morg, grab his legs. We'll carry him over to the hotel."

Virgil lay in bed with sweat pouring from his forehead. He moaned as his pain increased in intensity. Lamps had been brought from all over the hotel to try and create as much light as was possible. Doctor Goodfellow measured the morphine in the syringe and let a few drops spurt from the top. Virgil closed his eyes as the needle entered his arm. The morphine stung as it entered the bloodstream. Virgil gasped at the sensation then exhaled. The pain eased and his eyelids grew heavy.

Wyatt recoiled at the sight of the needle.

"I'm going to cut out the shot. Stay calm, it's going to hurt a little."

The doctor cut the sleeve of Virgil's shirt with a pair of scissors and pulled the fabric as far away from the wound as he could. It was clear that part of the bone had splintered. The blood spurted on to everything including the bedclothes. Wyatt noticed that some blood had dripped onto the cuff of his shirt. He turned his head away so that he couldn't see the doctor cut into his brother's arm.

The scalpel entered and cut the skin. Despite the morphine, Virgil rose in the bed from the pain, sucking air and gasping. Allie clutched his hand until her knuckles grew white. She stroked his forehead. "It won't take long. Trust me," she said.

The doctor continued in his efforts. Every piece of shot required a separate cut to be made. After fifteen minutes the doctor raised his head to mop the sweat from his eyebrows. He sighed, cut another line into Virgil's arm, stopped and raised the scalpel up into the air. He dropped it on to the metal dish full of bloody shot and rubbed his eyes.

"This isn't going to work."

"Why? What's wrong?" said Wyatt.

"Perhaps Allie should wait outside. This isn't anything she needs to hear."

"Why?"

"Trust me it would be better if she leaves."

Allie looked from one man to the other, "I ain't going nowhere. I'm not leaving Virge like this. I got a right to know what's happening."

"It's for your own good," said the doctor.

"You can say it all you want, I ain't leaving."

"Let her stay," said Wyatt.

The doctor sighed, "I don't know how to put this but there's more shot in Virgil's arm than I'm going to be able to get out without cutting deep into the bone. I've all ready removed a great deal of shot."

"Can't you cut deeper?" said Allie.

"He's lost a lot of blood. I can't guarantee I'd get all the shot removed in a safe fashion and even then the chances of him losing the arm later are very high. I don't want him to suffer from blood poisoning."

"So what are you going to do?" said Wyatt.

"I need to amputate his arm."

The room was silent. Wyatt stared at the bed clothes, with his chin against his hand. He tried to think clearly about everything but there was nothing that he could think about. He could feel his eyes burning with tears and fought hard to remain calm.

"Will he be okay?" he said.

"I don't know Wyatt. Sometimes it works out, sometimes it don't. He's lost a lot of blood."

"What if we leave it be?"

"He won't stand much of a chance that way. Believe me I wouldn't take his arm unless I thought it necessary."

"Please don't take my arm," said Virgil. "Please just leave it be."

"I don't know what to say Virgil, I don't think I can get all the shot out."

"Please."

"Even if I do get it all out, it's unlikely you'll have use of the arm."

Allie leaned against the bed and sobbed. Virgil heard her crying and put all his effort and strength into moving his other arm towards her. She dropped her head to the mattress and felt his hand caress her hair, "Don't worry Allie girl, I still have one good arm to hold you with."

She opened one eye to her husband and smiled up at him, "I love you," she said.

"I love you too honey."

Doctor Goodfellow looked at the couple. "We really shouldn't waste any more time."

"Go Allie. I'll be all right," said Virge.

"I want to stay with you."

"No you don't."

Allie rose from the bed and wiped her eyes with her handkerchief. Morgan helped her out of the room.

The doctor cut deeply into Virgil's arm below the elbow and removed piece after piece of splintered bone and shot. He worked for the best part of an hour. Wyatt sat beside the bed and tried not to watch. Morgan helped to remove the bloodied sheets and bundled them up. "I'll take them downstairs. I dare say someone will know what to do with them."

Wyatt watched Morgan leave and was jealous that his brother had made himself useful.

The doctor wrapped Virgil's arm and tied the ends of the bandage tightly in a double bow. "You can ask Allie back into the room now if she likes. Perhaps she would like to help in remaking the bed, make Virgil more comfortable, that sort of thing."

Wyatt nodded and went to fetch Allie. He brought her in to see Virgil and then found himself walking from the room and out into the corridor. He passed Morgan on the stairs, carrying a bundle of clean sheets.

"Where you going?" said Morg.

"Out. There's something I need to do."

"Will you be long? I'll come with you. Don't go out there alone."

"I won't be long. You go and keep Allie company."

Wyatt rushed down the stairs before his brother had a chance to ask any more questions. He hesitated as he reached the front door. Perhaps Morgan was right, maybe it would be safer to stay indoors. He felt anger bubble up inside. He was tired of hiding. He almost wanted the cowboys to shoot at him so that he had an excuse to shoot back.

He strode over to the Wells Fargo office and banged on the door. He watched a light move from the top room to the front of the office. There was a rattling as the door was unlocked. A man pulled the door ajar and peered at Wyatt through sleepy eyes.

"What do you want?" he said.

"I need to send a telegram."

"At four o'clock in the morning? Can't it wait until later?"

"No, I need to do it now."

"Then you better come in."

The man placed the lantern down on the table beside the machine, yawned and sat down in the chair.

"I want to send this to Marshal Williams," said Wyatt. "It should read, 'Virgil Earp shot.'"

"Hold your horses. I ain't awake yet. Now from the beginning."

"Virgil Earp has been shot. Odds are he won't live. Request the rights to deputise in his absence and the funds to raise a posse."

The man's finger tapped the lever in a regular rhythm. His finger stopped.

"That's it. I don't have any more to say."

"I'd say that's plenty. I'm sorry to hear about your brother."

"So am I."

"You want to wait here for the reply?"

"No I'm going to try and get some sleep. Bring

me the reply when you get it."

"Is there anything I can get you? It won't take long to make some coffee."

"That's okay."

Wyatt left the office and stepped back out into the darkness. He walked through the empty streets, exhaustion and depression weighed him down. The giggle of a woman and the familiar voice of a man, floated down to the street from a window at the Grand Hotel.

"Shit, what the hell am I doing here? I live up the street. I got so carried away after the shooting I forgot where I was."

There was a familiarity to the giggling laughter and the voice. Wyatt watched the hotel doors from the shadows and waited for the man to leave. The doors opened and out stepped one of the cowboys. The light from the hotel illuminated his face.

"Pete Spence," thought Wyatt.

The man looked back towards Wyatt, turned and strode on down the street.

"That son of a bitch! My brother's lying dying and he don't look like he has a care in the world."

With surprise Wyatt found his frustration and curiosity get the better of him. He started after the cowboy and did his best to follow him down the dark street, walking stride with stride, footstep for footstep, shadow with shadow. He knew that he should turn and go back to the hotel but he couldn't bring himself to. He grew bolder and more curious with every stride. The cowboy walked down Fremont Street until he reached the Crystal Palace Saloon. He turned down a side alley and went through a rear entrance into a back room. Wyatt stopped short.

"Where you been all night Pete? We thought you got lost."

"I was over at the Grand Hotel with a bunch of the others."

"Spending time with your little girlfriend were you?"

"She ain't my girl."

"She ain't nobody's girl, she's a stinkin' whore."

"You take that back, she ain't a whore."

"Ah so she is your girl then?"

Wyatt tried to get closer to the door to hear.

"Where's your hat Ike?"

"I lost it after we ran. Damn near went back for it but Johnny wouldn't let me."

"Wouldn't do if someone saw you."

"Hell, everyone thinks it's me that did it anyhow."

There was a long pause. Wyatt tried to breathe as quietly as he could.

"Do you think Virgil's dead."

"Sure as hell better be. Behan won't pay us otherwise."

Wyatt almost choked. He realized his mistake and moved away from the door.

"What was that?"

"I don't know, go check."

Wyatt stepped into the shadows. He made his way down the other side of the alley and hid behind a pile of wooden crates. He saw the outline of Curly Bill peering down the alley. His long hair hung roughly around his shoulders. Curly stared at Wyatt, saw nothing, shrugged his shoulders and went back into the room, closing the door behind him with a bang.

Wyatt rushed back along Fremont, taking no time to stop in the dark. He welcomed the sight of the warm glow coming from the hotel. He climbed the stairs, went back to his room and locked the door.

CHAPTER TWENTY-SEVEN

The rattle of a ball riding the roulette wheel caused Doc to lift his head. He looked over at the party of miners and whores that played the table and turned his attention back to the faro game that he was dealing. He moved two counters on the case keeper over to the right and dealt another game. The rattle lifted his head for a second time and roars of laughter came from the winners at the roulette wheel. Doc knew the sound and peered over the top of his brown tinted spectacles to get a better look. There in full view of everyone was Kate, drunk from too much whiskey, her silk dress, pulled down over her shoulders. She was smiling and laughing with her arm around Frank Stillwell's waist. Frank put more money on the table and Kate's eyes gleamed under the lantern light. She kissed her chips and pushed them to the croupier.

Doc sighed and returned back to his game. He tried to ignore Kate, but the ball started to move around the roulette wheel with a loud rattle that rung in Doc's ears until his head ached. He concentrated on the stack of cards but his thoughts remained on Kate. He called the winner and loser and began another game.

At the far end of the Bird Cage the first act took to the stage. The noise of a squealing viola and cello filled Doc's ears. The noise exploded into a rendition of a Russian song. The thumping and thudding of the bass took a marching rhythm and the devilish rich tone of the viola rose into the air. Doc raised his eyes from his spectacles to watch a line of almost naked beauties high-step in time to the music. Feathers lined their flimsy costumes. They stomped and pranced in their cowboy boots. Doc almost felt they were taunting him.

The miners and cowboys hollered at the stage, fired their guns into the air and wolf whistled. Doc took a swig of whiskey and turned his attention back to Kate. She leaned against Stillwell, beaming with joy and liquor. The whiskey in Doc's body fueled his anger and added to his torment. He stared at the cards until the colors on the figures blurred together. Kate's tinkling laughter rang in his ears. He rose from his chair and made his way over to the roulette wheel. He approached Kate, his eyes intense. She turned around. Her smile vanished.

"What are you doing Doc?"

"I want to talk to you."

"Maybe some other time huh I'm busy playing roulette."

"Now."

"Don't make a scene. I'm having plenty fun, please don't ruin it for me."

Stillwell grinned and pulled Kate into his arms, "She's mine Doc. She told me of how you and her was apart and didn't care no more. Leave her be."

"Go away Doc. I don't need you no more."

"Let me talk to you alone."

She looked at him with a smug smile, "Why the hell would I want to do that?"

"I guess everything's straight, you're staying with me sweetheart," said Stillwell.

"You son of a bitch!"

Doc dropped his hand to his hip but his gun was with the bartender. He reached for the derringer deep in his vest but as his hand clenched the mother of pearl grip, the other members of the cowboy gang turned and stared at him. His hand released the gun and dropped down to his side.

"What you going to do Doc?" said Stillwell.

Johnny Ringo looked at Doc and laughed, "He hasn't got the nerve. Even his girlfriend could beat him up."

"This is none of your business Ringo."

"He doesn't even know."

"Know what?" said Doc.

"I had your girl Doc. She's as much mine as yours. I let Stillwell here borrow her for the night. Everything on the level, cowboys are brothers, we share everything, even our women."

"I don't believe it."

"It's true Doc. You weren't interested any more."

"Why?"

Kate smiled, "Can't I have a little fun?"

"Get the hell out of my sight!"

Ringo smirked, "He doesn't want her boys, Kate's one of us now."

"As for you Ringo, I'll meet you outside."

"Are you suggesting I waste my time fighting with a consumptive?"

"Get your gun!"

Doc turned away from the cowboys and made his way to the bartender. His head throbbed from his anger and his chest was so tight he could hardly breathe.

"Give me my gun!"

The bartender looked at him with concern.

"Give me my damned gun!"

The bar tender handed over the ivory gripped colt to Doc. The dentist strapped the gun to his hip, turned and walked into Morgan.

"Where you going?"

"I'm going to kill them bastards!"

"Now hold on. What are you talking about?"

"I can't take any more from Ringo and Stillwell. I'm going to get this over with."

Morgan shook his head, "Don't, I won't let you. We're all in enough trouble as it is."

"Let go of me! I know what I'm doing."

Doc pulled away from Morgan and returned to the cowboys. He pulled the gun from his hip as he reached the table and pulled back on the trigger.

"Now you finally get what you deserve."

Stillwell laughed, "I don't know what you mean Doc."

Ringo pushed Stillwell aside. "He means me Frank. C'mon Doc pull that trigger."

Doc smiled, "Do you think I'm stupid? You go first."

Ringo reached for his belt and pulled a Bowie knife out. It gleamed in the lantern light.

"I don't have a gun, I only have my knife, but if you take one step closer, I'll cut you so deep, you'll drain blood for days."

"You really think you can beat a gun with a knife?"

"Yes, I'm sure of it."

"You're crazy."

"I know."

Doc pushed the gun into Ringo's chest. Ringo lifted his knife to Doc's throat. Morgan took the barrel of his gun and slammed it over Doc's head. The dentist collapsed on one knee. Morgan grabbed Doc by the shoulders and dragged him away from the cowboys.

Doc opened his eyes and looked around. He lay on top of his bed at his room in the Cosmopolitan Hotel. Morgan sat at one side of the bed talking with Wyatt and drinking coffee. Doc sat up as best as he could and felt the blood rush to his head. He lay back down.

"I'm sorry. I must have hit you harder than I thought," said Morg.

"That's all right. Am I bleeding?"

"You were. You're bandaged up good though."

"I'm sure that's a pretty sight."

Wyatt pulled a chair over to the bed and lit a cigarette.

"That was something else you were getting into with Stillwell and Ringo. What on earth possessed you to start such a fight?"

"Kate."

"I thought you and her had split up?"

"We had, but it still hurts to see her."

Morgan smiled, "Well look, why don't you get

yourself tidied up some and we'll hit the town. Me and Wyatt was planning on seeing a show when you started that ruckus out there."

Doc sat up slowly, his hand clutching his head, "What were you all planning on seeing? Maybe a show will take my mind off things."

"Stolen Kisses."

Doc looked at Morgan and did his best to smile, "I think I'll have to pass."

"Oh come on Doc. Where's you sense of irony?"

Doc smiled, "I really don't want to go back out there, not tonight. I think I'd be happier staying here for a while. My head's hurting pretty bad. I may take some laudanum and call it a night."

"When's the last time we all got the chance to do something together? We've been walled up in this damned hotel for way too long. Besides tomorrow's Wyatt's birthday what you say we get him drunk?"

"I'm sorry. I just can't do it. If I see one of those bastards in there, I may have to kill one of them."

Morgan took a swig of coffee. "What about after the show? You could meet up with us afterwards. We're going over to Campbell and Hatch's to play some pool and drink some beer."

Wyatt gave Morg a strange look, "I thought we was coming back to the hotel after the show. I don't want to stay out any longer than we have to. No need to give the cowboys an open invitation."

"Oh Wyatt you ain't no fun. The cowboys haven't done anything in months."

"All right, but only one game."

"What time?"

"Half past ten."

"OK, I should be good by then."

Wyatt shook his head with a smile, "Lord Morg, you never can let things be."

"Come on we better get going. Last chance Doc, you sure you don't want to come along?"

"I'd rather stay here and fester. Oh and if you see Kate, tell her from me to burn in hell."

"I'll remember that."

CHAPTER TWENTY-EIGHT

Doc woke and checked his pocket watch, he had overslept by an hour. He rose, took his overcoat from the chair, and placed his hat over his bandaged head. He hurried across the street and along to the saloon where his friends were waiting. A dog barked in the distance. Doc cut across an alley to get to the back entrance of the bar. He squeezed past the garbage and crates. A bottle fell and smashed to the ground behind him. He turned with his hand to his holster. A black tabby cat jumped down onto one of the boxes and hissed at Doc. It switched its tail backwards and forwards. Doc sighed and climbed up the back step of the pool hall, peered through the glass and opened the door.

"Well look who's here," said Morg with a grin. "We was getting worried you wouldn't show. You're kind of late for this game but you can join the next. George here came along and made another player. You met George? Of course you know Texas Jack and Dan Tipton."

"Of course, I remember them from Dodge City." Doc reached his hand forward to shake, "nice to see you again Dan, I hope you haven't had any more trouble with horse thieves?"

"No, I can't say I have."

The men sat down beside Wyatt on the chairs at the side of the pool table. Prospector lifted his head from the ground and wagged his tail from side to side, sniffing Doc's hand.

"You sleep good?" said Wyatt.

"I sure did, I slept better than if I was dead. I thought you'd all be heading back to the hotel by now."

"I would have done but Morg here is on a roll, this is his third game. He's won two already. I don't suppose we'll get him through the door, his head's so big. The whiskey on the table's for you. Morg bought the round."

"Thank you." Doc lifted the glass to his lips and took a swallow, "Dang, this is prime bourbon."

Morg laughed, "I wasn't going to get you no gut burner."

"Thank you."

Morg reached over the table and potted the eight ball, "My pleasure, I figured I'd soften you up before I kick your ass."

Doc laughed, "What makes you so sure you'd beat me. I was a fine player back in Georgia."

"You was, you ain't worth a dime no more. You boys want to see a trick shot?"

Wyatt sighed, "You better say yes he's going to do it any way."

Morgan walked around the table, angled the cue, over his left arm. He tapped the white ball. It rolled along to the end of the table and bounced across the corner. It crossed the table again, bounced the corner and crossed the table in the opposite direction. It then came in behind the pink and knocked it into the middle pocket.

Everyone cheered, Doc whistled, Morgan laughed and took a bow.

"I ain't never seen nothing like that," said George.

"Hey George, you better chalk that cue up. I might let you play here in a bit."

Wyatt smiled, "I'd take him up on that, your opportunity might not come again."

George got up and made his way to the pool table, he reached for the chalk. Morgan watched him with a grin, "Now then, you might not know the rules so I'll run over them for you. This here is the pool table and these are the balls."

"Yeah I know that part."

"Hey Doc, you want to play?"

"Sure why not?"

"Well get you a cue. Don't use that one to the left, Wyatt says its broke or something. Personally I think that's a load of bullshit."

Doc stood up to get a cue. Prospector got up and stood with his hackles raised, a low growl emanated from his chest.

"What's wrong with the mutt tonight?" said Morgan, "You ain't got any need to growl at Doc, he ain't going to hurt you."

The dog wagged its tail at Morgan's voice but remained were it stood with its ears cocked and its back stiff. The deafening boom of a shotgun rang out in the alley. The glass panel on the side door shattered into thousands of pieces. Prospector lunged forward towards the door, barking and snarling. A second shot ran out. Everyone ran towards the door with their pistols drawn. The sound of footsteps echoed down the alley. Wyatt pushed his way outside. He ran out onto Allen Street with Dan Tipton following close behind. People from neighboring bars came out on the street to see where the shots had come from but there was no sign of the gunmen. Jim came out from the hotel and ran over to where Wyatt was standing.

"Are you okay?"

"Did you see them?"

"No I didn't see nobody."

"C'mon we all best get off the street. It might not be over yet."

Jim, Dan and Wyatt went back to Campbell and Hatch's. They picked their way across the shards of broken glass. In the far corner, George lay on the floor clutching his leg. Blood oozed through his pants and he rocked to ease the pain. On the floor beside the pool table was Morgan. He lay face down on his stomach, covered in blood and broken glass. Wyatt knelt down beside him and was relieved to hear him still breathing.

It seemed to take forever for Doctor Goodfellow to make it to the pool hall, despite him hearing the shots from across the street and running over as fast as he could. He pushed through the crowd of people that had gathered, to the back of the bar and knelt down beside Morgan. He slipped his fingers against Morgan's wrist and counted his pulse.

"Is he still breathing?" said Wyatt.

"I think so. Help me lift him onto the couch in the poker room. There's no point in him lying on his face like that."

Morgan cried out as he was rolled over.

"It's all right Morg, hold steady."

"Okay let's lift him."

Morgan whimpered as they lifted him, broken glass pressed into his body.

"Please don't. I can't bare it."

Wyatt and the doctor tried their best to be gentle but the pain registered in Morgan's face. He was pale and quiet the whole time he was being carried. The men lowered him onto the fainting couch in the card room. Wyatt brushed broken glass from his hands. One of his fingers was bleeding but he didn't care. Texas Jack moved the crowd back out on to the street. The door to the card room was closed and a strange quiet fell over everyone.

"That's better, least now we can see you," said the doctor.

Morgan's blood flowed readily and it wasn't long before the velvet fainting couch was covered in patches of red. The doctor studied the gunshot wounds and measured the depth of each one, making a note of the amounts of shrapnel. The largest was over four inches long and had cut cleanly through Morgan's back. Doctor Goodfellow looked at the wound and shook his head sadly. He put his hand under Morgan's leg and lifted the left and then the right in turn, flexing the knee and hip joints and letting each leg drop.

"Does it hurt when I do this?"

Morg shook his head. "I can't feel a damned thing."

The doctor opened his case and removed a syringe, loaded it with morphine and shot the substance into Morgan's arm. He got up from his patient and closed the bag.

"What's wrong, can't you get the buckshot out?" said Wyatt.

"No."

"But there must be something you can do?"

"There's nothing. I'm sorry Wyatt."

"That's it?" said Doc.

"I've done what I can. His spinal cord is shattered, it's only a matter of time. I'm sorry."

Morgan looked up at Wyatt with quivering lips. He tried to smile, "It's funny, I never figured it would end like this. I guess this is the last game of pool I'll ever play."

Wyatt smiled at Morgan's attempt at humor but the light in his eyes soon vanished.

There was a knock at the door. Jim opened it and let his brother Virgil in. He walked unsteadily, his face was ashen and a blanket was wrapped around his shoulders. Allie supported him as well as she could for her small size, her arm barely reaching across his back. She led him over to Morgan and helped him sit down beside his brother.

Wyatt knelt down by the couch and clutched Morgan's hand. His brother reached up and made his best attempt to hug him. Wyatt grabbed him and clutched him tightly.

"I'm going to miss you," he said.

Morgan whispered into Wyatt's ear and then dropped his grip. His arms grew limp and his hand loosened from Wyatt's. His eyes closed and his face grew expressionless.

Wyatt grasped his brother's hand.

"If I'd known this was to happen, I never would have come here."

"It's not your fault Wyatt," said Virgil.

"I'll never forgive myself for this. He was our little brother."

The brothers stood next to Morgan's body. From beyond the doors of the card room Prospector whined and yelped in a pitiful manner. He broke into a heartfelt session of baying and howling. A heavy feeling of disgust and desperation washed over Doc until the situation was unbearable to take. He walked out of the card room door without saying a word.

"Doc, where you going?" said Wyatt.

He walked on without turning back.
"Don't go out there alone. Please Doc."

Doc walked on ignoring Wyatt and sought out the shadows. He walked down every alley and every dark corner with his gun clenched in his hand. He climbed up the back steps to the room at the back of the Grand Hotel and banged on the door.

Wyatt chased after him.

"What are you doing?"

"I'm going to kill them for this. I'm going to find them and kill them."

He banged on the door. A man in a nightshirt answered, "What's going on?"

"Where the hell are they? I know they're in here."

"Who's in here? What are you talking about?"

"Doc, let's go," said Wyatt.

"I'm not going anywhere. I know this is the cowboy's meeting room. Where the hell are they?"

Doc lifted his gun to the man's chest. "Tell me where they are?"

The man looked perplexed and he raised a shaking hand to Doc, "Please, I don't know what you're talking about. There's nobody here bar me and my wife. I work at the hotel. This is my home."

Doc slammed the door in disgust and went outside. Wyatt ran after him and grabbed him by the shoulder.

"Get away from me!"

"Please think this through. You're not helping anything."

"I'm going to kill those bastards."

"Doc please?"

Doc turned and walked down to the reception at the Grand Hotel. He pounded the bell at the desk until a clerk rushed through from the back, to help him. Doc lifted his pistol to the man's face.

"What do you want?" he said.

"Stillwell, Spence and Brocius, I want you to look them up in the register for me."

"Yes sir, right away. Do you know which room they're in?"

Doc engaged the trigger, "Look them up!"

"They're not here Sir."

"What do you mean?"

"They checked out this afternoon."

Doc swept the book from the counter and knocked it on the floor. He ran up the stairs until his breath was knocked from his lungs. He wheezed and choked, trying to get his breath back while walking from door to door, searching.

Lodgers opened their doors to look out on the ruckus. "What in hell is going on?" said one person. "It's that Holliday, he's crazy," said another.

Anger filled Wyatt. He took a swing at Doc, punched him under the chin and knocked him to the floor. Doc got up on one knee and tried to stand. Wyatt punched him down a second time.

The people gawked at Wyatt, chattering and gossiping about what they had seen. Wyatt glared at them, "It's late. Isn't anyone tired tonight?"

The crowd of people drifted back to their rooms and shut their doors.

Doc squatted on the floor, his leg bent at an odd angle, his expression dazed. He got up, faltered, and wobbled, then fell back onto the floor. Wyatt reached his hand out to him. Doc looked up into Wyatt's disapproving eyes. He felt ashamed and tears swelled up inside of him. He fought them back but to no avail.

"Oh God Wyatt. I'm so sorry. I never wanted for all this to happen. Please forgive me."

"Get up," said Wyatt.

Doc reached for Wyatt's hand and let his friend pull him back on his feet. He wiped tears from his face and swiped a line of blood from his nose.

"I'm sorry Wyatt."

"It's okay. Let's go home."

CHAPTER TWENTY-NINE

The following afternoon, Doc left his hotel room and walked down the stairs to the front parlor. He wore a black suit and clutched his hat in his hands. His skin was colorless and so transparent that the veins in his forehead were showing. His eyes were bloodshot and shadowed from lack of sleep. His nose was swollen. He peered through the stained glass of the parlor door and knocked. Texas Jack opened the door, a shotgun resting on his shoulder. Doc nodded at Jack and entered the dark room with some hesitancy.

The casket lay open on a table surrounded by flickering candles. Wyatt stood in the darkness, his face reflected in the soft candlelight. He turned to face Doc and although it was hard to tell in the dim light, Doc thought that Wyatt's eyes were still wet from crying. Doc looked down at Morgan and wished that he was elsewhere. He had spoken with Wyatt the night before about the arrangements but it hadn't seemed real at the time. Now to see everything in the light of day was heart breaking.

Morgan wore one of Doc's suits, his own ruined during the shooting. The sleeves of the suit were an inch too short. Sunflowers surrounded his body. The cheerful yellow of the flowers stood in stark contrast to the darkness. On hearing of Morgan's death, everyone had wanted to contribute something or offer sympathy. There were cards and notes of condolence covering the far end of the table.

Wyatt stood behind the casket with a pained expression on his face. Doc looked up at his friend and down at Morgan.

"I should be the one lying there. It was me that Stillwell wanted."

"Don't Doc. It's not worth tormenting yourself over. Morgan wouldn't want that."

"It wasn't even his fight."

"He told me one time back when we was looking that hit list over that he wanted to be the one to die. He said, he couldn't bear having to watch one of us get killed, that if one of the Earps was to die that it would be him."

Tears ran down Doc's cheek, he covered his face with his hand and bit his lip to stop himself from crying.

Wyatt could see his friend falling apart in the dim light.

"Please don't," he said, "I can't take it right now. You'll have me crying again and I don't want none of the women to see."

Doc sniffed and wiped his eyes with the back of his hand, "I'm sorry Wyatt. It's hard not to."

"I know that. As soon as this is over, we're leaving. I'm taking Morg home to California. I'll have guards to watch the train."

"What about the cowboys?"

"I've spoke to Marshal Williams about getting money to form a posse. I'm going to string up every damned cowboy in the territory if needs be. I need you along for the ride. Will you do it?"

Doc looked surprised, "Yes," he said.

"Good be ready."

Outside in the streets the fire bell tolled long and low, the noise reverberated in the wind. Doc looked up to the window and shivered at the eerie noise.

"You know once this is begun there'll be no easy way to finish it?" he said.

Wyatt nodded.

Jack opened the door. Behan entered and took his hat from his head. Wyatt raised his head and turned to meet the uninvited guest.

"I came to pay my condolences and to see you Wyatt. How are you're doing? I need to talk to you about my deputy, Mr. Stillwell. It appears there has been some talk around town. I'm concerned that his reputation is being unfairly tarnished."

"I have nothing to say of Stillwell. The way I see it, he's a dead man."

"If you dare touch my deputy, I'll haul you back here in shackles and have you hanged before the day is over."

"Johnny, the way I intend, you won't get to see me again let alone catch me. Now get the hell out!"

###

Holliday watched as the pallbearers lifted

Morgan's casket onto the train. He stubbed out his cigarette with the toe of his boot and climbed on board. He followed the pall bearers into the closest carriage. The men lowered the casket down onto one of the tables, supported by the back of the seats.

Allie watched the men leave the casket. She tried to smile and turned her attention to making her husband comfortable. Virgil sat beside her with his shoulder and side strapped together. His face was pale and despite his large frame, he was slow and weak, relying on Allie's help. He looked over at the casket with a pained expression and then down at the pistol that lay against his wife's side. He smiled at the strange sight, the large gun rested in a strange fashion against her checkered dress. He reached his right hand across and squeezed Allie's hand.

Doc walked up to the casket. Despite the company of the Earps, he felt alone. He placed his hand up against the wood, wanting to be closer to Morgan. In his mind, he almost expected to see him board the train with a smile, walk over to where he stood, and lay a hand on his shoulder. There was nothing, only the light from a lamp reflected on the wood paneling.

Wyatt walked up from behind and startled Doc at his appearance.

"I didn't mean to scare you."

"That's okay I was just thinking about Morg."

"I know." He took a long look at the casket, "C'mon, it's getting dark out and we need to let everyone get going."

He walked down the length of the carriage, Doc

followed closely behind. Wyatt stopped in front of
his brother. Virgil looked up at Wyatt,

"Take them out Wyatt. You've got my blessing."

"I'll do that and more. I'm going to get every
damned cowboy in the territory if needs be."

"Be careful, last thing I need is to lose another
brother."

"You won't. I won't let them have the pleasure.
Look after Morg, give him a fine funeral."

"I promise you he'll be well looked after. Safe
journey Wyatt, God willing we'll see you back in
California."

"I'll be back home before you know it."

"Goodbye Doc it was good knowing you. I don't
suppose we'll see each other again."

"I figure not."

"Sorry to interrupt," said Texas Jack, "but Dan
said he saw Stillwell and Ike entering the lunch
room on the other platform."

"Has anyone seen them leave?"

"We haven't seen them but there's been word
that someone is moving about in the shadows out
there. We think Stillwell's on the opposite platform
watching the train."

"I ain't going to sit here and make him a pretty
target."

Wyatt followed Jack out into the darkness. Doc
walked closely behind. Wyatt stepped down onto
the tracks. The noise of the train blowing smoke
was deafening. Each man filed down the track and
walked along the body of the train until they could
see the opposite platform. There on the other side
was Stillwell edging his way around looking for a
clear shot through the train window.

"Stillwell!" shouted Wyatt.

The deputy looked up, stunned. Wyatt walked down towards him and he raised the shotgun under his arm until it was level with Stillwell's face. Wyatt expected the deputy to run but he stood trembling in the lantern light that shone down from the front of the engine. Wyatt walked closer, until the light from the lantern painted a hazy aura around him. The men stood less than two feet from one another but despite the closeness, it was hard to see details in the dark. Wyatt pressed the gun into Stillwell's body.

"I know what you did that night. Don't think that you're going to get away with it."

Stillwell's eyes grew large and contorted. He trembled in the darkness and stared up at the gun. The light shone in his eyes.

"Oh my God Morgan!"

Wyatt drew back both pins on the gun and eased back on the trigger. Stillwell screamed. The noise of the shot echoed around the station. Stillwell fell backwards on the tracks, his coat burning from the close impact. Wyatt looked down at the body and released the second load of buckshot. A shot was fired from behind, he spun around. Ike Clanton was running for his life. Dan was chasing him as fast as he could.

"What's happening?"

"Ike tried to shoot you in the back," said Doc. "He saw you shoot the hell out of Stillwell, he turned and ran. So this is Stillwell?"

Wyatt nodded.

Doc pulled his pistol from his coat pocket and fired two shots into Stillwell's head. Wyatt gave his friend a questioning look.

"I'm sorry Wyatt. That bastard deserved to die more than once."

"At this point I don't care any more - one for Morgan."

Doc smiled in the darkness. Wyatt walked by the window of the train and raised one finger up to the window. Virgil looked out the window and caught Wyatt's gesture and smiled. The train bell rang and the train pulled out of the station, puffing and blowing. Wyatt watched the train pull away until it was hard to distinguish the back of the train from the darkness.

"That's the last we'll see of Morg."

"C'mon Wyatt, we need to get going."

Wyatt followed Doc to the side of the train station and strode up onto the platform. In the darkness a man walked towards them, his face hidden in shadow. He stared at Wyatt for a long while but walked on and disappeared down a side entrance to the platform.

"That man seemed strange," said Wyatt.

"What about him?" said Doc.

"He stared at me as if he knew me."

"If I'd just seen you turn Stillwell into a colander the way you just did with that gun of yours, I'd probably be staring too."

"So you don't think there was anything strange about it?"

"Not under the circumstances I don't."

CHAPTER THIRTY

Wyatt took one last look at Morgan's old room at
the Cosmopolitan Hotel and checked that nothing
had been left behind. He stood at the window and
gazed down onto Allen Street. A crowd of men
had gathered, some were mounted, nearly all of
the horses had a rifle holster on the saddle. Wyatt
looked to the far corner of the window shade and
thought he saw Behan sitting up straight on his
horse smiling and giving orders.

"What's going on?" said Doc.

Wyatt startled and turned. He relaxed when he
saw who it was.

"It looks like they're putting together a posse."

"For us?"

"Yes, I'm guessing that's what they have in
mind."

"Is that Ringo and Spence?"

"I don't think Spence is down there but that's
Ringo all right."

"That slime bucket was too scared to go it alone
then?"

"I guess he thinks he'll be safer in Behan's company. I heard someone say he wanted Behan to arrest him."

Doc laughed, "I've a good mind to go jig that spineless toad and see what he does."

"You'll leave him alone. Best we ride out of town quiet and alive."

Doc looked around the darkened room.

"It's still so hard to believe."

"I know. I can't hardly stand to be in here but I couldn't bare the thought of leaving anything of his behind. I came for one last look."

"It don't seem right. I keep wanting him to walk in that door and say he was only fooling that night, that it didn't happen."

"I know."

The noise of horses hooves on the street outside diverted both men's attention.

"Come on we'd better get going."

Wyatt and Doc walked out into the corridor. They met Wyatt's older brother Jim on the landing. He hugged Wyatt.

"Take care. Give them hell. I'll be waiting for you in California."

"When are you getting out of here?"

"Today hopefully."

"Be careful."

"Don't worry they've got no gripe with me. I served free beer to those boys plenty of times."

Wyatt smiled, "I don't think they're thinking of free beer today."

"Go on Wyatt. I don't want you all to get holed up in here."

Wyatt nodded and gave his brother one last look.

He turned and walked down the stairs. Doc nodded at Jim and followed Wyatt. He met with the rest of the posse by the door of the Grand. Texas Jack stood with his shotgun, relieved that they were finally ready to leave. To his right was Jack Johnston, behind was Dan Tipton, Wyatt's youngest brother Warren and finally to the far side was Sherm McMasters. The group walked out to where the horses were tied. Doc slung his saddlebags over the back of the saddle of Wyatt's chestnut Thoroughbred and Warren took Virgil's dapple-gray. The odd man out was Jack Johnston who unhitched his little, piebald mustang and swung his long legs into the saddle. His heels hung far below the pony's belly.

"Kind of small ain't he?" said Wyatt.

"He's tough though. He don't bellyache like a Thoroughbred does. I rode him clear all the way from Texas and never once did he get sore on me."

"Well, if you think he can keep up, you're more than welcome to bring him along."

"He can keep up with them pedigree knuckleheads mark my words we ain't going to fall behind."

"Let's get going then."

The men turned their horses and rode down the center of Allen Street away from Behan's posse. Doc glanced over his shoulders at the men that were gathered in the center of the street, still listening to Behan talking, too busy to notice them all slip away down a side street, out onto Fremont and out to the desert and the Dragoon Mountains beyond. The horses broke to a canter, feeling the desert floor beneath their hooves. Doc spurred his

ISOLATE

horse forwards, still glancing behind. He felt excited to be so close to the mountains after so little riding but nervous at the thought of being brought back to Tombstone by Behan. It was sad that they were finally leaving but in the same breath it was a great relief to be gone.

For hours the riders climbed further into the Dragoons, winding through a maze of boulders, ocotillo cactus and creosote bushes. They crossed up across the mountains and down along a river bed and a thick swatch of cottonwood and sycamore trees. The horses needed no invitation to go to the water and happily walked across the river's shallow bed to take a drink. Wyatt let the reins loose and kicked his feet free from the stirrups, letting his legs dangle. Doc pulled his horse up beside Wyatt's and let it drink.

"How much further do you think we have to go?"

"We're practically there."

"Do you think Pete will be here?"

"There's only one way to find out."

Wyatt pulled up his horse's head and set off up the dusty road at a steady trot. The rest of the posse followed as close as they could. In a clearing there stood a small wooden shack with log piles laid out on either side. Wyatt dismounted and gave the reins to Doc. He knocked on the door. A skinny Mexican man answered. He looked worried when he saw Wyatt, but stood silently waiting for Wyatt to talk.

"We're looking for Pete Spence. Is he here?"

"Que?"

"Where is Pete Spence?"

"No entiendo."

Wyatt cleared his throat and spoke hesitantly, "Donde esta Pete Spence?"

The man shrugged and swatted a fly from his face. Wyatt was frustrated.

"It's all right Wyatt. I can set him straight," said Sherm. He brought his horse over to the cabin and explained the situation to the man in polished Spanish. The man smiled and nodded his head in understanding.

"Él no está aquí," he said.

"He's not here," said Sherm.

Wyatt sighed. "Does he know where he is?"

Sherm asked and the Mexican laughed and answered.

"Well that beats all!"

"What did he say?"

"He said that Pete Spence is in Tombstone. He had Behan arrest him under one of his previous stage robbing charges. Behan's protecting him right now."

The Mexican continued to talk with a grin.

"He said that Spence is a coward to run and hide and not brave like him to stay out in the open. He says he saw Spence the night he killed your brother."

Wyatt's eyes lit up, "What does he say about that night? How did he see him?"

"He said that he was in the alley behind the saloon. Por qué estabas allí?"

The man's eyes lit up and he laughed.

"What did he say?"

"He was paid to hold the horses while they shot Morgan. He said they paid him twenty-five dollars to do it and he was glad of the money. He bought himself a beer after wards."

Wyatt grew quiet and pale. He took the reins of his horse and mounted. The Mexican sensed the atmosphere changing and realized that he had said too much. He looked up into Wyatt's eyes, turned and took to his heels, running as fast as he could up the hill behind the cabin. Wyatt was surprised at the man's reaction and kicked his horse into a steady canter. He reached the crest of the hill in no time and watched the man stumble and trip his way down the other side, puffing and panting all the way. Wyatt pulled his revolver, lined the gun up with the man and shot him cleanly between the shoulders. The man yelled out and fell to the ground.

Wyatt cantered over to where he lay and dismounted. He rolled the man over onto his back. The man's eyes stared up at him with a shocked gaze. Johnson rode up along with the rest of the men.

"He's dead," said Wyatt.

"Good he deserved it," said Doc.

"Come on let's get out of here. It's getting late and I sure as hell don't want to have to camp any where near that bastard."

The men broke their horses forward to a trot and made their way out from the trees and across the hills.

"What time was that money getting dropped off Wyatt?"

"Three o'clock. Warren said they would meet us out at Iron Springs. They didn't meet up with him last night. I have to hope they'll be there today. We need the money."

"Damn straight," said Doc, "I'm tired of sleeping in the thicket like some demented alley cat. I'd give my eye teeth for a bed right now."

"It ain't so bad," said Jack.

"I'm tired of checking the bed clothes each night and checking my boots every morning for creatures. Right now I'm craving a steak, a glass of bourbon and some clean sheets."

"Well I'll buy the bourbon if it will keep you from whining," said Jack.

"This is the last night in the wilds Doc, I promise," said Wyatt. "Tomorrow night we'll be back in society again."

The riders rode along the side of a line of pine trees and down along a sandy rise. Wyatt loosened his gun belt a couple of notches and steered with his other hand. He kicked his feet free of the stirrups and let his long legs dangle.

"I'll be glad of a break," said Dan.

"You're not the only one."

"Any chance of me bumming a cigarette, I'm out of smokes?"

"Sure Sherm I'll loan you some. Mind and pay me back when we hit town."

"No problem."

Doc threw Sherm his silver cigar case. The cowboy caught it easily with one hand, flipped the top, put a cigarette in the corner of his lips, struck a match against his chaps and lit the end. His horse smelled the smoke and snorted but kept a walk and shook its head, making the bit chain jangle. Sherm took a puff and blew out. He rested his hand on his leg with the cigarette close to his

chaps. He swung his leg up over the horse's neck
and sighed with pleasure. He closed the case with
his steering hand and flipped it over.

"August fourteenth. What the hell's that mean?"
he said.

"It was a birthday present from Kate."

"Thought you two had split?"

"We have, but I can't bear to part with it."

"I didn't know you cared so much."

"Damn straight I do, that case is pure silver."

Sherm grinned and threw it back to Doc, who
caught it one handed.

Wyatt shook his head with a smile. He rode
closer to the rise. His stallion snorted and sucked
air like it had spied a snake. Its eyes rolled in its
head. It dropped, twisted its shoulders, slid in the
soft sand, raised a front leg and snatched at the bit.

"Quit that!" said Wyatt. He rubbed his spur into
the horse and patted its neck. The stallion
hesitated, gave a gruff snort and slid further back
onto its haunches. Wyatt kicked with his heels but
the horse wouldn't move.

"Okay, have it your way. If I have to lead you
through this damn rise, then so be it."

Wyatt dismounted and flexed his stiff legs. He
took the horse by the rein and walked a stride
forwards. The horse snorted and pulled
backwards. Wyatt turned and saw Curly Bill stand
up from behind the rise, a shotgun raised in his
hands. A group of cowboys stood up with him.
Curly fired the gun and the noise of the shot
echoed around the gully. The stallion roared and
reared. Wyatt moved to avoid the metal shod
hooves that flailed near his head. He reached for

his Winchester, but the horse spun in the opposite direction. It backed up and twisted around in a tight circle with its head high in the air. A second shot tore through Wyatt's open coat, ripped the material to shreds, broke the saddle horn and knocked it to the ground.

A third shot from Curly's friend tore across the gully and shot Johnson's horse in the chest. The little mustang screamed, roared, and collapsed on its side, pinning Johnson's leg to the ground. He sunk his hands into the sand and dug a hole from around his leg and slid out from beneath the dying animal who still kicked the air in spasms. He looked around and saw the rest of the posse beat a retreat behind a line of bushes. He pulled himself free. Texas Jack turned and saw that Johnson was out in the open, galloped back and hauled him up onto his horse and away to cover.

Wyatt stood alone in the gully. He gave one last effort to reach the Winchester, the horse moved in his favor and the gun pulled loose from the saddle sheath. He lifted the rifle and tucked it under his shoulder, sighted Curly Bill's shadow and fired. The cowboy folded clean at the waist and dropped to the ground. Wyatt fired a second shot. Curly's friends saw him fall and took to running. Wyatt saw his chance, pulled his holster up and vaulted onto the back of his horse. He rode back to where the rest of the posse was hiding.

"My God Wyatt! Are you okay?" said Doc, "Your coat's torn to pieces."

"I'm not shot. I thought you were behind me and I turned and you'd all gone."

"I figured you'd do the same Wyatt," said Texas

Jack.

"Well you figured wrong. I'm sorry about your horse. We've time if you want to get the saddle."

Johnson nodded in appreciation. The posse watched and waited looking out for Johnson as he made his way back to his horse. He bent down in the sand, next to the horse's belly and lifted the saddle flap to untie the girth from the saddle. The knot was easy to release but the cinch wouldn't budge under the horse's weight. Johnson let go of the girth strap with frustration and tried the bridle instead. He undid each strap in turn and with some effort got the horse's mouth open far enough to remove the bit. He cradled the horse's head in his arms, pulled the bridle off its head and sobbed. Texas Jack and Dan Tipton walked over to the horse and bent down. They spoke words to Johnson and helped him move the animal to where they could cut the girth free. Johnson took the saddle from the back of the horse and stood back up. He looked the mustang over for the last time and walked back with Dan and Texas Jack to where the rest of the men waited.

"I'm sorry Jack," said Wyatt. "He was a fine pony."

"That's all right. These things happen. I'm just glad none of us is dead."

"We'll get you a good horse from Hooker. God only knows we all need a chance to rest up any how."

Jack nodded, "Thanks." He took Texas Jack's hand and pulled himself up behind the saddle of his horse.

"We'll take it in turns," said Wyatt. "There's no

point in wearing out any one horse over this. If we have to walk in stretches, then so be it."

CHAPTER THIRTY-ONE

Wyatt placed his fork on his plate. "That was a fine meal Henry. That's the best steak I ever tasted."

"It should be, it was eating grass just this morning."

"I'm sure the boys thank you for your hospitality."

"Oh no problem, it was the least I could do for you, I don't know if I approve of your style but either way it's good to know that Curly Bill won't be causing any more bother. You know there's a reward don't you? The cattleman's association put forward the money. I can arrange to have a part or all of it wired tomorrow."'

"That's not necessary, I didn't do it for the money."

"I know you didn't. Another one for Morgan huh?"

Wyatt nodded, sighed and got up from the table. He pulled his pipe from his top pocket and opened the door to the back porch. Henry's dogs rushed to

the door, sniffed Wyatt's legs and wagged their
tails. Wyatt pushed them away and walked outside
onto the porch. He sat down on a bench by the
window, watching the light dim over the lake.
Henry looked out at the shadowed figure.

"There's a lantern out there, it's getting dark."

"Thanks, I'm fine."

"I'm sorry for everything that's happened. I
didn't know Morg too well, but I've never heard a
bad word spoke against him."

"These things happen." Wyatt pulled his pack of
tobacco from the top pocket of his shirt and
dropped a pinch in the pipe. "Can you sell me a
horse? Sherm had his horse killed back in the
gulch."

"Sure it's the least I can do. Tell him he can pick
a horse tomorrow morning. I'll have one of the
men run them by. There are some good colts from
last year just broke."

"That would be fine."

"Have you had a chance to read the newspaper
yet?"

"No not yet."

"Ike is claiming that you're all dead."

"Really?"

"Yes, that's what he's saying. Doc was so mad
when he heard he's writing a letter to the Editor."

"That sounds like Doc for sure."

The men grew silent. Wyatt puffed on his pipe.
The red embers glowed in the darkness. Henry felt
awkward and thought of things to say but nothing
that came to mind seemed to be the right thing.

"Well," he said finally, "I suppose I better get
back inside. I've a stack of papers on my desk and

dust ain't going to clear them."

"Thanks, Henry."

"You're welcome. Yell if you need anything."

The screen door slammed shut and left Wyatt alone with the crickets and the dark. Wyatt sat back on the bench and crossed one knee high over the other. He stared into the darkness, watching ripples on the water beyond. He felt something cold rub against his leg and then the warmth of a wet muzzle against his hand. He looked down at the long body of a dog that was neither greyhound or beagle but a strange mixture of the two. The dog nuzzled Wyatt's hand and whimpered. It sat down beside the bench and offered a paw. Wyatt looked down at the dog, he placed his pipe into the corner of his mouth, reached down and took the dog's paw and shook it gently. The dog raised its head, its dark brown eyes, sad and intense, and whined. Wyatt stroked the dog's head and thought of Prospector. He had been Wyatt's dog at the start but had loved Morgan. The hound had ridden the train from Tucson and sat next to Morgan's casket during the journey. Tears fell down Wyatt's face. The dog cocked its head sideways, one ear raised, listening. Wyatt moaned and wrapped his arms around the dog and hugged it. The dog sat still, as if it understood.

The screen door opened and closed with a bang. The dog spooked at the noise and ran away into the darkness, disappearing into the gloom. Doc walked outside and fiddled with the lantern. A gradual glow grew from the bottom to the top and light spilled across the boards and across the bench.

"Don't turn it too bright."

"Wyatt? I didn't know you was out here ain't no point in sitting alone in the dark, the boys have got a poker game going in the parlour, some of the ranch hands have joined in, it's shaping up to be quite a night."

"I haven't got any money."

Doc chuckled, "Shit, we're not playing for money, everyone's broke. The pot at the moment is a pair of chaps, a silver ring and an old saddle."

Wyatt shook his head with a smile and casually wiped his eyes with his finger.

The clouds drifted from the moon and a faint wash of blue light shone down onto Wyatt. Doc looked up at the full moon and beyond to the clusters of stars that lit the heavens.

"My Lord, but that's a fine sight."

There was no reply from Wyatt. Doc looked down and saw the vague glimmer of tears in his friend's eyes.

"Are you okay?"

"Seems funny, it hasn't bothered me so much until now."

"It ain't been quiet until now. Things are nice and comfortable here at the ranch. I hate to say it but things seem normal and that hurts pretty bad."

"I never thought of it that way. For once we don't have to watch our backs or expect Behan to come after us. It's almost like none of this ever happened and things are just the way they always were. Then I get to thinking about everything that we've lost."

Wyatt swallowed hard and puffed on his pipe. He gazed up at the stars.

Doc pulled out his silver hip flask from his inside jacket pocket. The moonlight gleamed and reflected off the metal surface. "You want a drink Wyatt?"

"No, I don't take whiskey."

"I wasn't asking you're preferences."

Wyatt took the flask, unscrewed the top and slugged back the liquor. He twitched at the bitterness of the taste.

"Thanks."

"My pleasure you looked like you needed it. You don't mind sharing do you?"

Wyatt gave the flask back to Doc and the dentist drank heartily.

"I didn't think you'd mind."

"You know, when I think about it, you don't hardly seem to cough as much as you used to."

"It's the air here in Arizona. My lungs are healing, the climate's doing me good."

"You know we'll probably have to leave Arizona and go to Colorado after this?"

Doc nodded and took another slug, "Everything else has gone to hell on a shutter, why not my health as well? Still it was fun while it lasted."

"Well, I've heard some people say that good mountain air does wonders for consumption?"

"Yes, that may be true and so does eating raw meat and eggs, sleeping in the freezing cold and drinking blood. It's all bullshit Wyatt."

"What about those new sanatoriums folks are starting?"

"Just a pretty idea by a bunch of crazy European medics who fell upon some cheap land in the mountains and figured a pretty view would fix everything. They're farming invalids Wyatt, its like cattle farming but you don't need to own so much pasture."

Wyatt smiled, "Do you have to be so sour?"

"Shut up and have another drink."

Wyatt took another slug of whiskey and looked back up at the night sky.

"You know the stars are pretty tonight. This reminds me of one night back in Dodge. I was depressed after one of the men I arrested died during an operation to remove the bullet I had shot into him. Bat took me into a saloon and got me drunk."

"Was that the night you were sick as a dog and I gave you laudanum?"

"Yes I thought the world was coming to an end. I thought I'd hit rock bottom."

"Had you?"

Wyatt smiled, "Nope, not nearly."

"Lord that seems a long time ago."

"Yes it does. I'll be glad to be out of Arizona. I know we're safe here at the ranch but I don't trust some of the men. You'd be wise to do the same."

Doc sighed and turned away, "I don't see how you can indulge in such paranoia."

"I'm just being careful."

"I ain't got time to be careful, I want to enjoy my life, what's left of it."

"I just want to make sure we all make it in one piece, doesn't that mean anything to you?"

"I care as much about the rest of the group as anyone but I'm not going to compromise as a result."

"You'll do what needs to be done, if that means

you have to do some compromising, well you'll damn well do some compromising."

"If that's the way it is, then I need to cut loose on my own for a while. I'm not going to squat in some piss-ant town in Colorado, I'm heading to Denver."

"Are you crazy, we need to hide low for a while, you want us all to get arrested? As soon as one of us shows their face in Denver, there'll be detectives crawling all over the place."

"I don't give a shit any more Wyatt, I've had more than enough."

"I just about lost my entire family and that's all you have to say?"

"That wasn't my doing Wyatt. Don't pin the blame on me I didn't do a damn thing."

"What about the gunfight?"

Doc gave Wyatt a look, his eyes black in the darkness.

"If that's how you feel than there's no reason for us to keep talking."

He turned and walked back into the ranch house.

CHAPTER THIRTY-TWO

Doc walked down the street, swinging his jacket over his shoulder. He had spent most of the day at the Denver races with Dan Tipton and had met up with Bat Masterson after lunch. A chestnut mare in the two o'clock race had won Doc two hundred dollars. It felt good to be in a large city again. He had spent several weeks shacked up in Gunnison trying to keep a low profile. It had been boring but at least he'd been in comfortable quarters. Wyatt had arranged accommodation with some of his more influential friends that lived in town. Wyatt wasn't happy when Doc jumped on a train to travel to Denver for the racing. Now Doc took strolled easily down the streets. He looked forward to an easy night, catching up with Bat's news, eating a good dinner and playing some of the gambling tables. Doc had always enjoyed playing Monte with Bat in particular. He was the only person that Doc knew that heckled the cards after a few drinks. "The Queen of Hearts is such a slut," he used to say. Then he'd lose another game and call the Queen of Hearts a "fat whore" and so it would go on until Doc would be laughing so hard he'd begin to choke.

A misty rain fell on Doc's back. He shivered and pulled his jacket on. There was a crowd of people lined up outside of the theater. The rain grew heavier as Doc walked passed. From out of the crowd a redheaded man appeared. He wore his hat pulled low over his forehead, so that it was hard to see his face. He walked with a strange waddling amble and hopped from one foot to the other if necessary, to pass people to catch up. Doc strode on down the street with his cane in his hand, oblivious of the man following behind him. They passed the baker's, two bars and a hardware store before the man caught up. Doc had his hand on the door of the saloon when the man caught up and pressed the revolver into Doc's back. "Mr. Holliday, my name is Mallen. I'm a bounty hunter working for Cochise County and I have a subpoena for your arrest."

"This is some kind of a joke surely?"

"No sir it's not. If you care to come with me down to the town jail, we can discuss this further. I'm sure you don't want to embarrass yourself in front of the whole town?"

Mallen prodded Doc in the back and pushed him down the street. Everywhere they walked, people turned and stared, gossiping and talking. Doc tried his best to ignore the faces. The bounty hunter grinned as he passed by with Doc. In his mind he was Denver's newest hero. Doc was relieved to reach the jail and walked forwards without much prodding from Mallen.

"Here's your prisoner, a Mr. Doc Holliday..."

The deputy looked surprised, "What's he here for?"

"What's he here for? He's only the most deadliest gunfighter in the west, more deadlier than Jesse James some say. There are hundreds of reasons to arrest him but the reason he is here today is for brutally killing a man in Utah. He cut him up good you know, slashed him from ear to ear."

Doc pulled against Mallen's grip, "That's a lie. I've never even been in Utah."

Mallen prodded Doc hard in the ribs, "That's enough Holliday. We don't have time for your lies and deceit, you can explain yourself in court."

The following days were spent by Doc watching people come in and out of the jail and listening to the same lies that Mallen had started, being repeated over and over again. The worst experience was when a reporter from the Denver Republican cornered Mallen and gave a large part of the newspaper over to an in-depth interview which included a history that Doc had never lived and a list of places that he had never been. Mallen enjoyed his new status as town hero but Doc had to endure constant visits from people who wanted to leer at him in his cell.

Doc lay on his bunk and listened to the rain falling outside. One of the things that frustrated him the most about the arrest was his hunger. He hadn't had a chance to eat that night and he hadn't had an opportunity to gamble. It was his first night of freedom since before Morgan's death and it had all slipped away because of Perry Mallen. Worst of all he didn't know if Bat knew where he had gone. Both Dan and Bat would think that he had stood them up. He sighed and remembered that he still had a letter from Mattie in one of his pockets. At least it would be a way to pass the time.

He pulled out the crumpled envelope. This time it had only been redirected twice, once in Tombstone and once in Colorado Springs. It was surprising to think that Behan had let a letter to Doc make it to Colorado. Perhaps one of Wyatt's friends in Wells Fargo had ensured the letter wasn't ripped open in Arizona. Doc sat up in the bunk and leaned his back against the wall. He ripped the envelope open and began to read.

There was all kind of news about Atlanta. He read about his cousins and the family farm. His uncle's dog had passed away. As usual, Mattie asked after Doc's health and showed concern for his safety. Doc smiled, he never told her anything of the violent side of his life and yet she always seemed to know when something was up. In a change from her usual letters, Mattie ended the letter with a paragraph about herself. 'I've decided to enter the convent,' it said and beneath there was an explanation. The aftermath of the war had affected her decision and she felt she would never have managed without her faith.

Doc sat back with the letter still clutched in his hand. It was hard to think of Mattie entering the convent but in a strange way it was a relief. He had always worried about her as if she was his little sister. Especially after leaving Georgia, he felt that there was no one there to watch out for her. He had never wanted her to get hurt in any way and he had feared that someone might take advantage of her good disposition and try to abuse her. Now, in a strange way she would always be safe. 'Sister Mary Melanie,' he read again. A strange smile crept across his face. The rain grew heavier and clattered across the roof of the jail, "My angel," he said.

"Doc, are you okay?"

Doc turned his head and looked over at Bat standing at the door of the cell. He got up and strode over to the bars.

"I'd offer you a chair and something to drink but I think you're out of luck this time."

Bat smiled, "That's okay, I appreciate the thought any how. So how come you ended up here? I thought you'd been behaving."

"Oh I have. Have you heard about Mallen yet?"

"It's hard not to. Just about everyone in Denver has, you made it to this morning's newspaper."

"Did he ever say what he arrested me for?"

"What do you mean? You don't know?"

"He said some bull about me killing his brother but I never did hear the full story."

"You're being held for killing Stillwell."

Doc smiled and shook his head, "Mallen doesn't have jurisdiction for that."

"But Behan does. Last I heard, he's on his way to Denver."

"Do they know about Wyatt and the others?"

"No, they haven't a clue about them."

"What about Dan?"

"I made him take the train back to Gunnison as soon as we heard. There was no sense in him staying. He wanted to come and see you, but it was too risky. They want to extradite you to Arizona."

"If they do that I'll be dead before too long. They'll shoot me in the back like Morg. I'll be lucky to make it one night in Tombstone."

Doc looked out at the rain coursing down in big drips from an overhang on the side of the building.

"Don't worry, I'll think of something."

Doc looked back at Bat, "I hope so."

CHAPTER THIRTY-THREE

The sunlight crept in through the shutters of the courtroom. Doc sat in the defendant's chair. It was early in the morning and he was exhausted. A cellmate had yelled and banged on the walls all night and kept him awake. At three-thirty in the morning Doc had drifted off to sleep only to wake minutes later to talk that a lynch mob was coming to get him. No mob appeared but that didn't do much to ease the tension. Doc was finally able to get some sleep only minutes before the marshal woke him and told him to get ready for court.

Mallen sat with a smug, self-satisfied grin on his face. He had a small pile of papers in front of him and he took great pleasure in shuffling and rearranging them backwards and forwards. At first it made Doc nervous but after a second study, he realized that Mallen was bluffing. The papers may even have been blank for all Doc knew. The jury assembled themselves, the judge being the last to take his chair. Doc had been to court many times before but he had never felt so ill prepared. He looked for Behan and was relieved that Johnny hadn't made the ride to Colorado. Bat sat at the other side of the court room with a sober look on his face. Doc looked over and gave a weak smile, but Bat was concentrating on other things and didn't look up.

The judge banged his gavel. Everyone stopped their conversations and turned their attention to the front of the court room. The court proceedings began and Doc waited for his turn to speak but it never came. There seemed to be some indecision about paperwork. Mallen took the stand and gave the same rambling tale about Doc shooting his brother in Utah. He rambled about trailing Doc up and down boomtowns all through the West to bring him to justice. Everyone listened to Mallen's story but before he could finish, the judge cut him short. The information was deemed irrelevant to the case at hand. He was asked several times to give information regarding the shooting of Stillwell and when it was evident that he knew little more than what he had heard in rumor, Mallen was told to sit down. He ignored the judge the first time he was asked and when he was told to leave for the second time, his eyebrows were peaked in frustration and his lip wobbled. Doc smirked at Mallen, his moment of fame was over.

Sheriff Shibbell took the stand to read a prepared statement. Doc thought back to the train station, to the shadows moving in the dark, the noise of the train, Stillwell's scared eyes and the sound of Ike's feet on the platform, as he turned and ran away. He was scared that Shibbell, in some way, might be able to see inside his head and read his memories but, as he listened to the statement, nothing was read that would incriminate him in any way and there were no witnesses in Colorado. The words 'extradition to Arizona' were read. The judge asked for the appropriate paperwork to be handed over and Shibbell obliged him. There was a pause, as the judge looked everything over. Doc's throat grew dry and he fought hard to stop a fit of coughing.

The judge finished checking the papers and handed them back. "It seems that the paperwork for extradition is in order," said the judge. "However, it has been brought to my attention that Doctor Holliday is under arrest for bunco charges in Colorado. Thus it seems improbable that Dr. Holliday can be extradited until he has been sent to trial for pending charges in this state. Once said charges are undertaken, the possibility of extradition with Sheriff Shibbell can be reconsidered. Until then, Sheriff Masterson will take custody of the prisoner."

Doc glanced over at the judge and then to Bat with a foggy sense of disbelief. Before Doc had a chance to realize what had happened, he was sitting next to Bat on a train bound for Pueblo.

"Are you ready?"

Doc looked up from shuffling cards. Bat was peering at him through the bars of the lone jail cell in the Pueblo court house. "For what exactly?"

Bat smiled, "What do you think bunco boy? Your bail's been paid."

Doc's eyes glowed in the darkness, he slid the

cards into his top pocket. "Good, let's get the hell out of here."

Bat unbolted the door. Doc dusted off his hat and adjusted it on his head, rubbing the brim with his forefingers. "So how long do you hope to keep up this charade?"

"As long as we possibly can, until those yahoos go back to Arizona."

"Thanks, I appreciate what you've done."

Bat smiled, "Don't worry about it. It would have been wrong to let them take you back."

Doc followed Bat out into the dark streets.

"Cigar?"

Doc smiled, "Sure."

Doc puffed on the cigar and strolled out into the main street of Pueblo. A cool, refreshing breeze blew down across Doc's shoulders. The mountains beyond were dressed in layers of blue and gray clouds. The first rumble of thunder cracked in the distance, a small fork of lightning jumped from cloud to cloud and the rain fell down. The rain fell in large, soft droplets. Doc took the cigar out of his mouth, tipped the brim of his hat backwards and let the rain drops hit his face. A wide grin spread from cheekbone to cheekbone. He laughed, pulled the brim of his hat down over his face and walked on across the muddy street, watching the rain bounce off the ground. Bat led him down an alley and up through a side door at the back of a saloon. They walked in together, tipping the excess water off their hats and coats.

"What do you want to drink Doc?"

Doc smirked, "You're my parole officer, what am I allowed to have?"

"Shit, I don't care, just don't make an ass of yourself."

Doc felt a hand on his shoulder, "Doc?"

"Wyatt?"

"I think I need to buy this drink of yours. Bourbon be all right?"

Doc grinned at Wyatt, "I've never said no before. God, it's so good to see you again."

"I'm sorry for what happened and for what I said."

"Don't be it's over now. These last couple of months in jail have been the longest of my life."

"Longest time you'd been sober?" said Bat.

Doc smiled, "That's not what I meant."

"I think you getting out of jail is something for us to celebrate. I won't make any corny speeches."

"I'll second that," said Doc, "let's drink."

Doc clinked his glass of bourbon against Wyatt and Bat's beer glasses and they all took a swig.

"You're not going to get sick again are you?"

Wyatt looked embarrassed, "No, I don't think you have anything to worry about."

"Good because I don't have any laudanum."

"Just as well," said Bat.

"It's funny to think of all we've been through over the years. Where do we go from here?"

"Oh mining claims, maybe get together a new string of horses, new places, head back to California."

"Just thinking about it makes me tired, it sounds like too much hard work to me. What about you Bat?"

Bat smiled, "I'm your parole officer remember."

Doc looked at Bat with almost black eyes,

"Seriously, what do you hope to do with your life?"

"Seriously, I'd like to go to New York eventually."

Both Wyatt and Doc gave Bat a stunned look.

"What ever would you want to do that for?"

"Well," said Bat putting a cigar into the corner of his mouth, "I've been reading the newspapers back East and you know New York sounds kind of exciting to me, it has the edge that Dodge used to have."

"High homicide rate to boot," said Doc with a grin.

"That's not what I meant."

"What about you Doc?" said Wyatt, "You're welcome to come to California with me if you want."

"I'd be out of sorts there. Some how I can't imagine taking strolls on the beach."

"Josie wouldn't like it that's for sure," said Bat.

"Actually, speaking of which, I probably need to get back to her."

"Whipped all ready," said Doc.

Wyatt smiled, "I'm leaving town tomorrow but maybe we'll meet up soon."

"One day we will for sure."

"Goodbye then. You've been a hell of a good friend to me Doc."

"Goodbye my friend."

CHAPTER THIRTY-FOUR

Four horses strained and puffed clouds of cold air as they pulled the stagecoach up the side of a brilliantly sunlit snowy mountain. Tall pine trees stretched up to an icy-blue sky. The branches swayed in the growing wind and dredged little clouds of snow down onto the ground with a whispering rattle. Doc leaned his elbow on the window frame and gazed out at the passing scenery. He was glad of the sunshine for keeping the road clear. The route had been closed in the past for less snow. Deciding to leave Leadville had been a tough decision. Glenwood Springs was more of a health retreat than a boomtown, but Doc didn't care any more.

Despite his overcoat and leather gloves, Doc still shivered with cold. He reached for the flask of whiskey in front of him and took a swig. He welcomed the warmth and bite from the alcohol. He hoped it would loosen the muscles in his chest which had grown more constricted since he had left Leadville. Through the window he could see the blue haze of the mountains rising up in the distance. The coach rocked and creaked as the horses halted in Glenwood. Doc pulled his leather satchel up off the seat. He leaned all of his weight down against his cane and headed to the door. The cold air made him wheeze. He misjudged the step and stumbled getting down from the stage. A fellow passenger grasped him around the shoulders and helped him regain his balance. The man stayed with Doc until he had caught his breath and then, with a tip of his hat, left Doc standing in the street with his bag.

The weeks and months that followed dissolved into one another for Doc. It was hard to remember any particular day with clarity. The laudanum that initially had begun as a medical aid had become a crutch and was beginning to eat Doc's days and memories. Doc had a vague recollection of sitting in the Hotel Colorado's hot-springs. The yellow tinged clouds of sulphur rose around him. He had tried to swim at first but the water had been so hot that it had lulled him to sleep. He had dreamed about the Chattahoochee River in Georgia. He was fifteen-years-old and he was playing in the cool water with his friends. He dived below the surface, grabbed at his cousin's ankles and pulled him under. They'd resurfaced laughing. He'd relaxed and dived again into the water. He'd gone deeper and deeper this time, beneath the frogs and pond weed, down into the dark water. His mouth and nostrils had left trails of tiny bubbles floating upwards as he dived. Until his head hit something hard. He felt his body spring back to the surface until he was partially submerged and partially floating amongst the steam. He woke to a hand on his shoulder, clawing at him. Hotel attendants dragged his semi-conscious body out of the pool and laid him flat at the side. Someone was pushing on his chest, pumping the water out of his lungs until he spewed it all on the side of the pool. He took a shuddering breath of real air. He was more embarrassed than hurt when he finally came to. He sat up, thanked his rescuers, went to change out of his swimming trunks and smoke a cigarette.

In the following weeks he took a job as a faro dealer at one of the saloons off Main Street. The heavy smell of kerosene and the warm wet air in the bar irritated his lungs more than usual. The first evening he had only noticed a growl in his voice. The next evening his back and chest hurt enough for him to double his usual dose of laudanum. It caused him to lose track of the faro game once or twice but he didn't pay much attention to it. The third night he broke a sweat, grew dizzy and passed out completely.

He realized he had fainted and tried to get up, opened his eyes and found himself back in his room at The Glenwood Hotel. The white light from the snowy window pane blinded him. He closed one eye and felt the bed sheets with his hand to make sure they were real. They were warm and wet.

"I'll have someone come and change those for you, don't worry."

Doc looked up and saw a man in his fifties, with a well groomed, gray beard that came to a point, eyes that were pitch black, and gold spectacles.

"I'm Doctor Crook, from the hospital."

The doctor picked up a syringe full of morphine and pushed the needle deep into Doc's vein. Doc let his head sink into the pillow and closed his eyes.

The next time Doc woke, it was dark outside but hail was rapping the window. There seemed to be a shadowed figure standing next to the bed. Doc reached for his pistol that lay by his pillow. He hit the trigger over and over, the hammer hit empty chamber after empty chamber. The shadow loomed over the bed with glowing eyes, Doc slid deeper into the sheets, his eyes full of fear. He let out a muffled scream as the figure came up to the bed, then fainted away into another long slumber.

The creak of his hotel room door opening, woke him the next morning. At first, he couldn't place the noise and managed to reach his revolver, still empty from the night before. He lifted the gun with his arm wavering. New sweat trickled down his cheeks with the effort. He wouldn't let the shadow from the night before sneak up on him again. The bellboy entered the room, saw the gun and dropped the tray that he was carrying. A jug of water keeled over and crashed to the floor.

"I'm sorry sir. I'm so sorry! Please don't shoot!"

Doc lowered the gun, but the boy was so flustered he ran out the room and back down the stairs. Doc fell back to sleep.

The bellboy returned but this time with Doctor Crook and placed a bowl of broth next to the bedside. The noise woke Doc. He looked up at the bellboy and realized that the intimidating shadow he had seen earlier had only been a boy with large, scared eyes. The boy backed a step away from the bed. Doc reached a hand out to him but it only made the boy more scared of him. The effort of leaning over caused Doc to wheeze and a fit of painful coughing took him. He felt as if his whole chest was on fire. His eyes were burning. His lungs felt contorted in a way that was unnatural. He coughed and shook. Sweat dripped down his back. The fit ended after he vomited a slug of bloody phlegm. The boy had backed away to the door and it was Doctor Crook that stepped forward.

"Come on sit up," he said. He took a hot poultice that he had made with mustard and hot water. He slathered it onto Doc's back and rubbed the ointment until the surface of the skin felt like it was burning. It was difficult to tolerate, but in a strange way, it did seem to move something deep in Doc's lungs. He wheezed and received a slap on the back from the doctor which perpetuated the coughing until he choked with a deep bronchial bark. His chest felt as if he had swallowed razor blades. The doctor hit him again. Doc rolled his eyes in disgust at him. He choked on the blood at the back of his throat. It was thicker than normal and took a moment to snake to his mouth. With a strangled growl he coughed up the blood. Progress was slow and painful. He strained and retched until the greatest amount of blood and phlegm was out of his lungs. The pressure of the hemorrhage had pushed blood up out through his nostrils. He was a physical wreck by the time it was over. He sat on the bed in a pool of sweat. His mouth and nightshirt were bloody. Everything tasted salty and the air seemed warm and wet. He would have felt some relief if it wasn't for the headache. There was a constant buzzing in his ears that he couldn't shake and he felt that the light from the room made the pain worse.

Doc had been so preoccupied, he hadn't notice the bellboy returning to the room with a bowl of ice and water. Doctor Crook dipped a cloth in the icy water and pressed it up to Doc's forehead. Doc took the cloth with surprised relief. The doctor took Doc's hands by his skinny wrists and dropped them into the water. It felt pleasant at first but after a few minutes the numbness in his wrists became unbearable. He tried to pull his hands free but the doctor pushed his hands down.

Outside the window there were two loud bangs. Doc lifted his head upwards, flinched and struggled to release his wrists but the Doctor held them tight. Another loud bang hit the air and a ear piercing scream. Doc wriggled against his restraint. He tried to speak but he couldn't make any noise. Another explosion led to a cacophony of smaller bangs. This time Doc got his hands free and knocked the bowl of water over.

"Don't worry, it's just a fireworks display. It's to celebrate the opening of the new railway line in town. You're going to miss the celebrations unfortunately."

Doc relaxed his grip and slumped back on the bed with relief.

"If you like I can have Art bring you some of the food from the meal later tonight. Only if you're hungry of course."

Doc nodded his head and the gentle movement caused a trail of blood to drip down from one nostril. He erupted in coughing. A new pool of

blood dripped down onto the sheets. Doc looked at
the blood and cried. Tears dripped down his face
and ran into the blood below his nostrils, sending
streams of blood over his mustache and chin. He
wished the bellboy couldn't see him crying but the
boy seemed fascinated.

"Don't just stand there Art there are things to do
downstairs."

The boy apologized, turned and fled out the
door. Doc was relieved that he was out of sight.
The pain was excruciating. It was the exhaustion
that made the pain so intense. Doc knew what it
was like to get shot. There was lots of pain but
always adrenalin to get you through the first parts
of it. With this there was nothing. There was only
the headache, the pulsing of his heart beating faster
and then slower and the sharp spasms in his back
that led to coughing. He cried and didn't know
why he was crying. The blood continued to drip
from his face and it seemed hopeless, he just
wanted it to stop.

Doctor Crook looked on his patient with soft
pitiful eyes. He pulled out his pocket watch,
studied the time and then opened his medicine
bag. He took out a small envelope filled with
ergotine and loaded up a syringe. The needle
pierced Doc's arm. The agents in the fungus
coursed through his body and his pulse slowed.
He began to see his life with a strange sense of
clarity that he had never had before. He
remembered dental school for the first time in
years and he could almost smell the detergent on
the polished floors. He could remember the eyes of
his first patient.

The blood dripping from his nostrils, slowed and clotted. Doc wiped the blood off with the back of his hand and laid back on the bed. Doctor Crook took Doc's wrist and measured his pulse.

Doc remembered his first night in Dallas and he thought of his first poker game. He'd shown up hungover to work the next morning and his boss had sent him home after he'd thrown up over a patient. A few months later the dental office burned down. Doc hadn't cared as he had lost his job anyway. The memories kept coming. Doc wished he could understand why but despite the clarity of the visions, his thoughts remained muddled. His final memory before exhaustion caught up with him was of winning his first high stakes poker game back in Abilene. He smiled a blood-tainted smile.

"Feeling better?"

Doc looked up at Doctor Crook and nodded.

"Good, rest for a while. I'll be in and out to check on you."

Doc closed his eyes and drifted off to sleep. He was aware of people coming in and out of the room to check on him, but when he opened his eyes nothing seemed real. Everything had a surreal look to it that was disconcerting. It was hard to tell which people were real and which were part of his memory. He had seen Big Nose Kate enter the room at one point, but as she had reached him she had grown transparent and walked through his bed. He had also dreamed of his mother but he knew better than to believe that she was really there. Then there was the dream he had about Morgan. It was a simple dream, they were sitting having a drink and playing cards but it seemed so real. Morg had asked if Doc would come back to play cards with him again and Doc had agreed.

Doc had no idea how many days he had been in bed. The bellboy was no longer afraid of him and they'd formed a good friendship. Doctor Crook had begun rolling Doc into different positions on a daily basis to prevent bedsores. Despite being barely awake Doc had managed to growl, "You people flip me more than a damned pancake."

On another morning, Doc had sat up in bed without aid. He was able to look out of the window from his bed. Outside, snow drifted down over the fir trees, adding to the drifts of snow that weighed their branches down to the ground. The wind blew in gusts and tossed pillows of snow from each fork of pine needles, up into small clouds of snowflakes.

A letter had arrived from Martha and the thought of his cousin had made him aware of the outside world again. He was too weak to be able to understand what he had read but it didn't matter to him. He felt a strange warm feeling of love for her. She was his last remaining contact with Georgia and his family. She finally was happy with her life, and that was all that mattered to Doc. He pulled himself up from his bed and stood shivering by the window. He supported himself by wedging his body between the windowsill and the bed. He read the letter, or at least parts of it, then stood gazing out at the snow. He felt at peace. He thought about dying and for the first time in his life it didn't scare him. In fact, he looked forward to it. It seemed strange to meet such a peaceful end. There would be no adrenalin, no panic, no anger, no blood and no acrid smell of gunpowder in his nostrils. Instead he had a sense of peace, warm memories, a warm bed, and people that cared for him. Despite everything that he had been through, he knew that Martha still loved him.

He watched the snowstorm swirl in the wind. The flakes grew larger, until all he could see was the movement of the light reflected off each one.

Doctor Crook found Doc unconscious and slumped over at the window. He lifted him up into his arms like a child and carried him back to the bed. He covered him in a blanket and pressed his fingers to his neck to check his pulse. The waiting was finally over.

Note from the author~

I hope you enjoyed reading *A Gentleman in Hell*. Thank you for your support. I would be grateful if you would leave a review on Goodreads or Amazon and of course, it goes without saying, if you enjoyed this book, please tell your friends and family about it.

More About Elena Sandidge

Elena Sandidge is a Scottish novelist with a passion for the history of the Old West and the life of the legendary gunfighting dentist, Doc Holliday. Elena currently resides in Kentucky where she lives with her family, a goofy hound dog and a very furry black and white cat. If you would like to follow Elena's blog or just indulge in all things related to the Wild West please take a look at the following:

Website
www.elenasandidge.com

Email
elenasandidge@gmail.com

Twitter
@elenasandidge

Facebook

Elena Sandidge Books

Lightning Source UK Ltd.
Milton Keynes UK
UKHW021900050421
381470UK00017B/293